THE KEEPERS OF ARIS

THE KEEPERS OF ARIS

AUTUMN GREEN

Ooligan Press - Portland, Oregon

The Keepers of Aris

ISBN13: 978-1-947845-42-8

Ooligan Press
Portland State University
Post Office Box 751, Portland, Oregon 97207
503-725-9748
ooligan@ooliganpress.pdx.edu
http://ooligan.pdx.edu

Library of Congress Cataloging-in-Publication Data
[Names: Green, Autumn, author.
Title: The Keepers of Aris / by Autumn Green.
Description: Portland, Oregon : Ooligan Press, [2022] | Audience: Ages 15+. | Audience: Grades 10-12. | Summary: The human world has almost forgotten about Aris Magica, the secretive realm of magic that exists parallel to humanity, but when an evil presence returns to ignite a war between the worlds, sixteen-year-old Jay must challenge fate and reckon with her growing powers, or let Aris Magica and the human world perish.
Identifiers: LCCN 2022034995 (print) | LCCN 2022034996 (ebook) | ISBN 9781947845428 (trade paperback) | ISBN 9781947845435 (ebook)
Subjects: CYAC: Good and evil--Fiction. | Imaginary wars and battles--Fiction. | Magic--Fiction. | Fantasy. | LCGFT: Fantasy fiction. | Novels.
Classification: LCC PZ7.1.G73668 Ke 2022 (print) | LCC PZ7.1.G73668 (ebook) | DDC [Fic]--dc23
LC record available at https://lccn.loc.gov/2022034995
LC ebook record available at https://lccn.loc.gov/2022034996]
Cover design by Riley Roberts
Interior design by Savannah Lyda

Printed in the United States of America

Ooligan PRESS

Portland State UNIVERSITY

For you,

Dreams do come true, so don't give up.

Prologue

The door creaked as it opened. Moonlight shone through the window, casting a soft light onto the floor, illuminating the space between the four beds lined against the back wall of the rectangular room. A second door on the back wall opposite the first was wide open, leading to the bathroom.

Carefully, Jay tiptoed over to the bed directly in front of the window. The moonlight lit Dylan's face as he slept. Lightly brushing his brown hair from his forehead, Jay observed how much it had grown since they had first arrived here, now falling below his eyebrows. *He looks so peaceful*, Jay thought, even though she knew it not to be true. Ever since that fateful night of Dylan's parents' deaths, Jay could see how much he was hurting, even though he still refused to talk about it. She remembered a time when Dylan trusted her enough to tell her everything. A lot about him had changed since then.

They'd already been at the Institute for a few months since the incident. Yet Jay still couldn't get used to her room being so far away from his, especially while her dreams were still riddled with nightmares.

Jay climbed into Dylan's bed, and as she did, she barely missed a fatal blow from his dagger.

To take his mind off things, Dylan had enrolled in a weapons training class offered by the school. The Dylan she used to know would have boasted about his newfound ability to wield a blade with only a couple of lessons. He would have even laughed as he practiced his moves on her. But right now, the light from his stormy gray eyes had dimmed, and the look she received while he held a dagger to her throat terrified her.

"Jesus, Jay. You scared me." Dylan's eyes widened and his face paled an even lighter color. Jay saw the fear in his eyes as he realized what he had almost done. He withdrew his blade. The hilt of the dagger was wrapped in dark blue leather. Jay caught a glimpse of two tally marks and the letters *MC* engraved into the side of the hilt before Dylan returned his blade underneath his pillow.

Tears began to fall down her cheeks, landing on her hand, which shot up to cover her mouth. "Sorry," she squeaked.

They lay silently, side by side, the sound of the clock on the wall across from them slowly ticking by.

"Dylan?" Jay whispered.

He groaned, rolling onto his side to face her. "What?"

Jay bit her bottom lip. "Can we talk about what happened? Or at least talk about *them*?"

"Does it matter?" Dylan asked.

Jay shrugged, pulling at the tassels on his blanket. *It does to me.* "Why did . . . why did your parents die?"

Dylan hesitated, his words getting caught in his throat. "Dunno." Dylan's tone softened as he stroked her head of white hair. A weak smile faltered on his lips. "It's okay if you want to call them something more. They might not have been your real parents, but they cared for you like you were their own. And they are just as important to you as they are to me." Dylan cleared his throat. "Were," he corrected himself uncomfortably.

This was the most that Dylan had managed to open up about his parents' death since it happened. She was shocked. For months, she had tried to talk to him about their deaths, even the Institute's counselor had tried, but they'd both failed.

"But I wasn't theirs," Jay mumbled, squeezing her hands together. She would be twelve soon, the same age as Dylan. Another year would have gone by without word from her parents. Her own parents had abandoned her on her fifth birthday, six years before Dylan's parents died. All she had to remember her own parents by was her dark skin. Even when looking in the mirror she couldn't find them in her features: oddly colored blue eyes and unnatural white hair. As a child, she'd always been told she looked nothing like them.

She snuggled closer to Dylan.

"Alright," he sighed. "One more question; it's late."

Tears filled her eyes once again. "The sword." She recalled the memory of coming face-to-face with the Demon that now plagued her nightmares. "It pierced my heart, and its blade broke inside me. There was blood everywhere . . . I should have died. How did I survive?" Jay couldn't help but think it was all somehow her fault. Her body shook with uncontrollable sobs.

Before arriving at the Institute, Demons were just as imaginary as magic was. Aris Magica had been a world she knew nothing about, but Jay always knew that something about her was strange. To know now that she was descended from a hidden part of the world terrified her as much as her nightmares did. She never felt normal around other people, especially when her powers first manifested and created unnatural chaos. In elementary school, Jay had gotten into a fight with another kid, and the lockers had exploded. No one had known the cause, but Jay had suspected it had been her doing. For Dylan it had been different; he could pass as human, if he chose to. It wasn't until they had arrived at the Institute, weeks after his parents' deaths, was he made aware of his abilities. The professors had tested them both, discovering Jay to be a Pure breed and the Hybrid gene in Dylan. Shortly after, they narrowed his ability down to a Weapons Master. Dylan could use any weapon once and master it. After Dylan's parents had died, Dylan and Jay had severed their connection to the human world, no longer feeling a sense of belonging. Only now, the Institute was trying to slowly integrate them back into it.

Not much had changed, except for the fact that Jay now knew magic existed, and Aris Magica was intertwined in the same universe as the human world. Aris Magica was created by the very first Magician. Some described him as a being of light, while others said he was all races in one. His name was Aris, and there had never been another like him. After creating Aris Magica, he disappeared. History books said his essence flows throughout the land as Old Magic. Before, Aris Magica coexisted peacefully with humans, sharing the knowledge of magic, as Aris had planned. Now, Aris Magicians conducted magic in secret to help the human world advance, whether it was introducing new technology to the world, creating cures for diseases, or starting wars to cover up the wars happening within Aris Magica lands. But either way, magic, Demons, and the impossible existed. Jay pulled the blanket closer to her chest, wishing she could just wake up from the life that was now her reality.

"It was just a dream, Jay." Dylan pulled her into him.

Jay nuzzled her head into his shoulder. *At least one thing hasn't changed*, she thought. Jay could still tell when he was lying to her. It wasn't a dream; it was a memory. But she chose to let herself believe his words.

"I don't have all the answers," Dylan sighed, "but let's just keep everything how it is now. No more questions, no more trying to figure out what we don't understand. Never bring it up again. Deal?"

"Deal."

Chapter One

The metal chair tipped forward, then settled back into place. Jay pulled against the restraints tied around her wrists and ankles, getting nowhere. She was strapped to a chair, held down by locked chains. A single spotlight lit the area around her, forming one big circle. Outside of that was darkness.

Jay was on yet another mission, her third one this month. She wriggled her hands again to see if she could slip them out of the restraints, but they were strapped too tightly. All she did was burn her skin even further than she already had. She reminded herself to heal it later rather than go visit the Institute's infirmary.

Jay sighed, relaxing back in her chair. She stared up at the ceiling, not bothered by the bright light shining down from it. She closed her eyes, allowing herself to get lost in her own thoughts. *Why is it that I'm always the bait? For once, I'd like to be the hero, the one storming in to save the day.* If it wasn't for her powers, maybe she would be. As helpful as they were, they were also unpredictable. Plus, *adversaries tend to see the girl as weak and underestimate her*, Jay remembered her professor, Riley, saying. Each mission held a purpose: to find a way to coexist with the outside world while also using Aris Magician's powers for good—with the exception of this one. Jay had been assigned to this mission for a different purpose; the foe she was up against this time had harmed a student at the Institute early in the semester. It had been all over the news. "Student murdered in the Wallowa Whitman National Forest outside of Bull Run, daughter of a distinguished doctor. Murderer never found." Except the murderer had been found, but the police covered it up like they always did whenever an Aris Magician was involved.

It's not like the world forgot about Aris Magica by choice. After all, Aris Magica and the human world were forever entwined. It was just after the war between the two worlds that some Aris Magicians preferred to stay hidden, and eventually, humans forgot about them and their powers—good or bad—they brought to the world. When things happened that didn't make sense to humans, their natural instinct to pretend it didn't exist would kick in.

Jay smirked to herself. How could she use her powers for good when she wasn't even sure how she got them in the first place? Its not like either of her parents had anything magical about them, but she didn't have many memories of them to remember correctly. Her parents had abandoned her when she was five after seeing her hair turn white and her eyes turn red. Her parents had discovered when she used magic, Jay's blue eyes took on a crimson shade. Sometimes magic was enough to bring out the color, but there were a few times when her emotions controlled the change instead of magic. Once the magic was gone or she had calmed her mind, her eyes would return to their normal blue. Jay's smirk turned to a frown as she forced the thought of her parents from her mind.

Light footsteps approached from behind her, pulling her from her thoughts. The footsteps circled the chair, and a few seconds later, she was face-to-face with her captor. He wore a long, white lab coat without a name tag. His angular face was worn with wrinkles, and thick-rimmed glasses covered piercing, pale green eyes. He smiled, flashing a perfectly straight row of teeth. From his front pocket, he pulled out a pair of rubber gloves, snapping them into place over his hands. He lifted a strand of Jay's white hair, letting the pieces gradually fall back into place. Jay looked him over once again. He seemed to be calculating her actions before either of them had said a word.

A memory quickly flashed across her mind as she recalled Riley handing her a file. The man before her perfectly fit the description she had received. "Doctor," Jay snarled, deciding the title fit. He reminded her of an evil mastermind straight out of a children's cartoon. He was the one responsible for murdering the student at the Institute. According to Riley, it had been a pain to track him down. The doctor was known for experimenting on others, and his own daughter happened to be one of them. The doctor had publicly promised to cure all Aris Magicians from the burden of power they carry. He's made the declaration on national TV. Of course, no one had believed him. Aris Magicians kept their existence hidden from the world. The doctor had been stripped of all credibility by humans for believing in fairytales.

"If you didn't want to be found, then you shouldn't have broadcasted yourself so boldly," the doctor surmised. His voice was dark, yet whimsical, as the words left his mouth, sending a chill down Jay's spine. He took a step back. Jay scoffed, disgusted. "I apologize for the invasion of privacy." He gestured to her clothes, without an ounce of regret in his eyes. "But we had to take certain precautions when it came to restraining your powers." Jay's clothes had been replaced by a black leather bodysuit. The material was thick and slick, laced with a chemical that smelled like old eggs.

We? Jay looked around but saw no one else.

"You gave my security quite a fight before they knocked you out," he said.

While the doctor had been talking, she had attempted to summon her magic, but found she was met with an overwhelming emptiness. All she could feel was a slight tingle in her fingertips, but it wasn't from the doctor's suit. Her powers were unpredictable; sometimes they worked when she wanted them to, other times they didn't. At times, she thought they were tied to her emotions, and sometimes she believed they were tied to how much danger her mind believed her to be in. The bodysuit was comfortable, and for a second, Jay truly believed it was dampening her powers. *I wonder how long it'll last,* Jay thought, but she already knew the answer. No matter what the situation was, her powers never failed to come when she really needed them. Sometimes it felt as though they had a mind of their own.

"Magnificent, isn't it?" The doctor beamed, gripping the arms of her chair, caging her further. "You see," He pulled back, giving her room to breathe. "I haven't yet unraveled the depth of your powers, but I am close." He looked her up and down, admiring his work. "I wasn't sure it would work, but seeing it now, in all its glory . . ."

Jay raised an eyebrow, understanding the situation. He thought he had discovered a way to stop her from using magic. For a moment, she wanted to believe him. Had he really found the answer to the mystery of her powers? She yearned to find out more but knew it would stray from the mission.

The mission, she thought, annoyed, to herself. Jay regretted the moment Dylan convinced her to take on the extracurricular class at their school for the magical and abnormal geeks of society. The class was taught by Riley, who also taught the History of Aris Magica and Weapons Training. Usually, the mission was undertaken by five other students who also took the extracurricular class, but everyone else had gone home for break. Still, no one ever went on a mission alone. Dylan had been chosen to accompany her; it had been a while since the two of them had been alone on a mission. The students were chosen specifically by Riley for the class based on their high academic ranking at the Institute, as well as their performance in his training class. The course was to help teach them how to coexist with humans and use their powers for good. Riley was very strict when it came to his hands-on approach, hence the missions. Jay only agreed because it got her off school grounds—not that she felt any more comfortable in regular society, but sometimes, the Institute could feel like a prison.

Jay hadn't been listening to a single word the doctor had been saying, but she decided she would play his game anyway, at least for a little while longer. "I'm not some lab rat you can prod at to get answers," Jay said, as the doctor circled her like a vulture. "No matter what, I won't die here. Not like your daughter did." Jay knew it was risky provoking him like that, but she couldn't help herself.

"Precisely." He stopped in front of her. A wicked gleam reflected in his irises. "Perhaps my team and I can change that—discover the true reason for your ability. We . . ." His voice faltered, but only for a moment. "I failed my daughter. She wanted to be free of this hideous burden of magic, and I failed her. But her sacrifice can help so many more."

Righteous but crazy. Got it, Jay thought. "Did you lose any men?" Jay flashed a wicked smile. She had taken out at least seven of his men before they overpowered her. Of course, if she had been using magic, then his men would have not stood a chance of subduing her.

The doctor leaned in, trapping her in place again. She stared back into his sharp eyes. She could feel her power building up inside of her with nowhere else to go. Her powers were finally responding. The doctor leaned in even closer, his smile transforming into something sinister.

"The eyes change, but nothing will happen. My daughter told me about you." Jay couldn't even recall his daughter's name, so hearing that she had met her caught her off guard. "I'm in charge of your powers while you're here. Plus, I have an entire SWAT team within these shadows waiting to take you out the second your assistance is no longer required." He leaned in closer, whispering in her ear, "I would be cautious if I were you. My child, you are expendable. Do not think for a second that you cannot be replaced."

She glared at him, not saying anything. She watched as the doctor smirked before returning to his vulture-like examination of her body. Jay rolled her eyes, drawing into her thoughts.

She hated this plan of being used as bait, but kept reminding herself that it was all a part of their mission. Retrieve and encounter, minimal casualties, minimal exposure. Professor Riley had given Jay intel on the serum that was being kept in this building, but the only person who knew its exact location was the doctor. But why did every plan end with her being saved by *him*? All her life, it had been Dylan and her. He'd always taken care of her, even though she was now more than capable of taking care of herself. *I hate feeling like a damsel in distress.*

Jay was so lost in her own thoughts that she didn't notice the rounds of gunfire going off around her. The shots ceased, sending the room into deadly silence.

She slumped against the chair, frowning. "He's here."

The doctor looked at Jay then back to the shadows. He frantically pulled out a walkie-talkie from his back pocket and spoke into it. All that came back was static. "I said, 'Do you copy?'" he repeated desperately.

"What were you saying about that SWAT team, Doc?" Jay taunted. She watched as the doctor shriveled in fear as a dark shadow rose up behind him.

"You're late." Jay shouted into the darkness.

The tip of a blade wedged into the doctor's back, although it wasn't enough to puncture his skin. "I had a tough time finding my way. It's like a maze in here." Dylan grinned.

Jay smiled, rolling her eyes. The chains holding her down fell to the ground, and the cuffs on her wrists and ankles snapped open. She tossed the lock aside, smiling at the doctor's confused expression.

"You didn't seriously think your little science project had actually worked, did you?" Jay laughed. When her eyes had turned red, she had managed to undo the locks keeping her in place.

Dylan flipped the dagger so the hilt was now facing the doctor's back, and shoved him face-first into the metal chair. Jay didn't think twice before tying him to it. She snapped her fingers, and the doctor unwillingly turned his body to sit correctly in the chair. The cuffs snapped over his wrists, and the chain picked itself up and wrapped around his torso, pinning him to the chair. She made a fist, and the chains tightened. The doctor squirmed under its hold.

"Well, well, Doctor. What a sight."

His mouth was agape. The two teenagers towered before him.

Jay sensed the doctor's confusion. Two teenagers had made a fool of him. She smirked, satisfied.

"Don't panic. We only need one thing from you, then you're free to go." Dylan implored.

Jay shrugged, folding her arms over her chest. "Or we can just take his life," she suggested casually. "It's what he does to our kind; we should just return the favor."

Dylan ignored her. He took a step closer to the doctor, leaning in so they were inches apart. He held the blade to his throat. "The cure?"

A mask of dread fell across his face. "We have many cures in this laboratory. You'll have to be more specific." He managed to maintain a calm and collected edge to his voice, but it wouldn't last long.

Jay circled him, just as he had done to her moments before. "The one that was televised a few days ago, after your daughter's murder.

Very expensive." She stopped, grabbed his ear, and yanked his face in her direction. "That cure."

The chains around the doctor tightened again. Through gritted teeth, he said, "I will be obliged to hand it over in exchange for . . ." He glanced at Jay with wild eyes. She took a step back, disgusted. Dylan pressed the blade further into the doctor's throat. Drops of blood fell onto his blade. "My life! I—I get to live."

Dylan cocked his head to the side, glancing at Jay. "Fair enough."

"The code is seven three eight four. It's hidden in the X-file room down the hall, to the right of the stations."

"You better not be lying," Jay warned before loosening the chains. "Oh, and just so we're clear . . ." She spun on her heels, facing the darkness. "*Stige*," she whispered. Instantly, guns from the fallen security detail rose to aim at the doctor. His glasses fell down his nose and sweat trickled down the back of his neck. She curtsied, giving the doctor her best smile before leaving.

"Was that necessary?" Dylan asked, closing the door behind her.

She shrugged, not even bothering to answer his question. It's not like what she said mattered to him anyway. Whatever her response, they'd only end up arguing about it instead of him being proud that she was beginning to be able to fully control her powers. Occasionally, when her powers felt too overwhelming, she used harnessing words—magic words that helped focus her power on what she wanted to accomplish. A professor at the Institute had taught her this while Jay was learning to control her magic. Most of the time, using the words was helpful. Jay had the New Magic ability to control others, as well as objects. This was only a small portion of her powers, as she also had the Old Magic abilities of healing and bending reality. And still, new abilities were showing up all the time. New Magic didn't take much energy to use, and it didn't draw from another source, unlike Old Magic. The use of Old Magic was found in the purest of Aris Magician kind, while mixed blood Aris Magicians, or Hybrids, used New Magic. Old Magic pulled magic from anything with a soul. Jay's use of Old Magic was unpredictable, and whenever she used it, a price had to be paid. A piece of the object or person's soul the magic was drawn from was lost. If the source did not have a soul, then the user would pay the price. Jay tried not to use it because of that reason.

Jay and Dylan walked in silence down the hall until they reached the door. A plaque labeled *X-File* in gold lettering hung on the center of the door. Jay drove a bobby pin through the keyhole, picking the lock. With a soft click, the door swung open. A cold draft encompassed their bodies as they walked in. The room was small, bordered with stacks of black cabinets, with seven rows of computers at its center. There wasn't much to look at.

Dylan walked in, leading the way. He cut through the nearest row of computers to the other side of the room. "Spread out, the safe should be—"

Jay whistled, signaling him over. She was standing in the closest corner off to the right of the room, her arm resting on a small black safe jutting out of the wall. She spun the dial on the front of the safe's door.

7-3-8-4.

The safe opened with a soft beep, pouring out a thick cloud of gas. Jay held her breath against the foul stench. She exhaled as the smoke cleared the air, revealing a single vial filled with clear green liquid sitting alone inside the safe. The vial was a small beacon of light in the room full of darkness. Dylan came up beside her, peering at the vial. He appeared to be just as mesmerized as she was.

"It's so . . . tiny." Jay stared at it, confused.

Dylan reached for it, shoving it into his pocket. "Let's go."

Jay closed the safe door, backing up slowly. She followed him out, still thinking about the possibilities the cure held. The information about the cure's properties was strictly classified, but Jay liked to hope that it was meant for people like her. Maybe the students at the Institute would finally have a choice as to whether they wanted to live in secret, always fearful of being exposed. Jay loved magic, but the isolation that often came with it was sometimes too much to bear.

They took a different route, avoiding the room where they had left the doctor and dead guards. The path they took brought them to a set of stairs that lead to the rooftop. Dylan kicked open the door. A gust of wind blew, fanning Jay's curly, silver-white hair behind her. Up ahead, a ladder rolled down from an airborne helicopter. Following Dylan, she shielded her eyes from the glare of the rising sun.

Something the doctor had said had been gnawing at the back of her mind as soon as it had left his mouth. She had to shout to be heard over the helicopter's choppers. "Hey, were you considering it?"

"What?" Dylan shouted back.

They reached the ladder. "Letting the doctor test me! Figuring out the truth behind my condition." Although the doctor had been conducting experiments on how to rid Aris Magicians of their powers, perhaps he could have been able to discover more about Jay's past through her own gifts. Dylan didn't respond, taking hold of the rail and climbing up toward the helicopter. For as long as she could remember, they both had just accepted her powers without asking why she had them or where they came from. This could have been their chance to understand her abilities. "Dylan!"

"Just keep climbing."

A completely tattooed arm of pure muscle reached out from the cabin of the helicopter. The sleeves of tattoos snaked up the man's brown arms, ending under the gray, tightly fitted shirt he wore. As far as first impressions went, no one would ever assume that this gruff man, well in his forties, was a professor. Gray eyes looked down at them both. The man, Riley Burgeons, effortlessly hauled the two students up.

Dylan climbed the rest of the way in, and Riley clamped a calloused hand on the back of his neck. "Hah! Glad you're back, Dylan, Jay!" He slammed the cabin door shut, then ran a huge hand over his bald head, a wide grin on his face. He twirled his fingers in a circular motion over his head. "Let's get this baby on the road, Cap!"

The captain, in a black headset, flipped a couple of switches. Jay took her seat next to the window. The helicopter lifted higher into the air, leaving the building behind.

"Still can't believe y'all managed to pull that one off." Riley rubbed the back of his neck. "No back-up, huh?"

Dylan pulled out a handkerchief and began cleaning the blade of his dagger. "Professor Burgeons, come on," Dylan groaned.

Jay rolled her eyes. *When have they ever needed backup?*

Riley laughed, "Burgeons? What's gotten into you? Want me to add homework to this assignment?" Riley was one of the few professors at the school who allowed the students to call him by his first name, claiming his last name reminded him too much of his late father.

"I thought this assignment was the homework," Jay scoffed.

Riley stood at least two heads taller than the average man. He was the muscle of the group, with dark brown skin and piercing gray eyes. Just above his left eye was a huge scar that cut through the tail of his eyebrow. He also had a long scar on his right arm that he had covered up with numerous tattoos. He was a prominent figure at the academy, as it was he who convinced the Headmaster that the Institute wasn't just a school—it was also a home, and at the very least, students should be prepared to defend it and themselves if that day ever came.

"This it?" Riley held the small vial, examining it. "Thought there'd be more."

"Yeah, so did we." Dylan said.

Riley gave it one last look before digging out a small, black, rectangular case from the duffel bag at his feet. "Good work," he bellowed, ruffling Dylan's dark hair. Dylan responded with a cross look, dodging Riley's hand for a second time.

Jay watched the building grow smaller and smaller as they headed back in the direction of the Willamette Forest. The doctor had been hiding out near an abandoned power plant located in Bull Run, a ghost town if there ever was one. The building was a heap of barely standing concrete with many blacked-out windows, but the inside had been renovated for the doctor to conduct his research in. Outside the building was a river lined by rock cliffs. The water slapped against the base of the building. Trees surrounded the complex for miles. Jay hugged her knees to her chest, finally able to feel a sense of relief as they left it all behind.

Jay could feel Dylan watching her from the seat facing hers. She was half-listening to Riley ramble on about his days in the war. Jay calmly met his eyes and smiled—something that had grown to be a privilege to those who saw it. Dylan's cheeks turned red, and he quickly frowned, averting his gaze.

Today had put an enormous toll on them both. Jay's smile disappeared as she continued to watch him. He sighed, sinking into his chair, rested his chin on a hand propped on his knee, and stared at the floating clouds. *Tomorrow wouldn't be any better, either,* Jay thought. After all, tomorrow would be the fifth anniversary of Dylan's parents' deaths. She turned away from Dylan and stared out the window as well, her gaze wandering across the clouds they flew past.

"Great, one battle down, another to go." Jay uttered.

"What was that, kid?" Riley shouted.

Jay stared at Dylan quizzically.

Dylan avoided meeting her gaze. "Nothing."

It wasn't long before Jay could see the pointed roof of the Institute peeking from behind the forest trees. *Home*, she thought, knowing that she was using the term loosely. They were coming up over the mountains bordering the forest where the school was hidden. A grand waterfall fell between two mountain peaks into a small pool. Chunks of ice floated in the water at the base of the waterfall; it still wasn't cold enough yet for all the water to freeze.

"Aye, swing the chopper about a mile from the Institute!" Riley instructed the captain.

Jay looked up at him, confused. "How come?"

"Due to certain circumstances surrounding this mission, we're going to land a bit away. You see," Riley sounded almost embarrassed. "The Headmaster doesn't know about this one, nor should he until I'm ready to tell him. But something had to be done."

Dylan nodded in agreement, and so did Jay. It had bothered them when the Headmaster had refused to make a statement about his student after the murder, making it even easier for the police to cover it up.

"What about the cure?" Jay asked.

"Don't worry about it, I have a friend in Salem who will take care of it. She owes me a favor," Riley explained.

The helicopter sat down in a small clearing in the forest not too far from the Institute's grounds. The three of them disembarked the helicopter and watched as it flew off.

The trek back through the forest wasn't a hard one, only about a fifteen-minute walk from the Institute's front gates. Jay and Dylan had done it numerous times during their free time between classes. Jay felt a sense of familiarity as she walked beside Dylan and Riley.

"This brings back memories, doesn't it?" Riley said as if reading her mind. He smiled down at the two. The sun started to break through the trees, casting a bright glow around Riley's thick frame.

Jay tried to hide her sad smile as she looked away. It wasn't that long ago that Riley, Dylan, and she had walked this same path when he first brought them to the Institute, babbling on about Aris Magica, Hybrids, and magic. He had been the one to find them five years ago and had convinced the Headmaster to give them refuge. Before that, Dylan and Jay had been dividing their time between the streets of Eugene and the graveyard. After Dylan's parents' funeral, nobody had any interest in taking them in, and the last thing they wanted was to be separated by child services, so they ran and became orphans. Not long after, Riley had found them.

Much of Aris Magica could be found in similar places like the Institute. Aris Magica took root in desolate, forgotten places that humans often overlooked, so that Aris Magica could stay hidden from the human world. The Headmaster of the Institute had shrouded the building in a protective pocket dimension. A pocket dimension made it possible for two places to overlap in the same time frame, without disturbing the other. Although the humans that did stumble across the Institute's grounds could explore and wander, only an Aris Magician would be able to see and enter the pocket dimension. Aris Magica was all around the human world, as both worlds were entwined on the same red string of fate.

The trio walked up the final hill before coming to the tall gates. Jay recalled the first time they had seen these gates. When they first arrived, both she and Dylan couldn't see anything, including the gates. To them it was just a barely standing, dangerous structure taking up space in another empty clearing in the forest. Riley had told them to look again and really believe that magic could exist, and that was when they began to see the place that they would soon come to call home. Usually, an Aris Magician would easily have been able to see the pocket dimension and therefore the Institute, but Jay and Dylan had grown so distrusting to everyone and everything, they shrouded the truth from their eyes, even as it was staring right back at them. Riley had blamed it on them being disconnected from Aris Magica for as long as they had.

Even from afar, she could feel the strong hold the Institute had over her. Leading up the path was a stone fountain that sat in the center of the Institute's front lawn. The Victorian era building had stone and concrete walls with vines creeping up the sides, as if the vines were the ones holding the building up. The entryway was flanked by two grand pillars accompanied by a set of stairs that led to the front door. Along the pillars and walls were cracks that ran deep across the building's exterior. Along the fourth floor of the Institute was a block of marble attached to the front that read: *The Institute for Aris Magicians and the Gifted.* Below hung two banners bearing the Aris Magica emblem, an S with a diagonal slash through it. An endless and constant fog seemed to rise from the ground near the edge of the building's grounds. Before the Institute had become a school, it had been the Headmaster's home. Jay had recalled reading how the Headmaster had grown up in an orphanage that had been standing since the Victorian era, and once he became old enough, he bought it and transformed it into a school for the gifted. To the humans who would occasionally stumble upon it, the Institute would appear as an abandoned, run down, barely standing building that they would easily forget about. Later, Jay and Dylan discovered, in addition to the pocket dimension, the Headmaster had also laid enchantments around the grounds of the Institute: forgetting curses that only affected humans. It was another one of the Headmaster's tricks for rooting out Aris Magicians.

While the outside looked like any old mansion forgotten by history, the inside was a different story. On the exterior, the mansion seemed to be only four stories tall, but there were more rooms and floors than the naked eye could see. Jay had been here for five years and had yet to explore them all. She spent most of her time on the fifth floor, where the living corridors were, and on the 124th floor, where most of her classes were held when school was in session.

She often wondered how many rooms the mansion held; sometimes the staircases would appear to go on forever. Jay had once read somewhere about the Headmaster having the ability to create pockets within dimensions. These pockets provided sanctuary in dangerous times from the outside world. Many Aris Magicians hid in pocket dimensions today, where they could freely practice magic without judgment from humans. Most humans had no idea Aris Magica existed, and if they did, had kept the secret to themselves. Aris Magicians were too afraid to reveal themselves to the entirety of the human race given the dark history between the two worlds. At first, humans might be accepting of magic, but that acceptance could easily root into fear and the humans could once again turn on Aris Magicians. The Institute was as much a sanctuary as it was a school. Most of the students here had the same story: they were tossed aside and ostracized by the world until they were found and protected by the Headmaster. The school was home to almost every Aris Magician breed there was: Hybrids, Purist, Witches, Wizards, and Fairies. The only ones not allowed were the Demon and Faery races, due to their lineage and allegiance after the first Aris Magica War aligned them with darkness.

In their classes, students learned the basics about how to coexist with society, as well as how to control the growing powers or special abilities they wielded. Upon graduation, the students would be integrated into society. Some chose to live in secret among humans, while others went deeper into Aris Magica and found purpose there. The Institute made sure every student felt welcomed and looked after. It was as close to home as it got for Jay and people like her.

They arrived at the Institute around seven in the morning, welcomed by the loud silence of winter. Riley took the case that contained the cure from Dylan and headed inside. Dylan held open the front door, allowing Jay to pass through first. Everything was dark, with the exception of the dimly lit staircase not too far in front of her.

"Thanks," Jay mumbled.

Dylan and Jay walked in silence as they ascended the staircase. Jay slid her hand against the concrete wall as a guide. When they reached the top, she opened the door, stepping into the dimly lit hall. Warm energy engulfed her, relaxing her nerves.

The Institute was quiet, as most of the students had returned home to their respective families for the holidays. The Headmaster had decided Thanksgiving wasn't a holiday meant to be celebrated by their kind, much to the disagreement of the Hybrids and their non-magical parents. Other students didn't mind. Instead of having that week off, they had classes, and in return, they would be free from classes until the start of the New Year.

Usually, at this time of day, the halls were alive with the chatter of morning classes. But the hallway was empty now, and the wooden doors trailing along each wall were closed and locked. Somehow, it felt as if the mansion itself was asleep.

"Dylan," Jay whispered as they turned down another similar hallway. Hesitantly, she continued. "About earlier . . ."

Dylan came to an abrupt stop. The hallway split into three passageways. "Not right now," he stated.

Hint: "not right now" is equivalent to "not ever," Jay reminded herself, having known Dylan long enough to be able to read between the lines. Jay noticed a muscle in Dylan's jaw tightened, but he never responded. She frowned, staring ahead down the hall to the main room leading to the different levels of the mansion. "Fine," she sighed, taking the hall on the right, and leaving Dylan behind in his silence.

Chapter Two

It was snowing, and ice stuck to the panes of glass, creating a beautiful, thin layer of frozen crystals. Jay watched from the library window as Dylan crossed the icy lawn and mounted his motorcycle on the curb. Today was the day she dreaded the most. It was the anniversary of his parents' deaths, and every year, Jay couldn't bring herself to go with him to the cemetery. Part of the truth was that she blamed herself for their deaths and couldn't face the reality of it. Dylan never understood her feelings of shame, and it bothered her pretending everything was okay.

The library was an enormous haven for books. Countless rows of literature arranged on shelves stretched from one end of the room to the other. A glass dome composed of a beautiful mosaic of historic Aris Magica battles decorated the high ceiling. One half of the mosaic depicted Wizards and creatures of light energy fighting against Demons, Faeries, Witches, and other mystical creatures of darkness. At the center of these battles was a sphere of great light. This was the first war that separated Aris Magica into light and darkness. There had once been a time when all creatures in Aris Magica coexisted peacefully. Although after the battle, Witches became creatures of light, while Demons and Faeries remained evil beings. Soon after came the second war that would forever change Aris Magica. The other half of the mural demonstrated the battle between humans and Aris Magica. The war divided the world and made it what it was today. Most humans, unless directly affected by an Aris Magician in the family, forgot that the world existed. Aris Magicians, so damaged by the humans' betrayal, went into hiding.

The tall wooden doors across the room creaked open. Jay ignored it, sinking deeper into the pages of her book. The doors suddenly slammed shut, their sound echoing off the high glass ceiling.

Seven larger windows lined the back wall of the library, each with a boxed window seat stacked with pillows or books. There was said to be over four million books housed within the library walls. Only one person had read them all: the Headmaster. He was head and founder of the school. He had opened his home six decades ago, transforming these walls into the Institute for Aris Magicians and the Gifted. There wasn't really a difference between the two groups. The Pure Aris Magicians were students who hailed from a direct line of people connected to the Old Magic, whereas the Gifted were Hybrids who had unnatural abilities but did not descend directly from Aris Magica. Research had shown that the Hybrid gene was to answer for this, when either two non-magical parents, or one non-magical and one Pure bred, produced something of magic.

"Mind if I join you?"

Jay glanced up at the sound of an unfamiliar voice. A tall, lanky guy stood before her. His black hair hung straight, barely brushing his shoulders and he wore a dark suit that complemented his midnight eyes. The way he stood held a subtle, quiet confidence about him. With Christmas approaching, many of the students had left, and this was the first fresh face she had seen all week. She assumed he wasn't in her year, as she knew everyone who was, and his face was one she didn't recognize.

Jay smiled. She took a quick glance around the room, noticing the other empty spots near the windows.

"Ah, I just really enjoy the view this window has to offer. It's the spot I always come to in the library, but if I'm bothering you, I can go . . ." the boy said.

She stared at him a while longer, skeptical. She'd never seen him in the library before. They looked around the same age, too. Although it was a big school, she couldn't have missed him. Generally, the same people were always in the library. Jay shrugged. "I don't mind."

His mouth twitched into a smile. He crossed the room, disappearing within the bookshelves. Moments later, he resurfaced, hugging a thick red book to his chest. He sat down on the opposite side of the window seat, resting his back against the pillow.

Jay returned to her book, ignoring him.

> *The Way of Life: A never-ending ballad of verses lay before me. It had once again found a way into my soul. Love. I know one day will become our last. A time when I will have to say goodbye to this sweet sensation. The love that heals will one day fall into a forgotten abyss, taking me with it. For I, a person cursed with darkness, will not be worthy enough to be claimed by the power of love. I am an outcast who will only bring destruction to those I love. For me to live this way of life, the cursed ones must believe they will never be loved. Our paths have been set for us and follow them we shall. My only prayer is that those will understand the full truth I hold with these lost emotions. To truly live and love, this is something I must do. I must—*

Jay broke away from the book. The words on the pages had a firm hand, gripping her heart to the point where it was hard to continue reading. Slowly, her eyes found the boy's. His eyes reflected a deep concern for her. "What?" Jay lowered the book so her whole face could be seen.

"Were you . . . never mind." He shook his head, diving back into his own reading.

She continued to stare at him even though he avoided her gaze. "Was I what?" she pressed on, curious. She couldn't explain or understand his concern.

He shook his head again, not bothering to look up this time. "Trust me, it's nothing."

Jay rolled her eyes, letting out a heavy sigh. *In my experience, "it's nothing" usually means "it's something."* Jay smiled to herself, recalling a time when Dylan often used to say that to her.

She put her book aside, bringing her knees to her chest. "How can I trust you if I don't even know your name?" Jay asked. The boy ignored her again, flipping a page in response. "Come on, at least tell me your name."

He deliberated for a moment before finally meeting Jay's gaze. "You won't curse me with it?"

Jay scoffed. Clearly he had heard the rumors about her. Jay knew she was sort of an outcast, and people usually preferred Dylan's company over hers. Jay had a knack for not being able to always control her powers, especially whenever new ones would show up unexpectedly. The students in her year had grown fond of spouting rumors about her to scare the younger students about a magic they didn't understand. They even gave her the nickname "Witch," known for hexes. One year, she had accidentally cursed a girl named Ami. For a whole month, Ami couldn't walk properly.

Jay laughed. She picked up the nearest pillow and tossed it at him. He shielded his face with the book in his hands. "I"m not that kind of Witch!" Jay exclaimed, making the boy laughed. "I'm not even sure what I am. Are you still scared of me?" Jay asked.

"Taybeith."

"What?" Jay leaned forward.

"Taybeith. My name." He brushed back his hair, revealing a cuff on his left ear.

"Oh," Jay began slowly, "I'm—"

"I know who you are," Taybeith interrupted. He returned to his book.

Jay scoffed. "Okay." She bit her lower lip. "Are they that bad?"

"What?" Taybeith asked.

"You know what." When he didn't respond, she rolled her eyes, answering for him. "The rumors about my reputation."

Jay could see Taybeith struggling to ignore the presence of her power. Still, he refused to answer her question.

"Taybeith!" Jay snapped. She was tired of being ignored. She slid closer to him, pushing down his book. It fell into his lap.

"What?" Taybeith jumped, startled by her closeness.

Jay was inches away from his face. She could hear his heart picking up speed and his breathing shortening. Silver-white hair framed her brown face and fell to her waist. Jay watched as his eyes went through a range of emotions. At first, he seemed confused, but his expression quickly turned to a desirable, longing look. She noticed his eyes wander to her hair. Jay smirked; she could only imagine what he was thinking. Taybeith gulped. Jay parted her lips ever so slightly. She brought her shoulders in closer to her body leaning closer to him. Taybeith opened his mouth as if he wanted to say something.

Jay smirked. The charm magic was working; he was relaxing. It was a skill Jay had acquired and been able to summon without the use of a harnessing word. She was quite good at it. A little more and Taybeith would spill any secret she wanted. She suppressed her smile. She gazed back at him with blue eyes that were slowly changing.

"Red eyes?" Taybeith said in a daze.

"Never mind that. Why are you avoiding me?" Jay's words were laced with a powerful enchantment, giving her voice a slight vibrato. She needed answers to her curiosities about him. Normally, Jay couldn't care less if another student noticed her or not, but no one usually denied her answers to her questions out of fear she would use her powers against them. The fact that Taybeith did interested Jay. She had never seen this boy before, and out of all the empty seats in the library, he just so happened to choose the one she was sitting in. It didn't make sense. She was wary of him, though she wasn't exactly sure why. It was as if something inside her had called upon her magic as a warning.

"It's nothing." He was trying to fight against the spell, but his eyes couldn't break away from hers.

"Don't lie. You're evasive." Jay tugged a little harder, forcing him to spill everything.

"I know about your immortality." The word caught her off guard. She hadn't expected this to be the reason he was so distant yet curious about her. "I can help you discover more about yourself, if you want."

"How? Why?" Jay asked breathlessly. She lost control over her charm at his proposal.

Taybeith took a deep breath as the charm faded away. He watched as her eyes turned back to normal. "My gift. I'm a Tekhne. Anything and everything internet-wise, I'm connected to."

Jay had heard of them before but had yet to meet one. Tekhnes fell under the Pure breed class of Wizards. Each of the eight breeds of Magicians had many subclasses they were broken into. Whereas knowledge magic users usually fell under the Wizard breed, users who used any form of element fell under Witches. Healers were generally Fairies, while Purists dealt with breeds with more unconventional forms of magic. Sometimes Jay wondered why Tekhnes were still allowed to use their powers as freely as they wanted. Demons and Faeries had been banned by law against using their powers, but a Tekhne could be just as dangerous.

Jay narrowed her eyes, backing away from him. "Isn't that a bit invasive? Plus, I've done a pretty good job keeping myself off the internet, so how do you think you can find out about my past?" she said defensively. "And why do you even want to help me? You don't know me."

"I'm *that* good. No one's ever completely safe from the internet. And it's not invasive if it's a gift I can't control," Taybeith stated. "Plus, I've been wanting to talk to you for a while. I've been watching you from afar . . . sort of. I just want to help you not be misunderstood. I-I know how it feels . . ." His voice trailed off.

"You mean stalking me?" Jay asked, only half joking, but his shyness made her smile.

All at once, her eyes widened, terrified. The thought of finding out more about her past scared her, but it was also intriguing. She could finally know more about where her powers came from. Both of her parents, as far as Jay knew, were human. Jay recalled how much her parents had kept to themselves, making it difficult to find anything about them. The only friends her parents had were Dylan's parents. She didn't even know who her grandparents were. After Dylan's parents died, Jay and Dylan were left alone. Humans had abandoned them both, while magic had taken them in. But since being at the Institute, Jay felt as if she knew less about herself than she did before. "I distrust humans, but I think I distrust my magic even more."

"That's because you don't know magic or yourself," Taybeith said softly. "Let me help you."

Jay's mind wandered back to a few years ago when she and Dylan first entered the Institute. She had been eleven years old at the time, Dylan twelve. Jay remembered being scared of sleeping with a group of strangers who all had different abilities. She had roamed the dark, empty hallways that night until she had found Dylan. That night, they had made a promise never to dig into her past. Was she ready to break that promise now?

Jay looked out the window. She stared past the Institute grounds and above the trees to the mountains in the distance. They were beautiful; their snowcapped tops stood out against the endless green of trees. She was old enough to take charge of her own life; she didn't need Dylan's permission for everything. Jay rubbed her temples, thinking to herself, *This isn't the best idea, but what other option do I have?* She pushed back her hair, holding it against her head out of habit when things stressed or worried her.

"What?" Jay asked, noticing Taybeith staring at her.

"Your eyes," Taybeith spoke softly. She quickly looked away, irritated. Taybeith reached for Jay. "No," he said as he took two fingers, lifting her chin. "They're beautiful."

She met his gaze, surprised. No one had ever told her that before, not even Dylan. The hand over her heart squeezed. She pulled away from his touch, but Taybeith seemed unfazed. Jay felt an odd connection to him, beckoning her closer.

Weird. Jay rubbed her left temple again. "How does it work?"

Chapter Three

Dylan laid the bouquet of lilies on the single-stoned graves. His parents had been buried together in the city's graveyard in the farthest corner of the grounds, not too far from the forest that surrounded the city. His parents' gravestone had been covered in snow when he arrived, and the ground around it had been neglected.

Dylan stared at the words on the worn-down plaque:

Russell and Terrie McCoy
Beloved Husband and Wife, Parents, and Friends
September 12th, 1966-April 2nd, 2007
August 30th, 1968-April 2nd, 2007

Dylan tried to recall the good times he had spent with his parents before they died, but his memories always came back to the moment he saw them killed. His fists balled at his side.

"I made promises. Promises I intend to keep. I won't let anything happen to her or anyone else I care for." A gentle, cold breeze ruffled his scarf in the wind. "I'm sorry I wasn't stronger back then. Maybe . . ." He choked on his words. He took a slow deep breath, lifting his head to the sky. "Maybe things would be different today."

He rubbed his hands together. He had overstayed his visit; he needed to return to school before it got too late. Dylan gave one last, longing look at the grave before taking the winding path down the hill. He closed the frosted metal gate, leaving his parents' grave behind.

Dylan mounted his motorcycle and drove back on the backroad. His first instinct was to go back to the Institute—he needed to talk to Riley about what he and Jay had recovered on their last mission. He still didn't understand why Riley had withheld information from them about the cure's properties. It wasn't like him, and neither was the mission. Usually, every mission had a clear goal on how using their powers for good could still be accomplished, even when coexisting with the other world. This time, it didn't feel that way. Dylan glanced at the sky, noticing how clear it had become after the snow fell. *When was the last time I had a chance to relax?* His selfish desires won the best of him. Dylan couldn't remember the last time he had that chance.

The motorcycle hummed softly as it made its way along the curved road. It felt nice to finally have some time to himself. It gave him a chance to breathe without the feeling of watchful eyes. Sometimes, he felt as if he were suffocating behind the Institute's walls. He tightened his grip on the handles. Back at the lab, he had seen Jay was nearing an endpoint. Her powers were going to outgrow her. There was no stopping that, not anymore. She could potentially become a wild card and a threat to all of mankind if he didn't find a solution.

Dylan turned left onto a road surrounded by a thick canopy of trees. The sun barely touched the ground, bouncing off the leaves. It was as if time had stopped in an endless fall cycle here. It was a sore thumb in an icy place. Dylan tilted his helmet down to cover more of his face from the cold wind that burned his skin.

The road itself was as never-ending as the cycle the trees around him were trapped in. A howling breeze became present the deeper he drove into the tunnel of trees. Soft, enchanting voices rode along the breeze. Dylan could clearly hear the sweet melody the wind whispered.

He slowed his speed until he came to a stop. "Witchcraft," Dylan whispered, recognizing the ancient tongue. Dark shadows rose from the trees, looming over him and blocking every part of the sun. Dylan removed his dagger from the holster at his hip, holding it firmly against the bike's handle. He started his bike back up again, slowly continuing down the road.

A strange figure dressed in a long, hooded cloak suddenly appeared in the center of the road up ahead. The alluring melody seemed to be coming from it. Dylan sensed the chills of dark magic.

His motorcycle came to a stop a few yards away from the stranger. He carefully climbed off, palming the dagger in his right hand behind him. "You okay?"

The forest became deadly silent. Dylan tensed, taking a hesitant step back. "Who are you?" The stranger cocked their head in his direction and, in a graceful manner, began walking toward him.

Dylan took up a guarding stance with his knife out in front of him in case he had to attack. The melody began again, this time carrying a sorrowful tune. The sound paralyzed him as the stranger continued to approach. A pale hand revealed itself from under the cloak, reaching out to him. Dylan gritted his teeth, his body shaking in an attempt to break the curse upon him. The hood fell back, black hair fanning out around a pale face. Dylan's eyes widened, not able to take in the details of the stranger's face before his focus was on the strands of hair racing toward him. The hair wrapped around his body, lacing him in seething pain. It felt like needles rather than hair digging into his skin. Blood soaked through his jacket and down his shirt.

The strands of hair parted, revealing soulless green eyes. Dylan struggled to keep his eyes open, screaming in pain. The hooded figure approached him and spoke, "I have a message."

Chapter Four

Taybeith passed Jay a book titled *Immortality*. She smiled, grazing her hands over the bold colors, tracing the *I*. She sat the book in her lap and picked up the sandwich sitting beside her. Before starting their research, they had taken a break to grab lunch. The Grand Hall had food set aside for the students who stayed behind. Usually Jay would take her lunch back to her room and eat alone if Dylan wasn't with her, but she was eager to get started on researching about her past. She handed the second sandwich to Taybeith. He'd stayed behind looking for the book that now sat in her lap.

Taybeith took a seat beside her. He crossed his legs, set the sandwich aside, and leaned back on his hands. "I thought this would be the best place to start."

"I thought you were a Tekhne; didn't think starting with books would be your style," Jay snorted and peered up at Taybeith to find him carefully watching her. "How come . . ." She hesitated, knowing there was a chance that she was barking up the wrong tree. Most of the students at the Institute had the same sad stories she and Dylan carried. Taybeith took the book from her and began to roll it over in his hands before proceeding to open it. "How come you didn't go home like the rest of the students?"

A dark shadow fell across Taybeith's face as he said, "This *is* my home."

The air between them sparked with unsettling energy. Jay cleared her throat. "Yeah, same here." She tried to think of something to say to change the subject but couldn't come up with anything. It wasn't odd for her to see another student during break. There were still a couple of them left, despite the majority that had returned home, still frolicking in the Grand Hall with their endless parties. And on occasion, some would also be found hiding in the library, just as she was.

"How come we've never talked before now, huh? You seem cool enough. I don't even think I've seen you in any of my classes or just around," Jay said. She cursed herself for sounding like she was trying to pry more, but she couldn't help herself.

Taybeith avoided her gaze, his shy demeanor returning. He laughed awkwardly, closing the book. He pushed his head back and looked off toward the shelves of the library. "Why so many questions? It's like you don't trust me. I told you before, I just want to help, but I can leave if it makes you uncomfortable. I have that effect on people—"

"No!" Jay shouted, cutting him off. "It's just . . ." *Something about you that seems . . . different.* "I get nervous around *new* people, and tend to ask way too many invasive questions." Jay bit her lip. This time, she was the one to turn away.

Jay felt a pillow smack the side of her face. She gasped, then laughed, seeing Taybeith shyly grin. He'd taken the pillow he'd been resting on and used it against her. "For a minute there, I thought you were the one with the Tekhne abilities," he said.

Jay chuckled. She gestured to the book. "Back to business?"

Taybeith nodded and gave a small smile. He opened the book, but instead of reading its contents, he flipped to the very last page. "Here." He pointed to a picture on the page and tilted the book downward so that Jay could see more clearly.

She was staring at the *About Me* page featuring a picture of the author. The man looked to be well into his sixties. Even in the black-and-white photograph, she could see how startling white his hair was. His eyes were a dark color, though. He had a jolly smile and his arms were crossed high over his chest, as if the person behind the camera was the cause of his laughter. Next to the picture, in fine print, was a name: Morticai Alfonzo.

"We start here," Taybeith said.

"With a name?" Jay asked skeptically. She couldn't see how his name would help anything. As far as she could tell, Morticai was normal. "He only has white hair because he's old."

Taybeith gave her just as skeptical of a look as she was giving him. "You and I both know that there's no way to tell the difference between an Aris Magician and a normal human being just from a picture. Honestly, it's like you didn't listen to any of your teachers during your fifth year."

Jay scrunched her nose. "Everybody knows you don't have to start listening to your professors' lectures until the eighth year here, when you graduate."

"Oh, is that why you failed Intro to Aris Magica versus Realism your fifth year and have to take it again?" Taybeith teased.

"How did you—"

"I was in your class. I sat in the very back by the window. You just never noticed," he said, almost proudly.

Jay snorted, flabbergasted.

"Maybe we'll find something here in the dedication page." Taybeith began flipping the pages of the book to the very front.

"Have you even read the book to be sure this isn't a waste of time?"

"If there's anything helpful in the dedication page, maybe it'll hint at him knowing a little about our world." Taybeith passed her the book. "I know the rumor."

"What?" Jay asked, even though she knew what he was about to say. Because of her white hair and blue eyes, everyone around school, even the professors, assumed she was an Immortal or would eventually be. Immortals didn't age once they reached their full immortality. When and how that would happen was what everyone was waiting anxiously to know. If she were to be an Immortal before undergoing the transformation, the symbol of eternity should appear across her stomach. The symbol resembled that of the school emblem, an *S* with a diagonal slash through it.

"I don't think it's true, your being an Immortal. Your powers don't match up," Taybeith said.

"Yeah, well, we won't know till it happens," Jay mumbled. If she was an Immortal, that would just set her even further apart from the other Aris Magicians at the school. Immortals were rare, and their purpose taxing. They oversaw guiding dead souls back to their respective places: either heaven or hell, if that is what the Aris Magician believed in, or to the abyss where souls who hadn't decided on a religion go for eternity.

"It just doesn't add up," Taybeith whispered. "Once we find more about your past, maybe we'll gain some clarity."

Jay rolled her eyes and passed the book back to Taybeith. He was right, her powers didn't add up to being an Immortal. Although Immortals, whether Pure Aris Magicians or Hybrids, could use the Old Magic, they always had something to channel it through, like a weapon of sorts. Jay could heal herself, but she had to use Old Magic to do it, it didn't automatically happen.

As Taybeith began reading aloud from the page, Jay's attention fell toward the window. Snow still coated the driveway in a thick, white blanket. As Jay squinted out the window, she barely recognized Dylan limping up the path, dots of blood staining the snow in a trail behind him. His motorcycle was turned on its side and thrown against the curb. He clutched his side, the color drained from his face. Jay glanced at Taybeith, hardly listening to what he was saying, and returned to the window in time to see Dylan collapsed outside near the steps.

She pressed a hand on the glass of the window. He wasn't moving.

"Oh, here it says that he wants to 'especially thank the other world,'" Taybeith chuckled. "Well, that was obvious enough. Oh, never mind, he meant fictionally, but—"

"Dylan!" Jay screamed.

Jay slid to a stop, barely avoiding a collision with Riley. Taybeith nearly bumped into Riley as well in his attempt to keep up with Jay. Riley lifted his hand, which was holding a cup of coffee, spilling a few drops.

"Dammit, Jay!" Riley cursed as she pushed past him, causing more of the drink to spill.

Jay moved with incredible speed rounding the corner. "Dylan . . . he . . . he just collapsed outside," she shouted as she ran past.

Taybeith heaved in a breath. "Blood . . . lots of blood!"

The world seemed to momentarily stop. "Dammit, kid." Riley shoved the mug into Taybeith's hands and took off after Jay.

Jay burst through the front door and was greeted by a gust of wind that nearly knocked her back. She crossed her arms in front of her body and continued. Ice crunched under her socks, sending cold shivers throughout her body. "Dylan!"

Dylan propped his elbow on the next step, struggling to pull himself up. "Jay, get inside," he wheezed.

She fell to her knees before him and grabbed his arm, draping it over her shoulders. She rose to her feet, but the weight was too much, and they buckled. Dylan tried to push her away. Jay seized hold of the next step, dragging his body behind her to a higher level.

Jay looked down at Dylan and saw blood gushing from his stomach. She tried to call upon her magic, but nothing happened. She was too beside herself to focus.

Riley came rushing down the steps, two at a time. "Riley! Help me!" Jay screamed. Riley swung Dylan's other arm around his neck.

"Taybeith, go get the stretcher from the infirmary and tell Faith we're on the way," Riley barked as they reached the final landing.

Dylan leaned most of his weight on Riley as Jay pulled open the Institute's door. Seconds passed before Taybeith returned, pushing a lifted mattress covered in white sheets in their direction. Riley hauled Dylan up, carefully laying him down on the spread. Dylan moaned, his head falling to the side, his face contorted in pain

"Jay!" Riley shouted at her as she closed the main doors. "Bind him. Taybeith, get the hell out of the way!"

Jay jogged to the stretcher and cautiously climbed on. Riley commenced pushing the bed once Taybeith passed. Jay ripped open Dylan's jacket, peeling it from his skin. She lifted his shirt, exposing his chest. A fresh gash crossed from one end to the other, his swollen skin bordered by a dark purple. Her hands hovered over the wound.

"Calm down, calm down, calm down," she begged herself, repeating the mantra over and over. Jay took two deep breaths, and then another. She felt her eyes turning red. She placed her hand over Riley's, who was pushing the stretcher, and then let her other hover over Dylan's body. She opened her mouth to speak the words that would allow her to channel just enough healing magic to stop the bleeding, but Dylan grabbed her by the wrist.

"Don't," he struggled to say.

Jay's eyes slowly returned to normal as tears filled them, causing her to lose focus. She knew why Dylan had stopped her. For her to heal him, she had to take from another soul using the Old Magic. The closest thing was Riley. Usually she would take from a plant, but never a human. Dylan had stopped her from making Riley pay the price. She couldn't heal him, not that way.

Jay felt her heart drop to her stomach. She couldn't lose him. She leaned her head down closer to his. "Riley, hurry!" Jay cried.

With shaky hands, Jay removed the headband she was wearing to keep her hair from her face. Jay dabbed the tip of the headband in the flesh wound, clearing away some of the blood. Dylan winced. She was only making it worse.

"What happened?" Jay trembled as she worked.

Dylan played with the ends of her hair dangling in his face. He set his jaw. "Nothing," he said. His hand fell to his side.

Jay frowned, ignoring the fact that he was lying to her again. The last time he did that was after his parents had died. She peered down, noticing a mark burned into the surface of the inside of his left wrist. It was the bold outline of a trident with its forks facing him. "What's this?"

A woman in a white lab coat interrupted, blocking their path. Her glossy blonde curls were pulled back into a loose bun. Bags hung under her blue eyes from lack of sleep, but widened upon seeing her patient. Even during break, a nurse's job never ended. She was one of the three professors still left at the Institute during the off season, and for good reason too. Aris Magician parties sometimes tended to get a little too rowdy with the lack of instructors present to stop them. Taybeith moved from behind her, stepping out of the way.

"Off." Faith waved at Jay. "Bring him in, hurry!"

Jay gave Dylan one last concerned and confused stare before getting off. Riley rolled him past a couple of occupied beds before coming to a stop at the furthest one.

"Set him there," Faith called from across the room. "Anyone healed and just in here for kicks, out now!" Three students who were still awake, nosily sitting up from their beds, quickly rushed from their spots and from the room, closing the door behind them.

"Brace yourself," Riley alerted Dylan.

Dylan grabbed hold of Riley's forearms, and Riley heaved him from the stretcher, moving him onto the cot. A dreadful noise emerged from Dylan's mouth.

Faith hurried over, carrying a first aid kit. In a matter of seconds, Dylan had been hooked up to an IV and was already receiving the necessary fluids to keep his pain at bay.

The infirmary was a long, wide, and open space. Eight cots aligned the back wall, four on each side, fenced in by a blue curtain. The front wall was entirely dedicated to cabinets filled with medicine. Faith's desk occupied the lone corner near the door, papers and textbooks scattered across its surface.

Faith ushered Riley out of the way and leaned over Dylan to examine the damage. The wound was deep, but whatever had hit him had missed his major vessels. It was almost as if the attacker ensured he would survive, but still suffer. It would take a lot of time, patience, and mostly magic to heal this. Using magic, Faith could counteract the spell that had been used against him and was upsetting the balance inside him. The nurse slapped on a pair of rubber gloves, lightly brushing her fingers over the purple haze that was moving under Dylan's skin. Faith's eyes widened. Jay saw the urgency in her eyes as she stared at Dylan's injury. Jay turned back to the wound and recognized it instantly as dark magic. The boy had been cursed.

Faith was the nurse of the Institute. She was also a Fairy, making her a direct descent of Aris Magicians, like most of the professors, except for Riley and a few others. She used Old Magic to heal the students, but as a descendant of Fairies she had a special talent of being able to draw Old Magic out of the person she was wanting to heal without letting someone else pay the price. The toll from drawing straight from the healing source was small, leaving only a scar where the injury would be healed. It just took a lot longer.

"Son, what happened?" Riley demanded.

Dylan hesitated, his flickering between the people in the room. Riley's eyes narrowed.

Faith opened the kit, pulling out a needle filled with a glowing blue liquid. She had to remove the magic inside him before it spread beyond his wound and to his heart. "Out, everybody, now!" she commanded.

Riley didn't budge.

"What?" Jay protested.

Taybeith understood. "Come on." He gently tugged her elbow and guided her in the direction of the door. Jay glanced over her shoulder at Dylan just as the needle stuck his arm. The door clicked shut.

Jay stood for a moment at the soundproof door; she couldn't hear anything on the other side. She pressed a hand to the door and the other to her heart. She could feel her eyes turning red again as the tingle of magic warmed her body. Her heart pounded against her chest. She could barely breathe. She'd never seen Dylan this badly injured before.

If he dies... Jay instantly shut the thought from her mind, knowing if she let it continue, she'd lose what little chance she had of calming her magic and herself. "Just breathe, Jay," she whispered.

After a while, Jay slowly walked away from the door as Taybeith shoved his hands in his pockets and followed her. She retraced her steps back to the library. When they reached the tall oak doors, Taybeith broke the silence.

"Let's pick this up again tomorrow." He ran a finger through his hair. "A couple of the students are meeting in the Grand Hall. We're just going to hang out, drink hot cocoa, and maybe watch a movie. You should come, distract yourself."

Jay's hand fell from the knob. "Not tonight, okay?"

Taybeith nodded, backing away. "Yeah, it's no big deal. Next time though, alright?" He forced a weak smile.

"Next time," she mumbled, walking in the other direction. She couldn't bring herself to go back to the library knowing the state Dylan was in. She just wanted this day to be over.

She walked by the elevator, bypassing a small group of students, no doubt heading for the Grand Hall. Jay went through the corner doors leading to the steps. She climbed up, using the railing for support.

What was so bad that he didn't want anyone to know about it? Jay thought.

It bugged her that Dylan was keeping secrets from her. She shivered, still feeling the winter weather lingering in her wet socks. She rubbed her arms and reached for the door to the fifth floor. Her heart stopped, skipping a beat, causing her to pause. Jay took a step back down the stairs. Her breathing increased and a sharp sting beat against her rib cage. Her hand fluttered to her chest, while the other clung to the railing. Her chest felt like it was being ripped open. She bit down hard on her bottom lip, tasting blood. Jay gasped for air and sunk to the ground. She felt strangely weakened, and her body shook with violent chills from the sudden attack. She coughed into her hands, blood splattering her palms. The pain suddenly stopped, giving her just enough time to breathe before it started again. An explosive pain seized hold of her abdomen, broadening across her stomach. Jay hissed, feeling her left wrist burn. Tears formed in her eyes, but she would not let them fall. She grabbed the railing, biting down on the collar of her shirt. She suppressed a scream, allowing the pain to run its course. She couldn't focus enough to call forth her magic to do anything to stop it.

The pain continued for what seemed like hours until it suddenly vanished, leaving her mostly numb. Jay's hold on the railing loosened, and she slumped against the wall, out of breath. She lifted the hem of her shirt, revealing the tail end of a gashing scar. Jay stared at it in shock. It resembled the same injury she'd seen on Dylan, except without the trace of purple. Jay closed her eyes, giving herself a chance to get her labored breathing under control. Her wrist still throbbed with pain, causing her to open her eyes as she turned her left hand over. The top of her wrist was glowing with a burn that matched Dylan's.

A nauseating feeling grabbed her. Jay took deep breaths, using the railing as an anchor.

She made it to her room and pushed the door open. Her feet shuffled along the wood floor, searching her way through the darkness. Her knees buckled the weight of her body dragging her down. Jay touched a hand to the bed. Her legs finally gave out, and the darkness took over.

Chapter Five

Jay observed her reflection in the mirror. The dorm she shared with one other girl had been left a mess. Clothes lay scattered on the floor and their beds were left unmade. Magazines and makeup crowded the single desk against the wall below the high window. The only decently clean space was the small bathroom they shared. Jay prepared herself before lifting the bottom of her shirt. The scar stretched from one side of her stomach to the other, dark rings of bruises fencing it in. She brushed her fingers over the injury.

It could be worse, she thought. At least the wound on her stomach was already scarred over with new skin. Still, it hurt like hell.

Jay went to the small window that sat right over the bathtub in the corner. She grabbed the small potted cactus she kept on the windowsill and hovered her hand over it. "*Helbrede*," she commanded. Her hand lit up with a green aura. Jay looked at it, shocked by how easy she was able to call upon her magic. She hovered the light over her wrist where the trident-shaped scar was, but nothing happened. It was hopeless, she couldn't heal it.

Jay shook her head. She recalled learning how sometimes magic only works 99.8 percent of the time against certain types of offensive magic or curses, but Jay's magic had never failed her when it did reveal itself. Jay looked down at the trident scar. The skin around it was warm. Perhaps the scar was the reason for it. Jay scrunched her nose and held her hand out, palm first, toward the mirror in front of her. "*Confractus*," she whispered, testing her theory.

Sure enough, her eyes turned a dark red and her hand lit up with a gray aura as the mirror in front of her fractured. Jay squealed, excited, before covering her mouth and looking around, embarrassed, forgetting that she was alone. She focused again, holding her hand up to the mirror. This time she waved it, trying to fix the broken glass. Instead, it shattered.

Jay startled, shielding her eyes as glass went everywhere. After the glass shards settled, she collected herself. She sighed; she should have seen that one coming. Even though she was able to call her magic faster, she still didn't have control over it without using harnessing words to focus its center. She tried again. "*Opravit*." The glass shards collected, and the mirror mended itself.

Jay couldn't contain the joyful smile that overtook her face. She looked once more at the trident scar on her wrist. Cursed or not, it had appeared for a reason that seemed to be working in her favor.

Jay dug out a bandage and wrapped it tightly around her left wrist, covering the trident. Until she knew its purpose for sure, she thought it better to hide it from the others.

A knock came suddenly from the door across the room. Jay furrowed her brows, staring at the door like it would open itself. She wasn't expecting any visitors today. The only people who ever came to see her were Dylan or Professor Riley anyway. Jay slowly walked over to the door. "Who is it?" she asked in a standoffish tone.

"It's Taybeith!" He sounded nervous.

Taybeith? Jay opened the door. "How did you—"

"Ha, I used to stalk you, remember?" He teased.

Jay shook her head and laughed awkwardly. She felt slightly unsettled by him knowing which dorm she lived in, Jay still couldn't even recall ever seeing him around school before now. She glanced back at her room, seeing the mess. "Um . . . what brings you here?" There was no way she was inviting him in, but it was nice to have someone other than Dylan or Riley check up on her. Jay felt her face growing warm. *He's just a friend*, she reminded herself.

Taybeith shifted from one foot to the other, staring at the floor instead of at her. "You just seemed down yesterday. After everything that happened, I thought you could use the distraction." He finally looked up and gently reached for her wrist. "What happened?"

Jay didn't pull away as she thought she would once he grabbed her hand. When his skin touched hers, a wave of peace washed over her, calming whatever doubts or nerves she'd had about his unexpected arrival. It wasn't like when Dylan grabbed her hand or touched her. With Taybeith, she felt a sense of nervousness. "Um . . . uh . . ." she sputtered. "I slipped on the ice when carrying Dylan inside."

"Oh, should we go to the infirmary to get it healed? We can also check up on Dylan," Taybeith said, letting go of her hand.

"No," Jay said. "You know how Faith is—she refuses to heal minor cuts and believes we should learn to suffer a little like regular humans. As for Dylan . . ." As much as Jay wanted to see him, she couldn't bring herself to just yet. She was terrified to see him as he was yesterday. She'd known Dylan for a long time, but she had never seen him that vulnerable. She needed more time.

Taybeith chuckled, changing the subject. "Yeah, Faith's teaching methods are just as questionable as Professor Riley's. Should we go to the library? I figure the Grand Hall isn't much your style after you declined last night, so, um, we could always continue our research. Plus, I think I found something you might be interested in."

"Yeah?" Jay brightened. "I'll meet you there in ten."

"Okay! It's a date." Taybeith's face flushed. "No, no, no, not a date, but a study sesh. Yeah, a study sesh!" he rambled as Jay began to close the door.

Jay laughed. "Whatever you say, Taybeith."

Jay pulled down the first book she saw with the word *Immortality* written on its side and held it out to Taybeith. He took it, flipping it over in his hands.

"Harold Ranger, an Immortal himself," he mumbled. He met her eyes, his gleaming with hope. "Yeah, this should work."

"Whatever happened to that Alfonzo guy?" Jay asked.

"Nothing useful. In his dedication page, he just went on about how immortality keeps the fiction alive. Even on the internet, there wasn't anything helpful about him. A dead lead."

"Hmm. What exactly are we looking for?" Jay had no idea where to start, but Taybeith seemed confident nonetheless.

"As far as we know, you're not an Immortal yet because you're still growing. But you have the physical appearance of one, which can be mistaken by others when they first see you. Plus, Immortals are more like chosen soul reapers or something, I think. And your powers are way behind that, I imagine."

"Oh, you imagine." Jay smirked. She had gotten used to Taybeith's subtle teasing. She remembered him saying yesterday that he didn't believe she was an Immortal. But if she wasn't an Immortal, what exactly could she be?

"So, maybe there're more people out there like you. And since you know nothing of your history, we can dive into theirs, and that could help you become closer to finding yourself and understanding your powers more." Taybeith let out a long sigh as he caught his breath.

"You've been listening to Professor Minx and her nonsense. 'Learning oneself can help you control oneself,'" Jay said very slowly and high-pitched, mocking her previous year's professor. They both laughed.

"It's true though. When I first discovered my gifts before coming here, I was an outcast. Every time I looked at a phone, computer, or any screen, I would instantly know everything there was to know about the item I'm searching for and the device. Even things I didn't want to know." The dark shadow she'd seen before returned in his eyes. "My powers had control over me. It wasn't until . . ." His voice trailed off. He cleared his throat, continuing, "It wasn't until the Headmaster brought me here that I was able to find some sort of peace by getting to understand my ties to Aris Magica and my history. It's not perfect, but I can control them now,"

"If you want to talk about it . . ." Jay sighed. She had noticed Taybeith's voice falter. Something must have happened to him as well before the Headmaster had found him.

Jay wondered if her past really had the answers she was looking for. The only things she knew for sure about her past was her parents' abandonment and their apparent normalcy, at least in her memory. Maybe they couldn't handle having a child whose tantrums turned into bending reality, but maybe, there was someone else out there who could provide that connection for her, much like Taybeith had found. "Thanks for sharing."

Taybeith shrugged, turning the rolling chair around to face the computer. Jay nestled up into one of the armchairs behind him, immediately absorbed in the book. Today, they had the library to themselves. As usual, most of the students were still crammed in the Grand Hall, trying to pass the time. Taybeith typed in a passcode, logging into the computer. He tapped at the mouse, impatiently waiting for the desktop to load.

"Maybe I'm adopted." Jay smirked. She knew for sure she wasn't, Dylan had proved that to her a long time ago with a DNA test he'd found hidden away in his dad's study. Her parents had apparently checked before abandoning her.

Taybeith laughed at her joke. "I've been thinking, if you wanted to know more about your abilities, why haven't you researched them before?" He played with the ends of his hair, pondering his own question. "I know digging up the past can often be unbearable, but—"

Jay closed the book, interrupting him. "I don't want to learn about my past, just my abilities." Her past held so much sorrow that she wasn't ready to face just yet. She was convinced it would be a dead end. She laid the book on the coffee table between them, ignoring the other part of the question.

"Nothing?" Taybeith gestured toward the book.

Jay shook her head. "What's an Ancient?" She had come across the word at least twice in what she had read. "The author vaguely talked about how each Immortal is a soul reaper and an aide to an Ancient. Soul partners who protect the balance of reality." Jay explained.

Taybeith's eyes widened as if he knew, but the words that came out of his mouth instead made Jay sulk. "A what?"

Jay sighed. "An Ancient. Is that another Aris Magician breed?"

"Hmm," Taybeith pondered.

Jay was sure that none of her professors had ever mentioned this breed before. The only ones they ever talked about were the eight breeds: Fairies, Wizards, Witches, Demons, Faeries, Immortals, Purists, and Hybrids.

"What about the internet?"

Jay gave him a look of pure cynicism. "The last time I touched a mechanical device, the Institute was put on lock down. Do you seriously think I've used the web since then?" she challenged, crossing her arms and legs.

"That was you?" Taybeith laughed. "I thought it was another Tekhne first year in training."

"Not funny." Jay glared.

Taybeith pointed at himself proudly. "Well, I guess that's why you have me."

Chapter Six

"It was here." Dylan put his motorcycle into park at the entrance to the forest road. The wind blew past them, picking up the fallen leaves, a couple of them dancing in the air.

Riley slammed the door of his Ford truck. Gravel crunched under his boots as he walked over to where Dylan stood. "Kid, are ya sure it was here?" he asked. "I don't feel anything unusual."

"Positive," Dylan said as he picked up a rock and threw it into the entrance of the forest road. It disappeared.

Dylan took the first step and was immediately engulfed by the distortion. The familiar cold wave encased his body. The forest had a darker manifestation than before. Trees hung in thick canopies close to the road, the sun barely lighting the path ahead of them. A deep moaning echoed into the air, followed by the rhythmic calls of watchful ravens. Still, it was quieter than before.

"It's as if the place is sleeping," Riley said, letting out an impressed whistle as he took in their new surroundings. "A damn portal in broad daylight."

"She showed up farther down."

Riley clamped a firm hand on Dylan's shoulder, stopping him. Dylan winced as his damaged muscles twinged. "We aren't going in there alone. I need time to form a team and arrange back up. Whoever they are, they nearly killed you and judging by your experience . . . Hell, I got a feeling you didn't even have time to strike back." Dylan couldn't hide the look in his eyes when Riley had said *team*. "Of adults, other trained professors at the Institute. We'll look at it after the holidays pass."

Dylan's attitude changed. He was disappointed that Riley didn't trust him with more responsibilities. He was at the top of his weapons class, close enough to the top academically, and he already knew enough about coexisting with the human world—after all, he was raised in it.

"You're just a kid," Riley said, as if reading Dylan's mind. "These missions I send you and the other students on aren't supposed to pose real danger, they are meant to teach you a lesson. So don't go looking for this kind of trouble. Do you understand?"

The soft, alarming melody returned, silencing everything. Dylan stiffened. He rested a hand on the hilt of his dagger. Riley's grip tightened, digging into the bone of Dylan's shoulder. "I'll come back another day with a specialized team and a plan," Riley repeated.

Dylan hardly heard him; the music was wrapping around him, clouding his thoughts. It kept trying to lure him deeper into the forest.

"But if it's magic we're working with, we will need time to prepare," Riley said. "I'll talk with the Headmaster about bringing Jay in on this. It'll be good practice with her tracking magic she acquired last year, she can—"

"No!" Dylan retorted. The sound of her name brought him back to reality. "We will not bring her into this."

The melody dispersed, and instantly, the forest returned to its peaceful state. "What's going on between you two lately? Don't think I haven't noticed."

"Noticed what?" Dylan rolled his eyes.

"You two have been tip toeing around each other. I saw the way you were staring at her the other day in that helicopter," Riley smirked. "You like her as more than a friend now?"

"W-what?" Dylan's previous anger melted to embarrassment as he sputtered for a response. "Are you mad! Jay she's like a . . . like a sister to me! Nothing more, I don't feel anything. Oh, wipe that smirk off your face!"

Riley barked out a laugh. "It's only natural. The two of you are maturing." He raised his eyebrow at Dylan. "Things change."

Dylan shrugged off Riley's hand, pushing past him. "Stop Professor, please! My ears can't take it anymore."

Riley sighed, shaking his head as he followed Dylan back to the truck. "These kids." Another raven cawed from a nearby branch. From its high perch, the raven observed the pair of Aris Magicians, its glassy red eyes watching as they left the forest.

Chapter Seven

Google Search: Ancients. Humans possessing silver hair and red eyes.

Taybeith scrolled down the page, scanning the countless subtitles. Google provided vast amounts of information, bringing up links leading to topics surrounding albinism. Taybeith scrolled back up to the top and clicked on the first article. Jay paced back and forth as he quickly skimmed the pages.

"It says here that albinism is a genetic disorder portrayed by the loss of pigment in things like your skin, hair, or eyes; a defect."

Jay lifted a chunk of her hair, staring at it like it was foreign. She let the strands fall back into place. "This is way beyond that. Plus, I barely remember my parents, so . . ." she huffed, slightly irritated that they might have something to do with all of it. She didn't need a computer to tell her she was a defect. "Try something else."

Taybeith took a moment to try out different approaches. His fingers worked at an incredible speed. He flipped through the websites like he was flipping through TV channels. All Jay could see was a cloudy blur of words and numbers she didn't understand.

"Wow," she whispered. It was as if Taybeith's consciousness had drifted up and gone into the web itself. Jay watched him in amazement.

Suddenly, the computer screen settled, returning to its normal state. Taybeith leaned back in the chair, defeated. "Of course," he sulked.

"What?" Jay asked, falling back into the chair.

"I couldn't find a single thing about Ancients. Even on the dark web," he grumbled.

"Nothing?" she asked. She looked around the library and saw rows and rows of endless books. She wouldn't even know where to start to search for Ancients. Jay sighed, sinking deeper into the chair. "So another dead end."

"Maybe not." Taybeith quickly typed away on the keyboard, his attention slipping away back into the internet.

Jay caught a glimpse of what he typed before the screen became a blur. *Lost breed?* she thought. As Earth had evolved, so had the world of Aris Magica. Last year, she had taken a class about how many kinds of direct Aris Magician lines had gone extinct. Perhaps Ancients had been one of them and their record lost in history. Depending on when, their records would not be at the Institute's library. Everything in this library dated back a couple years before the first war broke out.

"This search would be a whole lot easier if Professor Minx was here," Jay said.

Taybeith spun the chair around to face Jay. "Right here, it states the ability to live forever: immortality." His face beamed with knowledge, each word filled with more confidence than the next.

Jay gawked, taken aback. "Are you crazy? Obviously, I already know that! I don't need someone else to remind me—"

"Just listen!" Taybeith snapped. He rolled his chair closer, grabbing her knees. "Here it states that experts believe that different kinds of immortality exist. The only consistent thing is that at a certain point in their life, an Immortal will stop living by heartbeat, and their powers will begin to either reach a limitation or exceed it. So maybe we were wrong about you not being an Immortal. You have the physical appearance, but maybe there're different kinds of Immortals, not just the soul-reaping, Aris Magician kind we learned about. Maybe an Ancient is just another version of an Immortal." Jay rolled her eyes. "Characteristics of those who acquire this power are ones with silver hair, and, get this, their eyes turn red in worst case scenarios. In your case, when you let your emotions control your magic."

Jay groaned, leaning her head into her hands. She pushed her hair back, overwhelmed with information.

"Scientists believe it's just a biological form of inheritance with various limitations that medical involvements can't even begin to fathom. It's also been theorized that immortality—"

"Stop!" Jay squeezed her eyes shut. She couldn't even comprehend the words coming out of his mouth anymore. "That's enough for today."

Taybeith tilted his head quizzically. "Are you okay?"

Jay rubbed her temples. "No. Who wants to be told all over again they're different from society, just with bigger and longer words?"

Taybeith patted her knee. "And experts."

Jay laughed.

The people who wrote the information Taybeith found were probably just a bunch of humans invested in the supernatural. "We already knew most of this information . . . This was a waste of time."

Taybeith took a deep breath. He shook his head, laughed, and put his hands back into his lap. "Alright, we can stop. This was a lot to take in for one day. Plus, you're right, we already knew that." He gestured to the book she had been reading. "Guess it was a dead end." He reached out and rested a hand on her knee. Jay looked at him questioningly. Taybeith still smiled. "No matter what we find, I'm on your side." It was almost as if he was warning her.

Jay smiled weakly. She opened her mouth to say something, but was cut off by the loud sound of a door banging closed. Dylan rounded the corner. He was in the process of removing his jacket when their eyes met. Jay's heart dropped to her stomach. It had been doing that a lot lately whenever he came around. He looked to be alright, in much better condition than before. *Alive.* Her breath hitched and her face warmed as she held his gaze. Everything around her seemed to be moving in slow motion, including him. *Have his eyes always been that dark? Since when did Dylan get muscles?* Jay found herself thinking as her eyes began to wander. She had never taken the time to notice before, but Dylan was fit beneath his jacket. It made sense; he trained every day. His dark brown hair was slightly wet against his forehead as if he had just come from getting caught in the snow falling outside. Jay's eyes found his again. She recognized the worry in his expression. Dylan set his jaw and looked away from her.

Jay's shoulders fell and she sank lower in her chair. Dylan took a place at the computer two desks down from them. Taybeith and Jay watched in silence as he booted up the computer.

"Hi," she said.

Chapter Eight

Dylan tried not to notice the boy sitting with Jay. He even tried not to care that she was hanging with someone new. He gave the stranger a quick once over. He was the opposite of Jay, at least in terms of looks. He appeared like he belonged in an emo gothic era, and, judging by how white his skin was, it looked like he spent most of his time in the shadows. "What are you doing here?" Dylan finally asked, growing annoyed by the other boy's company.

"Research," Taybeith squeaked.

Dylan faced them, and he glared at Taybeith, wondering why he was answering for Jay.

Jay folded her arms across her chest and cleared her throat. "I said 'hi.'"

Dylan ignored her. "Research for what? And who are you?"

Taybeith uncomfortably glanced at Jay. She met his nervous stare, and he fidgeted with his hands. "What brings you here, Dylan?" Taybeith asked, changing the topic.

"Research," Dylan answered. *How does he know my name?* Dylan had never seen the boy before. He wasn't even sure if he was a student at the school.

"Hah, you're kidding!" Jay mocked. "You've never researched anything! And he's a . . . friend."

Dylan sneered, noticing the hesitancy in Jay's voice as she mentioned *friend.*

"I'm Taybeith." The boy extended a hand toward Dylan. Dylan ignored it.

"Yeah, and I'd like to do my work alone, if you don't mind," he said with a sharp edge.

Jay narrowed her eyes, but rose to her feet. Dylan could tell he upset her. He sighed, preparing to apologize. He didn't want her to leave, he just wanted the boy to.

Taybeith jumped up, intervening. "Right! We were just leaving." He glanced at Jay.

The muscle in Dylan's jaw flexed in annoyance.

Taybeith led Jay out, lightly pulling her wrist, getting her to move. Dylan remained calm as she passed, drawing unnecessarily close, and he finally noticed the bandage wrapped tightly around her left hand. He glanced down at his own, seeing the faint trident scar imprinted in his skin. Jay shoved her hands in the pockets of her sweatpants.

"We need to talk," she whispered. "You're not going to like it."

Dylan unenthusiastically agreed. He had much to say to her, but he didn't know the right words. "Rooftop or—" The rooftop was one of their favorite places to run off to together. The other students had learned to keep their distance from their small corner under the stars.

"I'll come find you," she affirmed, moving on. The doors shut behind them, the loud sound resonating off the glass dome.

Dylan leaned back in his chair. He had spent over three hours on the web, searching for anything to help clear up the mass of confusion, but finding nothing. He grimaced, bringing a hand to his stomach. The pain was beginning to affect him once again. He would need another dose of painkillers in a few hours. He felt a buzz vibrate through his pocket. He pulled out his iPhone, looking at the screen. A blue rectangular box appeared with a brief preview of the message.

Professor Riley:

Get your ass down here! We need to . . .

Talk? Dylan assumed that was what the rest of the message said. Riley had been a father figure to him ever since he arrived at the Institute. He remembered the first time they met, Riley prying a freezing Dylan from his parents' grave when his other relatives wanted nothing to do with him and Jay. It was around that time that Riley decided to take the Headmaster up on his offer and start teaching at the school. Dylan had a lot to be grateful for when it came to Riley.

Dylan groaned. He still really wasn't in the mood to deal with anything that man had to say. All he wanted to do was take another dose of whatever Faith had prescribed and lie down, maybe even go relax in the Grand Hall with the other students, feel normal for once. Right on cue, his stomach let out a deep growl. Dylan frowned, shoving his phone back into his pocket.

Riley would have to wait.

A warm, comforting smell filled the hall, a combination of apple cider, cinnamon, and fresh hot chocolate. Dylan took it in, already feeling relaxed. He could hear the dainty voices of children laughing and conversing. Dylan pushed open the wide wooden doors to find other kids, ages eleven to eighteen, crowded in the main hall. Some sat on the leather couches pushed back to border the perimeter of the room, while others stood in small crowds. Long windows stretched along the far walls with snow sticking to the glass. Against the back wall, the huge stone fireplace extended up into the ceiling was alight, its burning flames providing warmth to the groups of students huddled in front of it. At first glance, it was hard to tell the difference between the students with Pure Aris Magician ancestry and the humans who were just Hybrids. It had been part of the Headmaster's plan when opening the school that there be no division between the two. Both groups of students were equally outcast by human society.

The Grand Hall was one of the biggest rooms within the Institute. The room had a high ceiling and fifteen long, glass windows. The moon reflected its light through the glass, bending at an awkward angle in the corner of the room. A long, wide table had been dragged in and placed at the center. Various assortments of desserts and drinks covered the surface with a sweet aroma that filled the air. The Headmaster kept it fully stocked during breaks to give the students who stayed behind a distraction from thinking about how they had no one or nowhere else to go during the holidays.

Dylan stepped forward, making a beeline to the refreshments. He ignored the kids casting random spells and the floating objects above him. His mission was the last chocolate cookie waiting to be devoured. Dylan approached the table with a controlled desire. He calmly reached for the cookie. A girl grabbed it first, cramming it into her mouth.

She had shiny blonde hair that fell to her shoulders and bright blue eyes. She swayed happily back and forth on her heels. She purred in delight, savoring each bite, and gave him a mischievous smile. His hand fell absently to his side, balling into a fist.

"Ami," he growled.

The girl licked her lips, giving him an innocent look. "What?" Pink blush glowed on her cheeks.

A muscle in Dylan's jaw twitched. Ami Ferrell was a Mist Caster, a subclass to a Witch, making her a Pure breed. She could manipulate the molecules in the air and create a gas formation out of them. This year they had four classes together, and in each one, they happened to find themselves sitting right next to each other. She was usually obnoxiously loud and confident. Anything she wanted, she wound up getting. But outside the Institute, she was only a rich man's daughter sent here because of her deformity.

Ami smiled, twirling her hand before him. A small, light blue mist formed, hovering above the tips of her fingers.

"Ami," Dylan breathed, trying to control his rising anger. He leveled with the girl, staring her down. She crossed her arms, and an arrogant grin formed on her face. She stood her ground.

If she wasn't such a pain, she'd be—Dylan gritted his teeth, abruptly cutting off the thought. "Ami."

"What? You've already said my name twice, I don't think I need to hear it three times," she answered with a haughty tone.

Dylan's muscles clenched, and pain shot throughout his stomach, crawling up into his chest. He decided to go with the tactful approach. "You're a very cute girl." His voice was still noticeably tight.

Her face turned red. She arched an eyebrow, curious. "I know," she said proudly. "But?"

Dylan sneered. "But you're utterly annoying."

The smile left her face, replaced by a crude frown. She placed her hands on her hips and took a step forward. Now that they were only a few inches away, Dylan could make out the faint freckles on the bridge of her nose.

"Excuse me?" she scoffed. "Annoying?"

The loud chatter had ceased, and a couple of heads turned to watch the commotion. Dylan rolled his eyes, avoiding eye contact. "Utterly," he confirmed.

Ami pursed her lips. She took another step forward and shoved him hard in the chest. Dylan stumbled a couple steps back. Shivers danced up his spine from her touch. "Maybe I just want your attention, seeing how most of the time, it's focused on someone else!" Tears glistened in her eyes.

Dylan knew Ami wasn't the biggest fan of Jay's, and she was the one responsible for most of the rumors about her. Their first year at the Institute, during their second term of classes, Jay had accidentally cursed Ami when they were arguing about whether Pure breeds should have to take math classes like the Hybrid students. Dylan knew Ami only wanted to take the math classes because he was required to, since he wasn't Aris Magician, just specially gifted in the art of weaponry.

Fake tears, Dylan thought.

He seized her right wrist, shoving her hand away from his body. She gasped, struggling against his hold. Out of the corner of his eyes, he saw a couple of wolfish girls snickering in their direction. A mixture of boys cocked their heads, knowing what was to come next. Dylan had built a reputation around here: no one crossed his path and left uninjured.

Dylan narrowed his eyes. They lost all familiarity, and his entire demeanor changed into that of a killer. Ami backed away wide eyed. "D-don't you dare give me that look!"

Dylan pulled her in by the loops of her jeans. She slammed hard into his chest. Her face drained of color. Astonished gasps spread across the room like wildfire.

"You aren't ready to handle someone like me." Whistles sounded, followed by a piercing howl. Ami flushed.

"Am I not good enough?" Her voice wavered as she spoke.

Dylan grinned sardonically, releasing her. "No," he whispered, barely loud enough for her to hear.

He picked up a cup of apple cider and took a long sip. Ami watched him, clearly beyond embarrassed.

"Hah, not so high and mighty now!" A student from across the room whispered. Dylan's ears picked up on the voices surrounding them.

"Should have known! There's only two people who can handle him, and she's not one of them." Another bystander said.

Dylan watched as Ami's cheeks flared red and anger exploded from her. She couldn't handle this humiliation. "McCoy!" She slapped the cup from his hand and pushed him hard into the table. He gripped the edge, preventing it from falling over. "You don't get to walk away from me without a fight!"

Dylan pushed off on the front of the table. He should have never come to the Grand Hall. He knew because of his relationship with Jay that there was bound to be someone he'd run into with a grudge against her, wanting to pick a fight.

A stabbing pain gripped his side. He groaned, half in irritation and half in agony. He was in no condition to fight back. Ami stood a few feet away from him in a fighting stance. Strands of her hair stuck out chaotically around her head. Her expression had lost all its glamour.

The unspoken rules of the Institute were to never run from a fight. Stand your ground, even if you can't win. Every student here learned how to defend themselves against the outside world and each other.

"Come on! Get up and fight me!" she provoked Dylan.

He grimaced as the pain increased.

Chants rose up egging them on. One person started, and the rest of the room soon followed. Dylan rubbed at the back of his neck. He'd rather not fight a girl, let alone break her any further.

Black mist enveloped her body, mimicking her emotions. Dylan smiled, instantly recognizing that she was scared. "Still putting on a show—"

The door swung open, cutting him off. "DYLAN! You better have worked up some damn good excuse because you're in a whole lot of trouble!" Riley's voice rang out.

"Great," Dylan sighed.

"You'll have to wait your turn, Professor Riley. He's mine!" Ami yelled. "I'll show you how good I am!"

Dylan ignored her and focused on the distance between him and Riley. He was getting closer, fast. Steam bellowed off him, his facial expression contorted with rage. He was furious. Dylan weighed out his choices—either fight Ami or face Riley. Both options sucked.

Dylan decided to take his chances. He knocked over the table behind him, blocking Riley's path. Then, he ran straight for the group of kids to his right. They parted, allowing him a path to the door.

"Dammit, Dylan!" Riley cursed, trying to shove past the wall of students.

"Dylan, you coward!" Ami screamed as streams of mist shot out into the crowd, branching off. Kids screamed as they watched those that the mist touched collapse.

"Dammit, Ami!" Riley yelled, exasperated. "Detention, both of you!"

Dylan reached the door, his eyes meeting Riley's. Riley looked from him to Ami, deciding which one he'd have to sacrifice getting away. Dylan shrugged, knowing who he'd choose, and slipped out.

Chapter Nine

Dylan stood at Jay's door, hesitating to touch the doorknob. He had no idea what he even wanted to say to her. He had so much he wanted to talk to her about, but the urge to protect her from experiencing anymore sorrow stayed strong in his mind. *Maybe Riley was on to something earlier.* Dylan cringed and tried to put the thought out of his mind. Even if he'd developed feelings for Jay, he could never pursue them. Things were just too complicated between them.

Dylan took a deep breath before finally opening the door with a soft click. Jay glanced up from the book she was reading. Dylan stood with his back to the door. He met her gaze and suddenly felt too embarrassed to look at her. He cleared his throat, looked away, then walked over and sat on the corner of the bed closest to the door.

"When will she be back?" he asked, referring to Jay's roommate. The two of them shared a small room with a single bathroom, one closet, and a miniature television set.

"She went home for the holiday." Jay pushed back a strand of white hair, continuing with the book she was reading.

"Good!" Dylan collapsed in relief, covering his eyes with one arm. Minutes passed with neither acknowledging the other. He stifled a groan, rising to his feet. Jay was in the middle of turning a page in her book. The cover of the book was deep blood red, and the pages within seemed fragile and old. She was only halfway done with it. She loved to read. At least that hadn't changed. He always knew he could find her in the library, and usually it would be him having to pull her free of a book's charm. He smiled.

"What are you reading?" He scooted closer to her and winced. The wound across his chest had yet to fully heal. He was still receiving treatments from Faith. She had told him the curse he had run into would take a while to leave his body.

Jay closed the book, flipping it on its back. She smiled, meeting his eyes. The color in her face drained as she saw the pain reflected in his eyes. "Dylan, are you okay?"

"I'm fine," Dylan lied. He didn't want to concern her with something she couldn't fix.

But it was Jay; he knew she could tell by his voice that he didn't want to talk about it, but she still pressed on. "You're lying."

"So what? It's okay for you to lie, but I have to tell the truth?" Dylan bluntly criticized. He groaned inside. He hadn't meant to say that. It just came out in frustration.

Jay gaped at him. "Not fair! Neither of us has been honest with each other."

Dylan started to stand but fell back onto the bed as pain shot through his body. The image of Jay and Taybeith together still tugged at his mind. He bit his bottom lip, cursing under his breath. He didn't understand why the pair of them being together bothered him to a point it hurt.

"Here, let me heal it for you." Jay's voice was calm as she gently reached for him.

Dylan pulled away. "You can't."

"I can. I can just use that plant over there." She pointed to the one sitting on her desk across the room.

Dylan shook his head again. "No, you can't even control your powers. Remember the last time you tried to heal an injury this big? You made half the school lose power because you drained the Old Magic from it." Before she could say anything, he continued, "And you said you were using a plant last time."

"That was an accident," Jay said softly. "Plus, I can control my powers better now."

"What? How?" Dylan asked.

Jay looked away and grew quiet.

Dylan groaned, frustrated. He knew she wouldn't talk until she was ready. "Jay! You can't keep going on like this. Doing stuff behind my back, keeping secrets. We're supposed to be a team!" Dylan wasn't just referring to her powers, but to why she had been with Taybeith earlier. He didn't like being kept in the dark.

Jay rose to her feet, towering over him. Her voice was small and on the verge of breaking. "I'm not the one keeping secrets or lying!" she shouted back. "I know who you are. You're my partner. I just don't know if I'm still yours."

She balled her hands into fists. Dylan clutched his stomach. "Jay—"

"Dylan, I'm a human being, too. I'm allowed to have a life outside of this!" Her voice continued to break. "I-I can't handle you keeping me at a distance whenever things get hard."

"What do you mean?" Dylan asked.

"You do this every time you think there's danger. You shut down and close me out." Jay explained.

"To protect you."

Dylan thought back to his parents' death. He wanted to keep shielding Jay from feeling that kind of guilt and fear again. He was afraid of losing her to herself again, and he couldn't bear that.

"Protect me?" Jay let out a sarcastic laugh. "I don't need protecting! Stop treating me like you did when we were kids."

Dylan looked at anything but her. How could he when she was right? "Your mind . . . I protect that," Dylan mumbled. He didn't expect her to understand. Jay didn't remember it because she was so young, but when her parents left, her powers manifested fully, and she nearly destroyed herself and anyone who happened to get near her. Dylan had been the only one able to calm her down. For some reason, her powers didn't feel the need to protect her from him. Jay remembered it as a simple tantrum, but what Dylan saw was how fragile her mind was and could be again when she was in danger.

Dylan felt his heart tighten. They had yet to talk about what had happened after his parents' death. He knew Jay still blamed herself, even if only subconsciously. He always assumed that was why she couldn't control her powers, because of fear holding her hostage. No matter how many times he reminded her that it wasn't her fault, he knew she wouldn't believe him. She would just smile sadly and tell him what he wanted to hear.

"It's not your fault," he said, catching Jay off guard. He hadn't meant to say it aloud as his thoughts wandered. Dylan sighed. "My parents, your parents . . . none of it is your fault."

Jay smiled like Dylan knew she would and said, "I know."

Dylan grabbed her by her shoulders; he had to make sure she understood what he was trying to tell her. "Jay, it's not. No one could have stopped what happened to them. And no one blames you—not them, and not me. So don't shut me out and try to figure things out on your own. I can't lose you. I can't! Because I love you too much. I—" He released her, his hands hovering in front of her as he took in the shocked expression on her face that reflected his. Dylan was suddenly lost for words. He loved Jay, he always had, but the way he said it, he meant it differently than before. He quickly backed away from her, hoping she hadn't noticed. "Ah, forget I said that."

Jay started laughing. "I know, I love you too. Always have and always will."

Dylan felt relieved but also disappointed at Jay not understanding what he had meant.

"Dylan, look at me," Jay said. "Please."

Dylan slowly returned his gaze to her. For the first time, he saw her in a different light. Jay wasn't the little girl he'd thought her to be—she was becoming a woman. His breath started to pick up and his body warmed. Jay's hair lay across her shoulders in perfect spiraled curls. Her blue eyes held a fierceness to them that drew him in. She was beautiful.

"I don't blame myself as much anymore, but it's still my responsibility to find out who I am and what I mean to the world, so that nothing like that ever happens again," Jay said.

Dylan looked away again, and she backed off, sitting down. She placed her hands in her lap and started unraveling the bandage bound around her left hand. Silence burned a hole between them. Time ticked away, passing on the clock. The sun had set, casting a dark, looming shadow over the room.

"Sorry," Dylan whispered. "Do you want me to leave?"

Jay shook her head.

She took a deep breath, rewrapping her wrist. "Are you in pain?"

He wasn't going to lie. "It comes and goes."

"Has it come?"

Dylan didn't respond. Jay stood up, disappearing into the bathroom. She came out holding a white cylindrical pill. Dylan took it, swallowing it dry.

"Thanks," he continued to whisper. Jay sat down beside him. He rubbed at his own hand where the trident symbol marked his skin. Each day it grew fainter, but it was still there.

He looked up in time to see Jay begin to put another bandage around her hand. "What's wrong with your hand?" He grabbed it, afraid she would dodge the question.

She didn't resist as he undid the ties wrapped around her wrist. The skin beneath the bandage was a pale brown. In the center was a black trident carved deep into her skin, almost as if it had been branded there. Dylan carefully ran his fingers over it.

"It's the same as mine," he mumbled, mostly to himself. "How long?"

She gently pulled her hand from his and clasped her other hand over the burn. "The night you came back. I know you don't believe me, but I think it's how I'm able to control my magic now." He waited patiently for her to continue. "That's not all—I got this too." She raised the bottom of her shirt, stopping a few inches before her bra-line.

Dylan examined the bruised scar stretching across her abdomen. It was mostly healed, but still in bad condition. Black and purple rings traced the line of gashed skin, darkening at the corners. When his fingers made contact, she shivered.

"How?" He asked softly.

Jay winced as Dylan's hands graze over her skin. "It just showed up. A searing pain coursed through my body and left these markings." She pushed her shirt back down.

"Why didn't you tell me?" Dylan whispered, more hurt than angry.

Jay apparently didn't hear him, as she continued explaining. "I'm not sure what it means, and you're the only one I've told." She quickly added, "I would have told you sooner, but lately you've been . . . unavailable."

She waited for him to say something. Dylan's gaze was fixated on the window across the room. The medication had helped ease his pain. He didn't know what to say, so he said nothing. His eyes drifted to the book lying on her bed. Jay rested her hand on his arm, holding tightly.

"So, tell me," she said, changing the subject. "Why are you here in the first place?"

Dylan relaxed but kept a suspicious eye on the book. "Ami. Riley." He gritted his teeth, remembering their recent encounter.

"Ami Ferrell?"

Dylan nodded stiffly. Jay fell into a fit of laughter. She hugged herself, falling back onto the bed. "What happened?"

Dylan smiled, glad to see her finally happy. "She exploded."

"Why?" Jay folded her hand over her stomach, falling back. Her chest rose and fell, settling from the laughter.

"I humiliated her."

Her voice became far off again, like she was there but not in the now. "Wish I could have seen it."

Dylan's eyes saddened. They had grown farther apart these last few days. Dylan eased back beside her, his arm pressing against hers. She didn't move, but his heart skipped a beat. Dylan hesitantly turned onto his side. Jay did the same, so they were facing. He grabbed a strand of her hair, weaving it around his fingers, distracting himself from her stare.

"You're so beautiful." He couldn't stop the words from leaving his lips. Jay scoffed. His eyes widened. "I'm serious!"

Jay arched her eyebrow, challenging him. She seized his hand—the one bearing a trident that matched hers. Her hand intertwined with his. "What happened to us?" she thought aloud.

Dylan frowned. "Life."

"Yeah." She looked away.

"What's going on between you and that kid . . . Taybeith?" Dylan squeezed her hand in his. Part of him feared her answer. It was weird for him to see her close with anyone else. Jay often kept her distance from the other students; he'd never seen her alone with anyone but him before.

"What do you mean?" The air around them suddenly became hot. Jay tried to pull away.

Dylan seized her wrist just as her hand slipped from his. He yanked her into him. She gasped, shocked. "Don't . . . please." She tried to pull away from him. The air was getting hotter by the second.

"Just answer the question!" Dylan said with a small laugh, trying to make light of it. Sweat trickled down Jay's forehead. She closed her eyes, shaking her head. She seemed to be in pain. Dylan loosened his grip. "Are you okay?" he asked, concerned.

"Please let go," she said tightly, not answering his question.

"Okay," Dylan said. He released her. She was breathing heavily. She rested her hand against his chest. "Are you sure you're okay?" Dylan asked again. He grabbed her by the shoulders and pulled her away so that he could look at her. She nodded but she looked slightly pale. "Jay, I'm starting to think I—"

"Taybeith and I are researching me," Jay confessed.

"What?" Dylan said tightly.

"Ancients," Jay said breathlessly. She grabbed her head in her hands and sat up. Dylan followed, keeping a close eye on her. "Have you heard of them?"

"You promised," Dylan mumbled. They promised when it was time to investigate everything, her past, her powers, they'd do it together, when the time was right. Dylan felt betrayed that she felt the need to go behind his back like that. "No," he said. Jay's face fell, but she didn't look surprised, as if she'd expected that to be his answer.

"Okay," she said.

Dylan scoffed. "Ancients," he repeated. He'd never heard of them before, but he didn't like the sound of it. Taybeith was putting unnecessary thoughts into her head. "Is that what he thinks you are?" Dylan asked, a little irritated.

Jay shrugged. "We don't know what I am. Maybe my parents did and that's why they ran."

The last part angered Dylan. Jay didn't remember much about her parents except for the bad parts, but Dylan remembered that they were good people. They must have had their reasons. "Taybeith doesn't need to be filling your head with false hopes and angers."

"He's not," Jay said defensively.

"He is! With these Ancients and—" Dylan gestured to the book on her bed next to them. The cover read *Immortality*. "—Immortals and promises, no doubt, that he'll help you learn more about your past."

He shook his head and reached for the book. Whatever was inside was probably everything they already knew about her powers. Dylan knew she would become an Immortal, all the signs were there—it was just a matter of when. Even without having magical parents, she could still use the Old Magic, her hair was white, and her eyes were as blue as the sky and changed whenever her powers were active. She was just wasting her time with Taybeith.

"Don't touch it!" Jay growled, her voice deep and powerful. Dylan flinched right before his hand reached the book. He looked back at her, alarmed and shocked by her anger.

"Now I'm even more intrigued." Dylan smirked. He reached for it again.

She drove her knee up into his groin. On instinct, he reacted, releasing his grip on her wrist, and bringing his arms down to block the attack. She didn't stop there. She flattened a palm to his chest.

"Hořet," Jay whispered. Dylan grabbed her wrist, pushing her arm hard to the right, redirecting her magic toward the pillow. His eyes widened when he saw the pillow burn to ashes, knowing that could have been him. Anger flashed in her eyes, and he nearly lost his breath seeing they'd taken on a red color.

What had happened? Something about the book had changed her. Dylan hadn't seen her this angry in a long time, almost as if her magic had taken full control over her again.

"Jay!" Dylan shouted, alarmed. "Jay!" But she didn't seem to hear him. He had no choice—it was the same as last time.

Dylan grabbed her other wrist, holding her down. He moved to a position above her, locking her body in place against the bed. Jay immediately reacted, driving her leg into his groin again. Dylan was faster.

Jay bit down hard on her bottom lip until she drew blood. She grinned and spat the blood onto his face, laughing.

"What the hell!" Dylan wiped his cheek against his shoulder.

Dylan dug his knee deeper into her skin. Jay thrashed beneath him.

"Who are you?" Dylan demanded. This wasn't her.

Jay flexed her hands from a fist to open palms. "Help me!" Jay cried, her voice breaking through the magic controlling her.

Dylan barely heard her at first. He noticed her trident burn was glowing gold. He stared at it, confused, wondering if it was the reason for her sudden behavior. His grip tightened. Her eyes were still red. "Jay!"

Suddenly, her eyes returned to normal, as did the trident. "Nothing. I'm fine," she whispered breathlessly.

Dylan pressed his forehead to hers, releasing her wrist. "Don't scare me like that." He grabbed her wrist again and stared at the trident. Had he imagined its glow? "What happened to you?"

"My magic . . . I guess I still don't have full control over it," Jay sighed.

Dylan glanced over her shoulder at the book, the red cover beckoning him. Jay's eyes followed.

Dylan released her and lunged for the book. Whatever was inside, he wouldn't let her have it, not like this. Jay rubbed the skin around her wrist where an imprint from his hold remained. She growled and held out her hands. Dylan picked it up, turning it over to its front. It was blank. He flipped through the pages. Nothing. Rage built inside him, threatening to explode. She was hiding the words from his view—magic. Dylan slammed the book shut with more force than necessary.

"Are you kidding me? Bring the text back!" Dylan faced her. His suspicion was right, the book had the answer he sought. "You saw what just happened! Whatever it was, happened because of that book."

"No," Jay protested.

Dylan flipped through the pages of the book again, hoping against hope the words would return. "Jay, please. It's for the best. I won't try to stop you, I just want to help."

The smug look fell from her face, transforming into a grimace. Her fingers curled inward, losing their hold on the magic. The words reappeared. Dylan flipped again and again through the pages. The book was written in an ancient text, something he had neglected to learn. He cursed under his breath. "You'll have to translate."

Dylan heard Jay moan from behind him, but she didn't respond.

A furious knock came from the other side of the door.

"Jay, open up!" Riley barked.

Dylan snarled, closing the book. It would have to wait. Riley banged his fist against the door a second time.

"Great," Dylan grumbled. How would he even explain what had just happened to Riley without Jay killing him, or Riley lecturing her? Dylan laid the book back down on her bed.

"Jay, open this door up or I'll kick it down myself!"

Dylan tossed his head back with a sarcastic laugh. He knew all too well that Riley wasn't joking. "I won't leave until you say some—" Dylan glanced up in time to see Jay's body fall against her bed. His eyes widened.

Jay was curled into a ball, her body shivering uncontrollably. "Jay?" Dylan croaked, barely managing to speak.

He dropped to his knees beside her. He yearned to hold her hand, to do something, anything, to help. She slapped it away. Thick curtains of her hair covered most of her face. His hands hovered there, unsure of what to do.

Something inside him broke. Tears clouded his vision. "Jay . . . Jay!" His pulse picked up speed. He was on the verge of having a panic attack.

Dylan screamed at the top of his lungs, not caring who heard, "RILEY, HELP ME!"

Everything was drifting away. Glimpses of the past were resurfacing: he remembered finding his mother in this state, curled in a ball in the corner of the room, her dark hair fanned out over her body, and her eyes were shut tight. A Demon stood above her, smiling with a dark malevolence. He recalled being frozen in place, unable to do anything—powerless. Dylan had backed away, fear consuming him. He had watched as the Demon picked up his mother's lifeless body in curled claws.

Dylan snapped back into reality, covered his ears and screamed. Sobbing fits exploded from his chest. Everything that had built up inside him collapsed, becoming a blur. The world was spinning. He had finally lost control. He couldn't lose her. Dylan screamed louder, the noise ripping from his throat. Strong hands pulled him back, shaking him by the shoulders.

"Don't get lost on me now, kid." Dylan blankly stared into Riley's assuring eyes. Riley stopped shaking him but continued to keep a steady hold on him.

"Breathe," Riley instructed.

Dylan breathed in deeply and let out a controlled breath. Dried tears streaked his face. A few seconds passed before he could put words into a sentence. "I'm fine."

Riley eyed him with a cautious look. Dylan shook his head, waving him off. "Alright." Riley's hands fell. "Now this one."

Jay was still unconscious on the bed. She wasn't breathing. Riley lifted her hand, placing two of his fingers on the inside of her neck. His face darkened. "It's happening sooner than we thought."

The transformation. Dylan and Riley exchanged a brief glance; they both knew it. According to the history books, the symbol of eternity should appear across her stomach. Riley unraveled Jay's other arm, turning her over halfway onto her back. Her eyes were shut. Riley pulled up her shirt and paused. He looked back at Dylan, startled.

"How did she get this?"

Riley showed Dylan the scar on Jay's stomach. The symbol was a curled *S* with a slash diagonally through it, connecting each end. Dylan recognized it as the same seal that hung outside the Institute's walls. It was the emblem of Aris Magica. As humans had their official flags, so did Aris Magica: a silver *S* with an arrow crossing diagonally through it. It stood for unity and eternity. Dylan looked away, ashamed, biting the inside of his jaw. Riley leaned his head close to her chest.

"You better fight, kid." Riley whispered in Jay's ear.

There was nothing either of them could do to stop what was happening. Jay was becoming an Immortal whether they liked it or not.

Dylan's hands tensed at his side. He couldn't bear the sight. He squeezed his eyes shut.

Remorse. Regret. He shouldn't have yelled at her. He should have been there, willing to jump in front of a train for her. He could hear his father's voice speaking to him, reassuring him:

It was an inevitable fate. His father had said.

I should have done something.

You have, you've done everything you can. You were there and still fighting. Those were the last words he remembered his father saying to them both.

Dylan sucked in a shaky breath. Riley grabbed his collar, forcing him to his feet. Dylan snapped back into reality.

Riley's face was inches away from his. "What happened?"

Dylan struggled to break free. "I don't know!"

Riley yanked him closer. Dylan could smell the salt and pine smoke drifting off him. "Don't piss me off!"

Dylan directed his rage toward Riley. "Piss you off? This is your fault! If you had let me take care of it, none of this would have happened. She wouldn't have that scar, and she wouldn't be suffering now!" His voice was as sharp as ice.

"What went down in the woods that night?" Riley's eyes narrowed, daring Dylan to defy him.

"I don't want to talk about it," Dylan stated with just as much stubbornness.

Riley shoved him into the wall behind them. "You damn sure will!"

Dylan cringed, pain shooting through his stomach. "I was given a message," he growled.

"What was it?" Riley pressed harder.

Each word was broken down, slowly breaking him. "I don't remember."

Chapter Ten

Glossy black curls drifted in the wind behind her. Fierce eyes outlined by black mascara shone bright in the dark. Her skin was a pale, almost white color. Cursive markings tattooed her shoulders, spiraling down her arms. She wore a dark red dress, its skirt dancing around her like fire. Her red lips curled into a malevolent smile. She held her hand out, beckoning. A single black raven with beady red eyes answered her call, taking its perch on her arm.

"You're finally ready to awaken." Her voice was beauty itself, hardly even a whisper.

Jay shielded her eyes with the back of her hand. A strong wind blew around them, producing a heavy fog. "What do you mean?" Jay's voice echoed in her mind.

"The ancient text has been written."

Jay hesitantly glanced down at her body. She was wearing a thin, white silk dress that stopped before her knees. Her dark skin was marked with symbols she couldn't read. The symbols faintly glowed a soft golden color outlined by a bold red. She'd never seen this form of writing before. Jay turned her arms over; the markings covered every visible part of her body. "Why?"

"Join me."

Jay shook her head. She had a bad feeling about the woman standing before her.

"We could do wonders."

"I-I can't." Jay took a step back.

"Oh, and why not?" the raven cawed, mocking Jay, while flapping its wings.

"This is wrong," Jay ran her fingers through her hair. "You're a Witch."

The woman chuckled, not the least bit surprised. "Don't look so shocked."

"Witch!" Jay repeated, backing away. She knew of the dark magic they possessed. There was a reason Witches were not accepted at the Institute; it would bring them to ruins. "No."

The woman advanced forward. "And you're an Immortal Witch. See, we are the same." She stood a couple of feet from Jay now. She grabbed a few strands of Jay's white hair, pulling her closer. "You and I will give this planet what it deserves: absolutely nothing."

Jay stumbled back. "You want to destroy Earth?"

She laughed again. Jay met her with a startling seriousness in her eyes. "No, just the part deemed unworthy."

"It's murder!"

"What has the human world ever done for us?"

Jay hesitated, "I—" Jay remembered the doctor, how greedy the man had been to cure his daughter who didn't need to be cured, how he had killed her trying to do it. Humans were foolish and controlling. She thought about how her own parents had left her. Humans were prone to betrayal. But then Jay thought about Riley. He was half-human, and so were Dylan's parents. They had shown her that the world could change and accept their kind. Not every Hybrid at the Institute came from a damaged human line. It'd be cruel of her to assume so and to take even the smallest acts of kindness for granted. "Plenty," Jay finally said as she met the woman's hopeful gaze.

The woman's eyes darkened as she smiled. "I will ask you once more: join me."

This time, Jay did not hesitate. "No." The symbols tattooing her body glowed a brighter gold, overpowering the red.

The raven flew from its perch on the Witch's arm. Her satin red lips downturned into a frown. She lifted her chin, raising the palm of her hand. Her voice was flat but powerful. Jay could feel the wind coming together, pushing her back.

"Fine."

Jay crossed her arms in an X in front of her, bracing herself for impact. The wind swirled, becoming a thick, black veil. She could no longer see but could still feel the unmistakable presence of the Witch lingering. The wind swirled around Jay like a tornado. For a moment, she couldn't breathe. It was as if the wind had hands that were suffocating her. The wind began to howl, forming a haunting song Jay recognized as magic. She closed her eyes, straining against the tone. She would not let herself fall under its curse. The wind suddenly stopped, disappearing along with the song. Jay shrieked, stumbling back onto her heels, and falling. A soft surface cushioned her fall.

Jay slowly opened her eyes to new surroundings. She stood in a vast meadow encircled by looming trees. The grass was dark green in the moonlight. The wide pond glistened, reflecting an image of the sky and moon. It was oddly quiet, and a red tint hazed over everything like miasma. Jay slowly released a breath, looking up. The moon was covered in a red film, one side fractured into many pieces.

"Where it began is where it shall end," a gentle breeze whispered.

Crimson leaves fell from the sky, covering the forest floor. Autumn was fast approaching. The Witch's song had returned, floating aimlessly in the wind, drawing out Demons and Faeries hidden deep within the shadows of the trees. Jay rose to her feet. More were coming out behind her, small and large. A horrific cry split through the night, then the sound of trees crashing into one another followed. Jay cringed, recognizing the sound.

Across the lake stood a beast nearly seven feet tall. In the red film, its skin was a pale shade of auburn with glowing purple veins. It walked forward on two legs, its body in the form of a wolf with two vicious horns protruding from its head. Obscured eyes glistened, looking in Jay's direction. Its tail swung side to side, and it let out another battle cry.

Another Demon of about the same height followed, veering close behind, its horns springing the trunks of the trees from their roots. Smoke puffed out from the Demon's snout. Jay retreated into the tall grass. A low growl stopped her. She felt hot breath on the back of her neck. Jay touched her skin, frightened, and slowly turned around. A tiger-like creature was behind her, its fur colored black and purple. Jay shook with fear, but the beast seemed to be looking past her, ignoring her presence. The terror she felt did not subside. Jay stared directly into its sea glass eyes. She gasped, falling to her knees as she realized that the creature before her was a Faery, one of the Demons from ancient times.

Jay frantically patted the grass around her for anything she could utilize as a weapon. Nothing was within her grasp. The Faery continued prowling forward, misting right through her. Jay caught her breath, stunned. She grabbed her body, pulling at her dress. No words or even thoughts formed. She unsteadily rose to her feet, unaware of the line of trolls passing through her like air. Jay glanced down again, astounded. She parted her lips, but her voice was gone. She clamped a hand over her mouth, even more alarmed.

Jay focused her attention on the event taking place across the pond. Her eyes froze on the woman who appeared, her long silver hair cascading down her back in one swooping braid. She possessed the same dark, rich skin as Jay. Pulsing ripples soundlessly emerged from underneath the woman as she stood at the center of the pond. A silky white robe covered her body, falling gracefully above the pond's surface. The sleeves hugged her arms, fanning out at her wrists. Familiar golden symbols lined the robe's hem and sleeves. In one outstretched hand she held a bronze staff. There was a red, egg-shaped stone resting in the center in a mounted hold. The light of the fractured moon reflected off it, casting a gentle glow over the center of the pond. A faint light outlined her body. Jay felt a sense of familiarity between herself and the stranger. It was as if she was seeing herself in another time.

The woman waved the staff in a repetitive circular motion above her head. A powerful pulse of magic flowed from its core. Jay crossed her arms in protection, planting her feet in the grass. The wave of magic was strong, pushing the army of Demons back. Jay let her arms fall to her side. The magic was not affecting her, but the monsters cried out, attempting to resist the power emitting from the staff.

"I call upon the power of old. Once more, allow me to use your power!" The woman's voice rang out, laced with an even stronger force of Old Magic. The glow around her intensified, turning a brighter shade of gold. With both hands gripping the staff, she drew it down vertically onto the water's surface, solidifying it. The water turned to glass-like ice beneath her.

Magic started to pour from every living thing around her and into the staff. The ground turned a crippled brown, and the nearby trees lost their leaves. "I hereby purify your souls, tainted with dark sins washed upon this world. Be at peace." The staff's end connected with the ice. The pond trembled, frozen waves rippling under the woman's robe. The light surrounding her split into multiple beams, shooting out rays that pierced the Demons surrounding them. Jay stood transfixed, fascinated by what she saw. Instantly at the light's touch, the Demons burned to dust.

A flock of ravens flew from one of the high trees deep within the forest. Dark winds gathered in the air. The woman raised her staff, pointing in the ravens' direction. "Show yourself!"

The ravens dove into the wind, transforming into the Witch from before. She glared fiercely at the enchantress with ember green eyes filled with an indefinite flame. Jay retreated to the edge of the woods, keeping out of sight.

"I shall seal you once again, Aturdokht. You shall not revive," the woman promised.

The Witch hovered in her spot over the pond. Her arms were crossed, and a smile twitched at the corners of her lips. She was neither saying nor doing anything in response. The enchantress's eyes changed to a golden red. The staff hit the ice and power surged from its end, traveling along the surface of the pond. The magic shot up, enveloping the Witch. Her power was absorbed, and her skin hardened to cracked stone.

Jay silently opened her eyes to a plain white ceiling. Various tubes were connected to her body, tracing back to a machine that monitored her heart rate. Thin lines moved in a straight, steady line on the screen. Jay carefully sat up in an upright position. A thick, light-blue curtain caged the side of her bed, boxing her in. All at once, she realized she was in the infirmary.

The curtain was briefly ruffled as Faith stepped in. She carried a clipboard and wore a mask that covered half of her face. "You're up!" Her voice came out muffled.

Jay managed a small smile. "Seems so." Fear engulfed her, and her eyes widened. "What happened?"

Faith crossed over to the heart monitor and jotted down a scribble of notes onto the clipboard. "You died," she explained.

"Died?" Jay repeated, unsure she had heard her correctly.

Faith rested a firm hand on Jay's shoulder. "Easy now," she sighed apologetically.

"How long was I dead?" she choked on the last word.

Faith took the stethoscope from around her neck and put it up against Jay's chest. "Forty-eight hours. You haven't missed much if that's what you're asking." Her forehead scrunched in confusion as she removed the stethoscope, writing something else down on her notepad.

"Why?"

Faith yanked down the mask, irritation taking over. "Honey," she sighed again and set the clipboard down. "You went through the transformation. Are you feeling anything abnormal?"

"What?" Jay cocked her head, befuddled. When she thought about it, something inside her did feel different—but it was too small and too deep to even realize it right away. For some reason, she thought immortality would feel different.

Faith leaned in closer to the monitor. She banged her fist on the top of the machine. The heart line had dropped flat. Jay's hand fluttered to her chest—it was utterly silent. She swallowed down the lump building in her throat.

"There is something that's a bit odd." Faith admitted. Jay looked at her curiously. "Your age receptors are still active."

"Meaning, I'll still age. But I thought—" Jay said, only to stop herself short. Maybe Taybeith had been right to say that there were different kinds of Immortals.

"So did I. Immortals usually stop aging after the transformation." She wrote something else down on her clipboard.

"Don't tell Dylan about this."

Faith gave Jay an astounded look before reluctantly giving in, placing her hands on her hips. "Alright, but the Headmaster will want to know, as well as Professor Riley. Gosh, he treats you kids like you're his own." Faith gathered her supplies and pushed a straggling strand of blonde hair behind her ear. "I'd like you to spend another day in the infirmary so I can run more tests on your . . . condition, but I have a feeling what I like doesn't matter, so you may go, if you wish."

Jay pushed the blankets back. Her clothes had been replaced with a thin, white, paper gown. Her face warmed with embarrassment. "Um," She cleared her throat.

"Don't worry, I'll bring you a change of clothes, as long as you promise to come in twice a week for a checkup," Faith bargained. "And this one doesn't count."

Chapter Eleven

Jay gave one last look in the mirror. She ran her fingers through the tangles of her silver hair. Her skin was freshly scrubbed clean, clear of any bruises and scars. The wound that had crossed along her mid-section was gone. It was as if nothing had ever happened. But it did, the trident on her wrist remained, reminding her of it. Jay recalled the dream.

Aturdokht, she thought, staring in the mirror. Who was she? Where did she come from? Why was it that the dream felt more like a memory? Her fingers gently grazed over her cheekbones, sliding down across her lips and chin. The enchantress had seemed so familiar to her. Unacquainted blue eyes stared back at her. Jay felt herself changing from the inside out. For instance, her eyes had a brighter shine than before, and she could see clearer than before, in both the spirit world and solidified realm. She also felt a stronger power taking form within her.

Jay shook her head, her face contorting with anger. She pulled open a drawer and searched through the mess of things. She found what she was looking for, carefully pinching it between her index finger and thumb. It was a small but sharp needle. Jay tightened her lip and dug the needle deep into her arm, tearing flesh. A thin line of blood poured from the small opening. Jay's breath shortened.

She held a steady gaze at her reflection in the mirror. "One . . . two . . . three . . ." She directed her attention back to her arm. Nothing. It was as if the needle had never punctured her skin.

There was a soft knock on the bathroom door. Faith's voice was on the other side. "You almost done?"

Jay wiped the sweat from her brow. She grabbed the navy-blue sweater hooked on the door and tied it around her waist over her jeans. The door opened and Faith pushed her way in, pausing in front of the mirror, taking her time to fluff her blonde hair. Jay shifted from one foot to the other. "Faith." She cleared her throat, horrified by her rough, raspy voice. "What did you give me?"

Faith applied more lip gloss over her puckered lips. "Nothing, why? You were on the brink of death, so I resorted to magic. All it did was make you look less dead and more alive, but you came back on your own. Oh, and don't bother thanking me for healing that nasty scar. You should have come to me earlier, it would have made healing it a whole lot easier."

Faith was known to be a great healer, but one with empathy to the outside world's ways. She tried to only use magic when it was absolutely necessary. During school hours, she also taught a class on the practice of medicine and healing used in both the human world and in Aris Magica. She believed that for humans and Aris Magicians to coexist, they must first learn and practice their ways. She would often remind her students it wasn't as though regular humans would use magic to handle every little accident they incur if regular medicine could fix it.

"Oh," Jay said, slightly disappointed. There went the logical answer to her problem. "I'm sorry. I thought I could use my magic and heal—" her voice faltered. It didn't make sense why her magic hadn't worked but Faith's had.

Faith glanced at Jay and her eyes widened. "Oh, no! Sit!" She pointed to the bathtub's ledge. Jay did as she was told. Faith opened the drawer, pulling out a comb and sat beside Jay. "This is a tangled mess."

Faith yanked the comb through Jay's hair. Gradually, the knots loosened, and her curls came back to life. Faith set the comb down and lifted strands of Jay's hair, weaving them into a braid. Faith was the closest thing some of the students had to a mother, or mother figure.

"You didn't have to do that," Jay mumbled.

"The Headmaster is back." Faith ignored her. "And Riley wants to talk to you." Jay slouched, clearly not welcoming the idea. "You owe them an explanation. The past few days have been brutal."

"I know," Jay said as Faith flicked the braid over her shoulder. "Thanks."

Faith pulled Jay to her feet. "Alrighty, get out!"

"Thank you!" Jay called. Faith waved her off as the door closed.

Chapter Twelve

Princess, the day to awaken is soon.

"Huh?" Jay glanced back over her shoulder. The hallway was empty. She shook it off and took a deep breath. She must have imagined it.

Jay stood in front of a tall wooden door located on the fourth floor, where most of the teachers and extra staff resided. It was bordered by intricate fringe designs that curled out in every direction, the wood was a dark hue, and the knocker looked like the talons of a large bird. Jay lifted the heavy knocker, letting it fall twice. She waited, then knocked again.

Jay turned the knob, and the door slowly swung open. It had been unlocked from the start. A small couch and a single oak desk faced the main window, and the fireplace against the back wall was lit with a warm flame. The first room was conjoined to a second room by another locked door.

Jay pressed her ear against the door farthest from the entrance. Voices could be heard on the other side. She inhaled, feeling a slight quiver of power rise throughout her veins. She willed it to her command, readjusting one of her eyes to the magic. She pulled the magic into her left eye, allowing her to see past the door.

The room was like the first room except for a huge bookshelf along the front wall. On one of the shelves was a row of glass orbs. Jay recognized them instantly as portable pocket dimensions, magic orbs that held the maps to other pocket dimensions around the Oregon area. The Headmaster must have kept them nearby in case of emergencies. She could see glimpses of various scenes within each one: one had rolling lavish green hills, while another had a tall silver skyscraper surrounded by the ocean.

Beside the bookshelf, three framed paintings hung on the wall. Each one was a painted picture of places within Aris Magica. Although Jay had never been, she recognized two of the locations just from the books she had read. The first painting was of the council building. A tall, pointed skyscraper surrounded by various egg-shaped rocks. Each rock was a gateway to another part of Aris Magica. The second painting was of tall, decorated oak doors, belonging to one of the secret libraries hidden within Aris Magica and the human world. The last painting Jay did not recognize. It was a tall black door shrouded in dark fog. Several hooded figures stood on a cliff overlooking the door. Looking away from the paintings, she could see Dylan and Riley standing with their backs to her. But the person that caught her attention was the older man behind the desk. His back was also to her, but she recognized him instantly as the Headmaster of the Institute.

"You think I don't care?" Jay overheard Dylan say.

Riley spun around, forcing Dylan to back up against the wall. He pointed his finger into Dylan's chest. "You're on lockdown. Believe it or not, people worry about you, kid. This must stop!"

"You don't know what you're talking about!" Dylan snapped.

"Son, it is for your own good." The Headmaster set down the glass ball he had been turning over in his fingers. "At the moment, you are letting rage control your actions instead of wisdom."

"We knew her fate was inevitable, but like I've explained before, she's a different kind of Immortal. We just haven't figured out the details yet."

"Taybeith?" Jay whispered, recognizing his voice. She spotted him leaning against the side wall with his arms crossed. A moment ago, she hadn't even noticed he'd been standing there, as he blended in with his surroundings.

From across the room, Dylan lunged at him. Riley slammed a fist into his shoulder, forcing him back. "Shut up! This is all your fault!" Dylan shouted accusingly.

"No, it's yours," Taybeith calmly responded. Dylan looked at him, unhinged.

"Enough!" Jay heard something slam against a hard surface. Silence descended over the room. The Headmaster's voice softened. "We have a visitor."

The door flung open. Jay stood there, bewildered. All eyes turned to her. Her eyes briefly met Dylan's, and she saw a glimpse of guilt reflected at her. He looked away. Soft eyes full of wisdom and strength met her gaze. The Headmaster moved from behind the desk and walked toward the bookshelf along the wall behind him.

He was a frail old man. His face was worn down by refined wrinkles that had been rewarded over time. He wore a dark green tunic with silver lining and black pants. A matching green amulet hung around his neck, capturing Jay's eyes. The amulet seemed to have its own separate magic contained inside. He stood a little over six feet tall, his gray hair slicked back into a ponytail at the nape of his neck. The Headmaster was known to be reclusive and introverted. She had only seen the occasional picture of the Headmaster but had never seen him in person. Only a few of the students at the Institute had claimed to have met him—and it usually was never for a good reason. But even now, the other rumors she had heard about him were true: she could feel magic radiating off him. His magic was almost overwhelming at first, but it changed into the feeling of a calm wave that washed over her the closer she got to him. The magic felt different, more pure, like the kind she'd learned about that existed in the heart of Aris Magica.

Jay straightened her posture and bowed out of respect. "Headmaster!" It was her first time meeting the Headmaster. She knew Dylan had met him a couple of times, but Jay had always been too scared. Even when she first arrived at the Institute, she refused to step into his office. Obviously, he had been a patient man until now. She wondered if he already knew this moment would come.

"It's good to see you up and about," he said with an arched brow. Jay nodded. She could feel the others' eyes burning into her skin—Dylan's, specifically.

"Jay!" Taybeith smiled, being the first to act. He crossed the room, drawing her into a tight hug. "So glad you're alive!"

"Ha, ha," she teased.

"Let me go," Dylan said, shoving Riley's hand away.

Jay avoided his gaze as he stalked over, ripping her from Taybeith's grasp and embracing her. Neither one of them said a word. Taybeith unwillingly stepped back.

"I thought . . . doesn't matter," he whispered into her hair.

She buried her face in the crook of his neck. She allowed herself to take comfort in his embrace and imagine that everything between them was back to normal. She felt Dylan squeeze her tighter, not wanting to let go of this moment.

Riley shared a look with the Headmaster, their eyes communicating with unspoken words. Not long after, the Headmaster cleared his throat, preparing to speak once again. "You came to talk, then?"

"Yes." She hesitantly pulled away from Dylan, letting their moment pass heavily between them. "Privately."

"Naturally." The Headmaster nodded.

Riley gestured to the door with his thumb. "Everybody out!"

Taybeith didn't argue as he headed for the door. He lingered, waiting for Dylan to follow. Dylan intertwined his hands with hers. "I'm not leaving." Jay's heart skipped a beat. She looked over at Dylan, who wore a determined expression.

Riley pushed up his sleeves, exposing the tattoos snaking down his muscular arms. "Damn it, you—"

"I wonder if Miss Raremore intended to say that *everyone* needs to leave," the Headmaster clarified.

Jay gently unwound her hand from Dylan's and offered a weak goodbye. Dylan set his jaw. "Save it," Riley grumbled, thumping the boy on the back of the neck. He grabbed Dylan by his shirt collar and forced him out.

"Sit, child." The Headmaster held out a welcoming hand to one of the chairs facing the desk. Jay settled in the armchair on the left, covered in a checkered print. The Headmaster took his seat behind the desk.

"I'm sure there is a lot you would like to tell me. Shall we start from the beginning?"

Everything began to pour out at once, from when she received the scar. "It was like a pain I'd never felt before. My entire body burned, and I couldn't stop it." She used light magic to draw the shape of the trident, tracing the faint scar on her wrist and showed the Headmaster. He examined it with a pensive stare but said nothing.

"There was another one too, across my chest and stomach, mirroring the same one as . . ." her voice trailed off, thinking of Dylan. She couldn't bring herself to talk about her death just yet, not after seeing the guilt in Dylan's eyes. "But it's not there anymore, Faith healed it." She quickly looked away. "There's something else too." Jay hesitated. "While I was dreaming, I met someone."

The Headmaster cocked his head to the side, his body language brimming with curiosity. "Do you think you are able to tell me more about this dream?"

Jay peered up at him through thick eyelashes. Nervously, she slowly nodded her head. "We were at a lake and the moon was fractured into tiny pieces. This place—it didn't feel of this world. Everything was so red." Jay looked down at the floor. "We weren't alone; there were other beings there with us. I saw . . ." She continued to stare hard at the floor. "The Demon from my nightmares from when I first got here. I think it's the one that killed Dylan's parents.

She wished the ground would swallow her whole. Her body fell under the heavy weight of pressure as she tried to recall more of the dream. A lot of it was hazy, except for the woman, whose emerald eyes burned into her soul. "Aturdokht," Jay said breathlessly. "And, I think, myself," she continued, sounding credulous even to herself. She quickly corrected herself. "Someone who looked very much like me stood over this lake, threatening to seal this Aturdokht woman once again. Professor, the darkness I felt from her was overwhelming," Jay said fearfully. She finally raised her head to meet the Headmaster's gaze. He was hanging onto every word she spoke with a spark of wonder in his eyes.

"Go on," the Headmaster gently prompted.

Jay shook her head, unable to. *I can't.* She had never felt magic like she had experienced while in her dream. Was that what true magic felt like in Aris Magica? Even though it was a dream, it had felt so real. *It was just a dream, right?* she wondered to herself.

"Sometimes dreams are just extensions of another reality, much like this pocket dimension we reside in while inside the mansion. It might not feel nor look like magic, but it is still an act of magic," the Headmaster responded. Jay wondered if she asked the question out loud, confused about how the Headmaster could seemingly read her mind.

The Headmaster folded his hands together, resting them on the surface of the desk. He leaned closer, pondering her tale. "That is quite the story, dear one."

Jay sat uncomfortably in her chair. She averted her attention to the stained glass mural hanging on the wall to the right of her; glass shards wove together to show a gruesome battle. A warlock in an ivy robe held a wand, blue sparks shooting from its tip. His opponent was a deformed black wolf. The beast stood on its hind legs with its snout ripped open, revealing sharp teeth and bloody drool. Surrounding the characters in the artwork was a swirl of blues, grays, and purples all moving together as one.

"Did this woman have the ability to control fire?" the Headmaster asked, bringing her attention back to the conversation.

"Aturdokht. Do you know anything about her?"

The Headmaster remained silent. His glasses rested on the bridge of his nose. He rose to his feet, striding over to the bookshelf, a look of contemplation on his face. He reached out his hand, and Jay felt the familiar spark of magic fill the room. From the highest part of the shelf, a book wiggled from its spot and fell into his hands. It was the color of brass. The paper was thinned and tattered, with nearly two thousand pages of knowledge stored inside.

"Headmaster?" Jay shifted to the edge of her seat.

He swiftly skimmed through a couple of the chapters before returning to his seat. He laid the book out in front of her. When he spoke, his voice rang deep. "There is a legend, one meant not to be discussed beyond these walls. Dark times. About a couple centuries ago, before the war that divided Aris Magica into light and dark, and before the raging war between humans and—"

"Aris Magica," Jay mumbled, finishing his sentence.

"There was a league made of the strongest ministers from four of the most powerful Aris clans. The Wizard Morbid, the Demon Lyist, the Fairy Aytox, and Serena, the most powerful Enchantress." All were long dead before the war against humanity took place.

Jay remembered learning about the big four. They were originally the start of magic itself. Later, other forms of magic began to develop based on their works and discoveries.

"The humans and Aris Magicians fought alongside each other against the dark forces. A Witch who had the ability to manipulate fire in a way we had never seen before led the Faeries and Demons. She was able to persuade the Demons into following her command."

The Faeries Jay had encountered had seemed unnaturally in order. "Headmaster, I know that part of history, but the woman, the one who . . . who looked like me?"

"I will speed up the story then," the Headmaster chuckled. "An Immortal was born on the seventh moon and second sun. Her rate of growth was incredibly fast, both mentally and physically. I have reason to believe that child was the start of the cycle. Even as a child, she knew her destiny and created her own forms of magic. She became the most powerful being within our forces, stronger than Serena. She was able to use the elements as her source of power, dark and light. The prophets divulged that to seal away the Witch, the Immortal would have to seal herself."

"So, the image I saw was the final battle between them?" Jay concluded.

"Not exactly, it could also very much have been the future. From that point on, we know her as the Immortal Princess, and on the next seventh moon and second sun, another was born."

Jay questionably pointed to herself. "Me?" She exhaled. "It's close, isn't it? That's why all of these changes keep happening to me?"

"I'm afraid so. In the meantime, I need to supply you a trainer to learn to gain control of your new power. It can be very dangerous if not handled by the right hands."

Just another new power to add to my never-ending list. "A trainer?" Jay asked.

"Each version of the Immortal Princess was assigned an Immortal that guided her to victory. It's been the same one since the beginning," the Headmaster further explained.

"Great," Jay sighed. "There is one more thing I'd like to ask you."

"Go on, child."

"After Aturdokht was sealed away, and the control the Witch had on the Demons shattered, they began taking human souls, and influenced their minds with poison, bringing upon the human versus Aris Magica War." Jay took a deep breath. She had learned all of this in her History of Aris Magica class last semester. "In my dream, I told you I saw the Demon that tore Dylan's parents apart, but I'm not sure if it was him . . ."

"Demons do not die," the Headmaster said. "The same concept applies to all evil. No matter how many battles rage, good and evil will continue to survive. That is the way the world is balanced. Good cannot survive without evil. But if it eases your mind, I will not relay anything we have discussed in this room to Mister McCoy."

"Thanks." Jay felt at ease. It was true what they said about the Headmaster—he was hard to talk to, but also the easiest person to confide in.

The Headmaster continued to explain while painting a picture. Silver dust trailed between them, rounding in the shape of a sphere. Three thin data streams circled the makeshift sphere. The dust fell, vanishing before hitting the desktop. "Regardless of being human or those belonging to Aris Magica, we all share one thing in common: the desire to live."

"To live?" Jay wondered. "To live or to survive with power." Jay looked down at her hands. She took a deep breath before meeting the professor's patient gaze. "Professor, have you heard of Ancients?"

The Headmaster smiled tenderly. "A breed of Aris Magicians that have been lost to history. Some to believe the Immortal Princess was one."

Jay pointed at herself. "Me?"

The Headmaster's eyes seemed to twinkle. "I wonder." He waved his hands again and another book came soaring through the air. He handed it to her.

Jay took it in her hands. It was a very thin book with a scaly, gray cover. The binding was old and tattered at the edges. Jay flipped it over to its front. The book didn't have an author, only a title: *The Forgotten Magic.*

Jay smiled and stood up from her chair. "Thank you!"

Chapter Thirteen

As Jay rounded the corner, a hand grabbed her tightly around her wrist, dragging her off to the side. Jay fought against the grasp that bound her. Her elbow went back, nailing the mysterious individual in the ribs. The person grunted, their hold on her loosening. A tiny shriek escaped her as their fingers tangled in her hair and they seized her yet again. Jay's captor shoved her into a dark room, slamming the door behind them, before finally releasing her. Jay stumbled on her heels and collapsed onto a plush cushion; the wind knocked out of her. She blinked, trying to adjust her eyes to the lack of light. Gradually, things started to come together. A tall silhouette loomed before her. Jay crawled back on her hands.

The tall figure bent lower, pulling her into them. "Thank God," her captor whispered, the familiarity of his voice sending a rush of relief through her.

Jay began to relax, wrapping her arms around him in return. "Dylan! Don't ever do that again or I might kill you," she threatened, slapping him in the arm and hugging him back.

"Stop talking," Dylan instructed. "I'm sorry for everything, okay? No more secrets, no more lies, and if you want to find out more about yourself, then let's do it together."

"Wow." Jay broke away, holding him back by his shoulders. "Who are you and what have you done with my Dylan?" A smile played at the corner of her lips.

Dylan rolled his eyes. He leaned past her to pull down the switch to the lamp on the stand beside them. A dim light illuminated their surroundings; she was in his dorm. Behind her was a bean bag she had fallen into, shoved in the corner. Four beds occupied the room—two on one side and two on the other. The other three beds were empty, for the moment, and neatly made. Two other doors hid in the back corner, one led to the bathroom. A tall window was shut with curtains drawn, blocking out the light from outside. A small desk rested beneath it, scattered with papers, pens, and manuscripts.

Dylan wrapped his arms around her waist, pulling her closer. He fell back onto the bed, bringing her with him. Jay giggled, turning on her back and nestling up beside him. The last time they were together like this, things didn't go well.

She tried to pull away, but Dylan didn't let her. She became aware of how close he was holding her to him. His hand was on the small of her back, gently caressing it. Jay cleared her throat. "Was Faith able to heal your scar, or . . ." She already knew the answer.

Dylan shook his head. "Not fully, no." Dylan took a deep breath. "We need to talk about what happened."

She knew exactly what he was referring to. "Part of me just wants to shut down and pretend what's happening isn't happening," Jay confessed, ignoring his statement. Dylan combed through her hair as she spoke. "But at the same time, it's not all bad," she said, meeting his deep gaze. His eyes had this effect on people, sucking them into a deep storm—dark, yet beautiful.

"I'm glad you're okay, but something's wrong, Jay. You're getting worse," Dylan said.

"It's only a phase."

"A phase! Are you serious?" He looked at her like she declared war against all of humanity. "Your eyes turned red, and for a moment, I wasn't even sure you recognized me! And then you died," he said breathlessly.

"Let's not argue tonight, okay? I feel like that's all we've been doing. Believe me, I know things are different, and that scares me, but I still don't want to talk about it," Jay confessed. The transformation had been a lot to take in.

Dylan held up his hands, surrendering to her wishes. "Alright," he relented. Dylan noticed the book still in her hand. "What's this?"

"Oh." Jay gave him the book. She smiled to herself. *Maybe if I'd just given him the last one as easily, then together we could've prolonged my transformation.*

Dylan turned it over in his hands but didn't bother opening it. "Did Taybeith give you this?" he asked slowly.

Jay shook her head. "The Headmaster did. I think he knows about Ancients and other magic lost to history."

Dylan's mood seemed to brighten at hearing the book came from the Headmaster. "Well, let's look through it together tomorrow." He sat the book on his bedside desk.

"Thank you," Jay smiled. Perhaps Dylan had changed. "And I'm sorry about before." Jay frowned.

Dylan stiffly nodded. "It's fine," he whispered, kissing her temple. "It's fine."

Jay rolled over to her side. She patted the area beside her. The spot was still warm but empty. She sat up in alarm. He was gone, no note. She reached for the book across the bed on his nightstand.

She ran her hand across the cover, tracing the letters of the title. "Okay," she whispered. *"Scire."* She felt her eyes change and magic course through her body. The book opened and quickly flipped its pages until stopping at the page she desired. Everything in the world had a soul, including books, meaning their soul magic could be accessed, used, and controlled, just as Jay had done.

The book stopped on a crinkled page, as if someone before her had considered tearing it out. The title of the chapter was "Ancients and Immortals." Jay flipped to the next page, titled "Shape-Shifters." The information she desired was limited to a single paragraph. She took a deep breath before beginning to read.

> *Here we come upon another lost breed. I have been able to find very little information on this topic. It's as if these creatures wanted to be forgotten by both humans and Aris Magica. Even in the grandest of libraries in Aris Magica, their telling is scarce. Different, but also confused for one another are Ancients and Immortals. Ancients were one of the very first Aris Magicians. Some think they started the acts of magic, being the first to pull magic from the land on which we stand, now called Old Magic. Neither Ancients nor Immortals are born, but chosen. How, I have not discovered. The transformation is different for each chosen. Some may die, while others may undergo changes in their personality or abilities, and some may go through both. While Immortals stop aging and live forever, an Ancient does not live forever in one body, but in many, as its soul infuses with that of its chosen. I believe only one Ancient existed, transferring their soul throughout history, saving us from a grave danger that the world may not know to fear.*

"Aturdokht." Jay whispered aloud to herself. The nameless author had been on to something. Jay closed the book and squeezed it to her chest. *Ancients*, she thought. Could she be one of them? It would explain why her age receptors were still working after undergoing the transformation the book talked about. Did the Headmaster know? Jay assumed he did, seeing how he had looked at her when she had brought up the topic. She wondered if Aturdokht suspected her to be one too. And the woman she saw over the lake, was that supposed to be her in a previous life? The unanswered questions raced through Jay's mind. Whenever she found a possible piece of herself, it felt as if she took a hundred steps backward from any other answers. Jay sighed. She wished she could talk to Dylan about this.

She looked up from the book and at the empty spot on his bed. It bothered her. Dylan never left without telling her where he was going if they were together for the night. Jay racked her brain, but the last thing she remembered was falling asleep in Dylan's arms. No, that wasn't right. The last thing she remembered was him whispering something about bringing an end to everything before leaving. She threw the pillow aside, slipping on her shoes. She didn't have a lot of time.

Jay charged into Riley's office uninvited. He was sitting behind the desk with a fresh cup of coffee and a newspaper. He was one of the only people at the Institute that liked to feel connected to the outside world. He also used the newspaper to keep tabs on possible human interactions he could use for missions. Jay noticed the open, yet neglected, textbook for their History of Aris Magica class off to the side. Covering half of the textbook was a list of possible missions the extracurricular class team would go on once the semester started. She saw her name and another student's, Adam, written next to the one titled, *Morris Bakery*. Jay banged her fist on his desk. Papers flew, and pens went falling to the floor.

"Oops." She hadn't meant to hit his desk that hard.

"What the hell!" Riley exclaimed, tossing the newspaper onto the desk.

"Sorry," Jay quickly blurted out. Riley gave her a strange look. "Where is he?" she demanded, cutting to the chase. She wouldn't dare pull this stunt with any of the other professors. It wasn't an unknown fact that Riley favored Jay and Dylan above his other students. In a way, he reminded her of what an older brother or father figure would look like. He was the one, under the Headmaster's guidance, who had brought her and Dylan to the Institute. Ever since then, he'd overseen teaching them how to control their "unchecked rage issues," as he would so eloquently put it.

"Where?" Jay gave him a glare full of promising threats.

Riley bared his teeth in her direction. "Damn it, it's seven thirty in the morning, Jay, stop harassing me!" Riley was not a morning person. His office hours were a strict 10 a.m.–7 p.m. Before or after, he didn't like being bothered, especially by Jay or Dylan, who usually found themselves in trouble. "You're working your way toward one hell of a detention."

Jay considered the idea, but she hadn't even begun to harass Riley yet. She rolled her eyes. "Where is Dylan?" she repeated.

"What, is he gone?" Riley asked, returning to drinking his coffee. "How the hell should I know where he is then?"

Jay shrugged and rolled her eyes. "Because he tells you everything."

"Not as of late," Riley said, taking another sip. He flicked his newspaper in the air and continued to read it, ignoring Jay.

Jay tapped her fingers on his desk impatiently. "So, he didn't tell you what happened in the forest that day?" Riley cleared his throat, but didn't confirm nor deny. Dylan had yet to tell Jay about the events that unfolded in the forest before he came back cursed, bloodied, and injured. They hadn't had a chance to talk about it. "I know you went back with him to check out the area." Jay pressed on. "Did you find anything?"

Riley continued to keep his mouth shut, pretending to be interested in his readings.

"Riley!" Jay begged. "Dylan could be in danger."

"When is he not?" Riley grumbled. He sighed, setting the newspaper down. He looked at Jay, seemingly contemplating what to tell her. "He met a Witch in the forest. Some delirious mage who can control pocket dimensions like the Headmaster. I'm looking into it, alright!" he said.

Jay's eyes grew wide. Her thoughts immediately went to Aturdokht. *Has she been watching me this whole time? Had she tried to use Dylan to get to her?* The trident on the inside of her wrist began to throb as if someone was poking it with a needle. Jay rubbed it, biting the inside of her lip anxiously.

Jay turned on her heels and began to head for the door. "Where the hell do you think you're going?" Riley shouted after her.

"I'm going after him. I have an idea where he could be. He takes the same road back to the Institute every time he visits his parents. The attack had to have happened there."

Jay stopped halfway to the door. She found herself staring at a prized weapon encased in a glass shadowbox, hooked to the side wall. It was Riley's mortar that he only took out on special occasions, usually to brag to the students about the great beast he'd taken down with it. Like Dylan, Riley was a Hybrid who excelled in weaponry. In Dylan's case blades, but in Riley's, it was guns. Riley never missed. She glanced back at Riley, who had followed her gaze. His back straightened.

"If you're coming with, you should probably bring that thing." Jay gestured to the mortar.

Chapter Fourteen

The wind faded as she stood yards from him. Dylan pulled out his weapon. He gripped the hilt of his two silver magnums. Although he preferred blades, he was just as skilled with guns. The air was quiet; even the wind had stopped moving. The trees seemed to lean inward, casting a dark shadow over the leaf-colored road. Colors of orange, red, and yellow surrounded him as more leaves fell from the trees.

Dylan took a deep breath. *Show yourself*, he thought.

He knew Aturdokht was nearby. He couldn't yet see her, but he felt her magic all over. A dark, suppressing feeling that floated through the air. Dylan raised an eyebrow as the magic revealed itself, becoming tangible. Dark, wispy clouds appeared from thin air, coming together before him further down the road. The magic came together, forming a whirlwind, until it took the shape of a figure.

Finally. Dylan lifted his guns, aiming them at Aturdokht.

The Witch drew back the hood of her cloak, revealing herself. She held out her hand, beckoning for him. Her lips moved in silence. Her hand began to produce a warm glow. A stream of fire emitted from the palm of her hand and launched out toward him. Dylan dodged to the side, avoiding contact. An ash-burned trail was left in his place.

Dylan fired his guns repeatedly, lunging from one tree base to another. The Witch was relentless, bringing more fire to the woods. A fierce wind picked up and a root rose from the ground, tripping him. A wicked smile spread across her face. The closer he got, the more he could see the palm of her hand illuminating with the symbol for flame. Dylan closed his eyes, ready to face the pain. He struggled to lift himself up, but a sharp pain shot through his left ankle and his side throbbed. He had torn open the stitches sown across his stomach, reopening his wound. Dylan cursed, feeling the heat of the fire quickly approaching.

"*Forsvinne*!" a familiar voice shouted. "Dylan, are you trying to get yourself killed?" The heat of the fire never came, bouncing off her counter spell.

"Jay," Dylan grimaced. "What are you doing here?"

"YOU IDIOT!" Jay fell to her knees and threw a protective arm around him. She pulled his arm up and draped it over her shoulder. She used most of her strength to pick him up and move behind the nearest tree. Beads of sweat broke along his forehead. Once they stopped moving, Dylan leaned back against the tree. He stared up into the smoke and red sky. An explosion went off behind them, sending pieces of tree bark and dirt flying in every direction.

"We've come to rescue you!" she shouted over the sound of Riley's machine gun.

"I don't need rescuing!" Dylan coughed as smoke entered his airway. He winced, clutching his stomach. He shifted his weight to the right.

Dylan looked up to see Jay peer around the trunk of the tree. The Witch stood unharmed. Riley was off to their side, loading more bullets into his weapon. Aturdokht met Jay's gaze, the Witch's amber eyes ablaze with a strong firelight. Dylan watched as Jay's entire body froze and panic arose in her eyes as she realized who the Witch was—Aturdokht. Jay dodged back behind the tree. Her breath was heavy and short.

"What's wrong?" Dylan asked, trying to support his own weight while standing on a sprained ankle.

Aturdokht waved her hand in a circular rotation. The tattered cloak she wore returned to the earth, replaced by a fiery red dress, its hem fanning out around her like flames of a fire. Her pale skin was invincible to the damage Riley had inflicted, the bullets passing right through her.

Riley let out a fool-hearted whistle. "Riley!" Jay shouted. He glanced behind him at the two students against the tree. Dylan's face paled, contorted with pain. Jay was doing her best to support his body.

Riley set the machine gun in place. "Jay, get him to the truck!"

Jay took an unsteady step from her protective spot behind the tree. Dylan caught her hand, yanking her back hard into his body. He grunted from the force. An arrow of fire whizzed past, nicking the side of the trunk. Dylan grabbed her shoulders, forcing her to face him.

"I'm fine," Jay assured him. "We need to leave."

Dylan wheezed in a long breath of air. "We need to fight." He reached for his knife.

"Dylan, you're injured!"

"I need to get close. Buy me a few minutes, will you?" He grimaced, attempting to stand straighter.

"Dylan, for once, listen to me! This is a battle we can't win. You have no idea who she is or what she's capable of. I've seen it," Jay said, searching his eyes. "The most damage you'll do is get yourself killed! Nothing's even hitting her," Jay protested.

"That's a risk I'm willing to take."

Jay's face darkened. She removed the dagger from her back pocket, ripping off a long piece of fabric from her sweater. She stepped closer to him and raised the hem of his shirt. The strings of the stitches were torn apart; he was bleeding badly. She wrapped the bandage around his chest.

"You aren't a hero," Jay said. She pointed a hand at his left ankle and then toward the tree they sat by. Her eyes glowed a pale red. "*Helbrede.*" Some of the leaves on the tree turned to a crumpled brown and dropped to the ground.

"Damn!" Riley growled. He bit off the top of another grenade, throwing it in the Witch's direction. Within a few seconds, it detonated near her feet. Using the smoke as cover, Jay darted past Riley across the forest floor. "Damn it!"

Jay held Dylan's two magnum guns in front of her. A fraction of power could be seen transferring into the guns' chambers as blue trails of light bounced from her fingertips. Up ahead stood a ghostly figure within the fog. Jay fired several rounds, and gold and blue streams trailed behind the bullets.

Dylan watched the smoke flash with signs of a battle. Crows and ravens took flight, cawing from the branches. The trees leaned toward the ground. The smoke began to thin into a lazy fog. Jay was in a raging battle with the Witch. She threw a fireball and Jay rolled to the side. Another followed, splitting in two. The heat singed Jay's skin as she continued to duck and dodge. A warm glow radiated from under Aturdokht's skin from her shoulders, traveling down her arms. Jay fired off one gun, tossing the other high in the air. She took out her dagger and threw it at her opponent. The airborne magnum landed in her hand, and she fired double the bullets.

The blade spiraled at an odd angle toward Aturdokht. She stepped back, clasping her hands together. She pulled them apart, spreading out a translucent wall of fire. The bullets ricocheted off the blade, going in every direction. Dylan watched as Jay flicked her finger, her focus seemingly aimed at one bullet, willing it farther and faster. He held his breath, watching the wall of fire expand around the Witch. The bullet passed through the remaining hole unnoticed.

"Yes!" Dylan cheered. The wall wavered, collapsing in a puddle of liquid flames. The single bullet had struck the Witch on the inside of her shoulder. She jerked back, gripping the spot. Blood soaked her hand, and she fell to the ground.

Dylan made his move as the magic Jay had worked on him eased his pain. Tiny, circular platforms aligned in a path before him. Jay was using her magic to help him. Every time his foot touched the light, his body moved faster. He readied his dagger, its blade pointing at his target. Jay covered the tip of his blade in magic. It was the only thing that seemed to have worked on the Witch, since she was bound to the laws of the space her spirit was confined in. Aturdokht gasped, seeing Dylan too late. He let out a battle cry as the cold blade sank into her side. She cried out in rage. Black wind surrounded her, blinding Dylan's vision. The last thing he saw was the wing of a raven.

Dylan glanced over at Jay, who was shaking her head, confusion written all over her face.

Dylan felt Jay's magic leave him and the pain from his stomach return. Riley was behind him before he could fall. "Can you stand?" Riley asked. Dylan felt exhausted. Riley steadied him, picking him up.

"Come on!" Riley grunted. "It's over."

"It's only begun," Jay countered, walking over.

Jay opened the door to the backseat of the silver Ford truck. Riley eased Dylan's body inside of the car. Jay followed, closing the door behind her. Riley hauled the rest of his equipment into the open bed, then climbed into the front seat. The sun was setting in the distance, painting the sky in rays of pink, orange, and yellow.

"That was *dangerous*," Riley announced with a ridiculing smirk.

Jay rolled her eyes with a mocking expression. "And you've never done anything dangerous."

Riley cracked a smile as he started the car.

Jay held onto Dylan's hand. His breathing was slow, but he was alive. He had fallen asleep, leaning on her shoulder.

Chapter Fifteen

Faith crossed her arms, glowering at the two. She held a first aid kit to her chest. "You've got to be kidding me." Her eyes shifted between the two of them.

Dylan and Jay sat side by side on one of the curtained-off beds. They shared the same wide grin. Bruises covered most of their bodies, and a mixture of blood and dirt caked their clothes and skin. Jay's clothes had been torn, her pant leg ripped in various places. Dark smudges scorched her face and hands. Dylan's smile wavered, turning into a grimace. He had reopened his wound and the blood was soaking through the makeshift bandage. He was in the worst state.

"Unbelievable."

Dylan shrugged. "We can't help it."

Faith rolled her eyes in dismay. "Yeah, yeah. Dylan, you're first. Jay, start healing yourself, there's a plant over there." Faith slammed the first aid kit on the counter by the bed. She didn't really need it, but it was a ready alternative. She gestured for Jay to move, gently pushing Dylan onto his back. "What happened?"

"My stitches tore, and my ankle twisted, but Jay healed it. It doesn't matter how it happened," Dylan explained. He took a deep breath, closing his eyes.

"Perfect," she answered, her voice lacking sympathy. "At least we know that even injured, your rude attitude is still intact." She lifted the lid of the kit, pulling out a needle and thread. She lifted his shirt, exposing his scar. The flesh was ringed with purple and black bruises, and blood seeped out.

"This'll sting."

Dylan's screams shook the infirmary as the stitches mended his skin back together. By the time it was done, he was breathless, cursing, and sweating. "Wasn't that bad, was it?" Faith patted him on the shoulder. "Now, let's have a look at this." She helped him sit up.

"Why? It's healed." Dylan frowned as she moved around the bed to his ankle. "Doesn't even hurt."

She examined it with her eyes. A soft glow came from them, shining on Dylan's ankle. "Huh? Jay did this?" Faith sounded proud. "She's gotten better, but unfortunately, she didn't heal it all the way. The bone has a small crack in it. Over time, it might get worse. You're sure it doesn't hurt?"

"No, can you just heal it?" Dylan asked.

"I thought maybe your stitches would be enough to serve as a reminder and teach you to be more careful. Apparently not—and I'm pissed—so deal with it," she snapped.

Dylan rolled his eyes. Jay called over from where she sat. She was pulling magic from the plant to heal her own small scrapes she had received. "How'd you see that crack? His ankle looks fine on the outside."

Faith scowled at her with keen eyes. "Just because I'm old doesn't mean my powers are gone." Faith was gifted with anything dealing within the art of healing. She chose to go about the human practice when dealing with students who only had the Hybrid gene. She had used her eyes to x-ray his ankle. Two bones were deeply chipped and jutting out slightly in the wrong direction.

Faith stood back, waving her hands elegantly in a flowing rotation. Green light and mint leaves swirled around his ankle. A white cast began to form around his foot until it became a solid boot. Dylan tried lifting his leg and frowned. It was heavy.

"Is the cast really necessary?" Dylan asked, slightly annoyed.

"Your turn." Faith faced Jay, ignoring Dylan.

Jay laughed awkwardly, backing away with her hands held up in surrender. "I'll pass."

Faith seized her wrist. "Not the slightest chance. Besides, you made me a promise."

Jay pouted as Faith pulled out a stool and pushed Jay down into it. She snapped her fingers and an oval-shaped pill and a glass of water appeared on the stand near Dylan. Without question, he swallowed it.

Faith tilted Jay's head up, turning it roughly around in her hands. She placed her stethoscope on Jay's heart. Still nothing, just silence. Faith examined the scars that scraped her skin. They were already starting to fade away.

Faith stepped back, slightly confused. "Well, you're fine, I guess."

"Besides the still heart, immortality, and everything else," Jay said sarcastically, reading between the lines.

"Ha, ha, very funny. Now get out."

Jay rolled her eyes, hopping down from the bed. Dylan could feel himself wanting to protest her departure, but his eyelids continued to grow heavier. The last thing he heard was the door clicking shut.

Chapter Sixteen

Jay slipped through the door, stepping into the library. There were quite a handful of people studying at the computers and tables in the back, each lost in their own world. Winter break was nearing its end and finals were approaching fast. More students had started returning to the Institute after being away for so long. Jay had decided that what was going on in her life was more important than school.

Taybeith collided into her, but instead of falling back, he wrapped his arms around her. He squeezed her so tightly that Jay felt like her ribs were being crushed. "You're back!" he laughed. It was the first time she noticed how strong he was. Even though his lanky body said otherwise, she hadn't taken notice of the fact that the black suits he wore hid the muscle he had beneath it.

The librarian behind the desk gave them a pointed glare. Taybeith wouldn't let go. "I thought . . ."

Jay eased her way out of his arms, taking a half step back. "Thought what?" Although she liked Taybeith well enough, she wasn't sure if his hugs were welcomed. It wasn't like they hadn't hugged before, but this time it felt different—wanting, almost. Taybeith smiled sadly in response to her quizzical expression.

"Look, I'm fine. Besides, I was only gone for, what? A couple of hours? In fact, I never want to hear those words again. Did you find anything new?" Jay quipped, changing the subject as she made her way to their spot at the window seat.

Taybeith seemed flustered, almost to a point of embarrassment. "Kind of. At least I hope it's useful." He opened his laptop that had been left there waiting for them. Jay pulled her knees to her chest, intent on listening.

"For one, you aren't an Immortal, just confirmation if you still had doubts." Jay figured as much, especially after reading the book the Headmaster had given to her. "But I found legends and stories about a Princess being sealed away—"

"Princess?" *The one from my dreams.* "Did it have anything to do with the seventh moon and second sun?"

"Yes?" Taybeith asked, puzzled.

Jay inhaled a troubled breath. "A couple of days ago, I experienced a dream. I—no, *my spirit* —was on the battleground of where the sealing supposedly took place or will take place. A woman I have never seen before stood on the lake at its center. She wielded so much power. In her hand, she held a staff and performed some ritual. I remember a seal wrapping around Aturdokht."

"Aturdokht," Taybeith said so quietly that Jay almost didn't catch it. Taybeith took the information in stride. "Perhaps there's a connection?"

Jay nodded. "Maybe. That's what I want to figure out." Her eyes lit up. "Oh, another thing. Maybe we should check the books without authors," Jay suggested. She knew there was a whole shelf dedicated to them in the back of the library. After reading what the Headmaster had given to her, maybe there was more information on Ancients and the Princess. Perhaps they'd just been looking in the wrong section, since the two were considered lost breeds.

Taybeith stared at something past her, looking out the window. "Hold that thought, will you?" he asked. Jay glanced behind but saw nothing. She turned back to him with a confused gaze. "I think I might have seen the book you're looking for," Taybeith stuttered, scrambling for an answer.

"Um, okay," Jay said. She watched Taybeith quickly get up from his spot across from her. He continued to keep his eyes on the windows. He headed toward the back of the library where Jay had mentioned.

Jay sat there for a moment, confused. She'd never seen Taybeith behave this way. It was true that he was a little odd, but he was always composed. But a moment ago, he had seemed startled. Jay tapped her foot impatiently, knowing she shouldn't pry. She bit her lip and began to twist a strand of her hair around her finger. She sighed and got up from her seat, following the path she saw Taybeith take toward the back shelves.

The farther she went into the library, the darker and quieter it became. She glanced to her left, checking the window seats. Most of them were empty. She checked to her right too, thinking he might have gone down one of the aisles. The smell of books grew stronger, and Jay knew she was entering the oldest section of the library, filled with books that had been around for many lifetimes. She loved books, but not so much the smell. Jay scrunched her nose as she neared the last window seat. Her eyes widened. Taybeith's back was to her as he stared out the window. On the other side was a raven flapping its wings to stay afloat. Ember green eyes stared fiercely down at him.

Jay gasped. She quickly covered her mouth and disappeared into a window seat. The raven looked oddly familiar. She and Dylan had both seen Aturdokht shape-shift into the very same thing. Jay remembered seeing shape-shifting as a lost form of magic in her book. Jay had seen ravens in her dreams as well when she had met Aturdokht. What was Taybeith doing talking to one?

Jay couldn't bring herself to peek around the corner again. She slowly and carefully slipped from the window seat and speed-walked back to her own. She began gathering her things in a panic.

The worst thought crossed her mind. *Was Taybeith in league with Aturdokht?* She had to find Dylan quickly.

"What's the rush?"

Jay froze. She slowly turned around. Taybeith was standing directly behind her. She searched his eyes to see if anything about him had changed, but he was still the same. She cleared her throat. "Oh um, nothing. It's just, I forgot . . . I forgot I was meeting Dylan!" she stammered frantically.

Taybeith nodded slowly, but if he noticed something was off, he didn't show it. "Okay. I guess I'll catch up with you later?" he asked. "Oh!" He grabbed her wrist, stopping her from leaving. "You had wanted to tell me something, about the authorless books?"

"Oh, no, it's fine. I'll tell you about it later," Jay lied. Taybeith nodded. He let go of her wrist and led the way to the door. Jay kept a small distance between them as they walked.

Chapter Seventeen

Dylan leaned against his crutch. He had been in therapy for the last hour. Professor Storwick, an older man with a shaved head, gray eyes, and a stocky figure, monitored him. Dylan was in the process of repeating the stretches as instructed when a knock came at the door. It creaked open, flying back on its hinges.

"Miss Ferrell," Professor Storwick said as he adjusted his glasses, pushing them further up the bridge of his nose. "What brings you here?"

"Riley and the Headmaster said . . . I wanted to see how he was doing?" she confessed.

"Yes, I suppose," he said, sounding uncertain. "I'll give you two a few minutes alone then." He stepped out of the small room and into the hall.

Dylan remained where he was, making no effort to approach her. "Hey!" She smiled as if they were longtime friends. Dylan stiffly nodded. "Mind telling me what happened?"

"It's none of your business."

Ami's lip quivered. "Yeah, okay. Is Jay alright?" She didn't seem too concerned, despite her best efforts.

"We're both fine." Dylan rubbed the back of his neck in irritation. "Ami, what do you want?" he sighed.

"Nothing, I just wanted to . . ." her voice faltered as she spoke. "I wanted to let you know that Professor Riley and the Headmaster want to see you."

"Thanks," was all Dylan said in response. He grabbed the crutch and headed for the door. Ami hung her head as he passed. "If you see Jay first, tell her to meet me," Dylan added, letting the door shut behind him.

It wasn't hard to find her. In fact, she was in the first place he looked. One of the students with blue skin, sparkling eyes, and studded horns held the door open. Dylan hobbled in, taking his place beside her. He wasn't ready for what he saw. Taybeith was inches away from Jay. The two of them were walking toward the door. Taybeith kept touching Jay, whether it was on her shoulder, or a light brush against her arm. Dylan had to resist the urge to storm over and yank them apart. He'd seen Jay with other guys before and couldn't have cared less. He couldn't quite figure out why, but for some reason, Taybeith made his skin crawl. He didn't trust the boy, and he didn't like how much time Jay had been spending with him. Was he jealous?

Dylan stopped himself in his tracks. His heart was beating faster than normal, and his breathing had quickened. He *was* jealous. Dylan suddenly had the urge to laugh. He was jealous! Dylan had never felt this way before—not about anyone. His palms became sweaty, and he felt his face flush from embarrassment.

"Oh, Dylan!" Taybeith called out his name. Dylan looked up and glared at Taybeith.

"Taybeith," he said coldly. His eyes fell to Jay's. Dylan just noticed how frazzled she looked. "Jay." He looked back at Taybeith. "What were you two up to?" His glare had returned.

Taybeith looked away suddenly, self-conscious. Dylan wondered why. Did Taybeith feel uncomfortable around him too? Dylan smirked at the thought. *Good.*

"We were in the middle of researching, but Jay said she had plans to meet you. Perfect timing." Taybeith gestured shyly to Dylan.

"Yeah, perfect timing." Dylan grabbed Jay by the hand. "A moment, please."

He pulled Jay toward the computers and away from Taybeith. "What's wrong with you?"

Jay gasped for air as if she had been trying to hold it in. "It's Taybeith," she said in a hushed whisper. "Something's off about him. I saw him talking to a raven."

A raven? Dylan remembered seeing one every time he'd encountered the Witch. He looked at Jay with shocked eyes. "Is Taybeith . . . her?"

"I don't think so, but I also don't know for sure. Something is weird about him. When he saw the raven, he freaked out."

Dylan looked over at Taybeith, who hadn't left yet. He stood there, fiddling with his fingers as he waited for Jay. Dylan groaned, then sighed, before he bowed his head. He knew what had to be done, but it didn't mean he liked it. He grabbed Jay by her shoulders and had her face toward him. He looked her directly in her eyes. A part of him wanted to pull her closer and just get lost in them. "Play along," he said. "Until we know for sure. Because right now, we're in the dark."

"Yeah okay." Jay's eyes became hopeful. "I might even be wrong, right?"

Dylan gritted his teeth and stopped himself from saying anything. *I hope so*, he thought.

Dylan and Jay walked back over to Taybeith. He looked down at their hands, still intertwined. Dylan didn't want to let go, but he knew he had to. Slowly, he let Jay's hand drop from his, but before he did, he felt her squeeze his hand as if she hadn't been the one to let go either.

"She's all yours," he said.

Taybeith beamed. "Well, we should take a break anyway. I hear they're serving lunch in the Grand Hall." Taybeith held out his hand for Jay to take.

Dylan saw as she hesitated before taking it. "Have fun you two," Dylan said sourly. He watched them leave together.

Dylan's blood was boiling. If Taybeith was a traitor, at least one good thing would come from it: he would be able to finally get rid of the kid how he pleased.

Chapter Eighteen

Jay felt relived now that Dylan knew what she did. If she hadn't told Dylan what she had seen, then perhaps she would have believed she'd imagined it. Shape-shifting was a rare and lost breed of magic. Although she'd seen Aturdokht do it a couple times, it was still hard for her to wrap her head around it. But it couldn't be a coincidence that Taybeith was talking to a raven that looked oddly like the one she had seen in the forest. Jay knew if she hadn't told Dylan, then curiosity would have eaten at her, causing her to act rashly and ask Taybeith himself. She glanced awkwardly up at Taybeith as they walked. She still couldn't believe what she had seen. Taybeith had been staring at that raven. After how many times she'd seen ravens in the past week, it was too soon to rule it out as a coincidence. Taybeith was hiding something. After a while of silence, she decided to do as Dylan had said and play along. Jay liked Taybeith, and she wanted to prove that he was just as much a victim in this situation as everyone else.

"Dylan needs to rest," Jay lied. They walked the halls on the main floor. "He wouldn't have admitted it, but I can tell he's still in a lot of pain."

"That, or he doesn't like me," Taybeith hinted.

"What?" Jay laughed awkwardly. "Not true!"

Taybeith sneered. "Sarcasm won't fix this one."

"Good morning!" Two girls waved, passing Jay. They glanced at Taybeith and Jay's hands. One of them snickered before looking away.

Jay gasped at the realization. They were still holding hands, and she awkwardly let go. She didn't even know why she had grabbed his hand in the first place.

"Jay!" They had absently wandered to the front door. Riley shook the snow from his coat. He hadn't been as badly wounded, just a few scrapes. "We need to talk, follow me," he ordered. Taybeith hesitantly inched back. "You too!" Riley looked back. "Where's Dylan?"

"I don't know," she said. She had to keep up with the lie she had told Taybeith. "And don't go looking for him either, he needs to rest."

"He can rest when he's dead." Riley scowled but didn't put any effort in going to find him. "Come on, someone wants to meet you."

Jay and Taybeith stepped into the room and the door closed behind them. They were in one of the smaller classrooms. Twelve rows of desks faced the only chalkboard. On the side wall next to them, four windows shone with bright rays of light. The Headmaster sat behind the main desk, flipping through a book. A boy leaning against the wall near the second window caught Jay's attention. He had snow-white hair, pale skin, and startling blue eyes. He looked at least a year older than her, around seventeen. The boy stared fixedly at a point beyond the glass.

"Ah, Jay, I hope you are doing well." The Headmaster closed the book with a simple wave of his hand.

"Well enough." Jay slouched into the desk closest to the door and furthest from the stranger, continuing to keep an eye on him.

"Headmaster." Taybeith bowed deeply before taking his seat.

Jay glanced at Riley, nodding her head toward the boy. Riley stood blocking the door with his hands shoved in his pockets. He shook his head, clearly just as confused as Jay was.

The Headmaster's demeanor instantly changed, settling in on a serious approach. "And Dylan?"

"Headmaster, who is this?" Jay asked, avoiding the question. Something about the boy put Jay's nerves on edge.

"Yesterday," the Headmaster began, rising to his feet and circling around the desk. "Describe what you saw." He towered over Jay, casting an eerie shadow.

Jay once again looked at Riley, who cleared his throat. "Headmaster, it's only been a day. The kid needs time to recover."

"I need all parts of the story," the Headmaster repeated, ignoring Riley. "Jay, we need you to cooperate. Was it her?"

Of course, she knew *whom* he was talking about. But she wasn't talking. She kept watching the boy. He must feel her eyes burning a hole in the back of his head, but still he refused to turn around. The Headmaster took notice of the distraction.

"I'm sure you have many questions about our guest, who I will introduce later, which will no doubt lead to more questions." His eyes narrowed, regaining her full attention. Jay had yet to see this side of the Headmaster. Although he appeared calm and gentle, his voice held a dangerous iciness to it that made her want to speak, rather than suffer the consequences of not doing so.

"It was her—Aturdokht." Jay leaned back in her chair. "She didn't seem to be able to talk like she had in my dreams. But the power we faced, it was real enough."

"It wasn't her." The boy peeled himself from the wall and faced them. His eyes, still startling against his white hair, were a paler blue than her own. Jay showed no hint of the emotions swelling inside her. "It was just a corpse of an animal, maybe." At his assumption, Jay recalled seeing the wing of a raven before Aturdokht disappeared. "Her spirit most likely borrowed it to do her bidding, and transformed it into what you thought to be human. A premature state—much like the one you're in."

"So, you're saying not only does this Witch use fire, but she also practices shape-shifting," Riley said, raising his eyebrows. "Shit."

Shape-shifting was another lost ability. Jay wondered if the lost breeds were forgotten for a reason; for how much fear, darkness, and power seemed to be wrapped up in their history. The more she found out, the more fear she started to feel. How was she supposed to be the reincarnation of an Ancient Princess who defeats Aturdokht?

The Headmaster explained, "Do you recall the discussion we had earlier about finding you a trainer to help control these newfound abilities? I'd like to introduce you to Cryis."

"You've got to be kidding," Riley snorted, saying aloud what Jay was thinking.

We are just alike. The thought appeared in her head, though it was not her own.

Jay stared at him, shocked, but his mouth had never moved. He narrowed his eyes, daring her to speak up.

"What the—" she stopped herself.

"Yes, I'm sure you have many doubts. But there is a reason he will be your trainer," the Headmaster responded. "As I mentioned before, the previous Immortal—"

"Ancient," Jay corrected. She looked up at the Headmaster.

The Headmaster looked at her with the same twinkle in his gaze when he had given her the book. "Yes, Ancient Princess." He smiled.

"Ancient what now?" Riley asked, looking between them.

"Ancients are a lost breed. I believe the Princess was one, making me one too." Jay looked back at Taybeith who didn't seem to be surprised. Riley nodded in understanding, but his expression was still confused.

"Every Ancient is assigned an Immortal who guides them and aids them in knowing how to defeat Aturdokht," the Headmaster continued.

Jay drowned out the Headmaster's words and looked at Cryis, who was smirking in return. This must be who the Headmaster had been referring to back in his office. She closed her mouth and spoke with her mind instead, seeing if he could hear her.

So, you're the one who's been with every reincarnation thus far, she challenged.

It's hard to believe you're the Princess.

Yeah, I know, I'm royal. What do you plan to do with me?

I've been sent to help.

Wait, are there others besides you and me? Jay asked, her curiosity getting the best of her.

His laugh tickled the corners of her mind. *You thought you were the only one?*

No, Jay lied, embarrassed.

He smirked. Jay responded with a bare of her teeth.

How the hell are you in my head? Jay snapped.

Cryis paused before answering. *It's my connection to your past lives.*

Jay opened her mouth to speak, but then closed it. That was right,

Cryis had been there with the very first version of herself. Perhaps the very first Ancient. She had so many questions for him. Suddenly a wave of comfort overcame her. Cryis would know exactly how to defeat Aturdokht, and he could even help since he'd seen her fight numerous times.

How many reincarnations have been before me? Jay quickly asked.

Not many. You're the seventh. Cryis sighed. *And hopefully the last.*

Jay took a deep breath. *How will we defeat her?*

There is no "we," Princess. This battle, you must fight alone, as always.

What! Panic rose in Jay at an alarming rate.

"Jay!" Riley snapped.

A golden light had begun to surround her body. She could feel intense magic surging through her. Everything around her felt surreal. Jay jumped from her seat, pointing a finger at Cryis. He stepped to the side, avoiding the stream of power that spilt from her fingertips, which struck the window. Glass shattered to the ground. Cryis looked at her with slight bemusement.

"Jay, calm down," the Headmaster leveled. Taybeith stared between the two, taken aback.

"Tell him what you told me!" Jay shouted. The fear she felt overwhelming her.

Cryis sighed, running his fingers through his hair. *Hush, you. They can't hear us this way.*

Don't tell me to shut up! You stupid psychopathic—

Immortal? he scoffed, pitying her. *Look, this isn't a position I'd wish on anyone, especially this young.*

The light around her strengthened. The power pulsed in waves inside her and she needed to release it.

"Miss Jaynie Raremore," the Headmaster's voice rose authoritatively. "I will not tolerate you demolishing the only safe place for us to be, nor will I have you wield this power without a steady hand. Calm yourself." Jay pursed her lips, frowning. "Mister Cryis was there when the first and previous Princesses had the chance to seal away Aturdokht, and he has come willingly to aid you."

"Professor, with all due respect, this boy you've brought in is only a kid. Let me call one of my contacts in Aris Magica. After catching him up to speed, he'll be able to help her far more than someone who should clearly be a student at this school can," Riley reasoned.

The Headmaster was not deterred. "Cryis is one of the few Immortals left from Aris Magica. He has fought beside the previous Princess and knows what Jay can expect and how her powers will help her in the coming months—if used correctly. He is the only one capable of helping and understanding some of what she will be going through."

The light around her flickered. Jay suddenly felt exhausted. Gray clouds hovered in the sky, blocking out the sun. The darkness, in some way, settled her. Slowly, the power drained to nothing.

"You will be wise to cooperate. It is not an option, but an order. Do I make myself clear? We do not yet know when this final battle will take place. Therefore, it's better for you to start preparing now."

Jay dug her nails into her skin making, a fist with each hand. Her fear was still there. She was afraid to fight Aturdokht alone. Up until now, she thought that she'd have Dylan by her side. They did everything together, so why should this be any different? The glow surrounding her vanished. She took a slow, deep breath. She couldn't lie and say that part of her didn't feel relieved to know the ones she loved would be safe. She bit down on the inside of her lip, trying to stop the tears she felt building in her eyes from falling.

A hand rested on her shoulder. Jay looked over to see Riley staring down at her. "You sure you're okay with this, kiddo?"

She knew if she said she wasn't, Riley would raise hell, even against the Headmaster. He was always looking out for her best interest. Now it was her turn to put everyone else first before her fears. Jay nodded stiffly.

Cryis looked pleased. "Good. Training starts tomorrow."

"Jay, meet me in my office." Riley nodded his head toward the door. Her shoulders dropped. Riley waited for her to exit first.

Jay looked back at Taybeith who began to follow her out. The Headmaster turned to Taybeith, stopping him. "Taybeith, it has recently come to my attention that one of Mister McCoy's roommates will not be returning this spring semester due to a family emergency. Since Jay will need a moment to come to terms with my decision, please escort Cryis to his room. You'll find him most grateful," the Headmaster instructed.

"Sir?" Taybeith began. He looked back at Jay. She could see the reluctance in his eyes, but only for a moment, before he complied.

Riley rested a hand on Jay's shoulder, guiding her out.

I changed my mind. Don't tell the others, she communicated sternly, lingering by the door before leaving.

Cryis didn't respond.

Chapter Nineteen

Dylan lay in bed, staring at his ceiling. His mind continued to wander back to the events that had happened in the forest. He had seen the bullet go through the fire wall and strike Aturdokht, but how was she still alive? They'd underestimated her. Dylan couldn't help but fear for Jay, knowing she felt a strong desire to have to face Aturdokht. Dylan had wanted to handle the situation before she had gotten heavily involved, but he'd failed again. Aturdokht was just too strong for them to face alone. Outside his door, Dylan could hear voices approaching. He turned to his side, his back to the door, hoping the voices would pass. They didn't.

"—don't trust you." Dylan began to put his pillow to his head but stopped upon recognizing Taybeith's voice. He sat up quickly, staring at his door in alarm. After what Jay had told him, Dylan trusted Taybeith less than he already had. "I don't know what you did to her but know this much: I will kill you." The coldness in Taybeith's tone did not suit him.

"An empty threat, Tekhne." Dylan heard an unfamiliar voice say in response.

Who is that? Dylan faced his doorway, not recognizing the second voice. The voice of the man was mocking and sounded too deep to be that of a student. Dylan reached for his blade that he kept hidden underneath his pillow. *An ally?* Dylan didn't put it past Taybeith to attempt to sneak one in.

"I also advise you to let go of your little crush. Friends don't make threats like that," the unknown man snickered. "She won't have the time."

Dylan wondered who they were discussing.

Taybeith's voice became muffled. "You know?"

Dylan debated getting up but didn't want to alarm them. There was no way he would be able to sneak around with the cast on his leg.

"I know everything," the man snorted. "Wait, was I right, you do like her?" He began to laugh out loud.

Dylan leaned forward, not hearing anything for a moment. He couldn't tell if they were still outside his door or if they'd passed. *Just get up already*, Dylan told himself, the anticipation becoming too much. He placed his dagger back where he'd found it and got up from his bed. He didn't want to raise suspicions with Taybeith.

Dylan was in the hallway to his bedroom door when the knock came. Moments later, he opened it. Exhausted, Dylan leaned against the doorframe. Judging by the expression Taybeith had on his face, Dylan knew he looked drained, and his dark hair was askew.

"Taybeith," Dylan said groggily, doing his best to act confused to see the boy at his door. The two of them weren't exactly close.

Taybeith moved aside. A boy with white hair, pale skin, and electric blue eyes held up a hand. "Yo!"

Dylan stared at him for a moment in shock. The man from earlier had only been a boy. He was lanky, yet his muscles were quite defined. Dylan could tell he would be fast in a fight.

In less than three seconds, Dylan had Taybeith by the collar, pinned up against the wall. "What the hell!" Taybeith cursed.

"What the hell is this?" Dylan whispered for only Taybeith's ears. He glanced over his shoulder at Cryis. Dylan knew an Immortal when he saw one. He'd taken a class on them three years ago to try to better understand why kids were calling Jay one. Whatever the reason was for this newcomer's presence, it couldn't be good, and neither was the fact that Taybeith had brought him. After what Jay had told him, he wasn't taking any chances with trusting the kid.

Cryis walked in uninvited. "Nice place you got." He plopped down on a freshly stripped, unoccupied bed. "I'm Cryis, by the way."

Taybeith didn't resist. In a quiet voice, he explained what the meeting was about, occasionally glancing over at Cryis. "It's only temporary, I think."

Dylan backed away from Taybeith. So, he hadn't been the one to bring the Immortal, but the Headmaster had. Dylan had been wrong about Taybeith's attempt to sneak in an ally. Part of him was disappointed, it would have been the perfect evidence to present to Riley. As much as he wanted to tell Riley and the Headmaster what Jay had seen, there wasn't any hard proof to back up their words.

"I'm afraid she'll destroy herself," Taybeith whispered. His words brought Dylan away from his thoughts.

Dylan ran his fingers through his hair, tousling it more. "We don't even have a full understanding of the situation."

"Why not? You guys have all the pieces," Cryis said from his position on the bed.

"What do you mean?" Dylan glanced at the relaxed boy sprawled out on the bed.

Cryis sat up, facing them, his voice lined with mockery. "You can't seriously think this all just started a couple of days ago." Blank stares. "Ah, man." Cryis tossed his hair. "This battle has been going on for centuries, way before you were born, and way before the battle between Humans and Aris Magica. Every event that has led up to this day in your lives is a part of this battle, even your parents' deaths."

Dylan's muscles tightened. "How do you know about that?"

Cryis shrugged. "The Headmaster filled me in. Look, a battle is coming, but this time, we can end it for good." Cryis beamed with excitement.

Taybeith glanced at Dylan, who didn't seem to be breathing. "How long have you been alive?"

The question seem to catch Cryis off guard. "Not long."

"You don't know."

Cryis gave Taybeith an amused stare. "Six thousand, seven hundred, and eighteen years."

Their eyes grew wide. "No way!" Taybeith gasped, and at the same time, Dylan scoffed. "You've got to be kidding me."

Cryis shrugged.

"So, how does the puzzle fit together? You said we had all the pieces?" Dylan asked skeptically.

"Close the door and sit down."

Dylan obeyed. Taybeith took a seat in the desk chair across the room. Dylan sat at the edge of his bed, his crutch at his feet.

"You're comfortable with him knowing?" Cryis asked, his eyebrows raised.

No, but Dylan held his tongue. He had a feeling if Taybeith didn't hear it now, he'd still find out one way or another. Plus, the more time he was here with him, the less he was spending with Jay, which bothered him more. Dylan nodded his head anxiously. "Go on."

"I'll tell you what I know. The Demon that killed your parents was a part of Aturdokht's army. His name is Phagos. There was a time of frenzy with the Demons and Faeries when they were fearful about being left behind. I studied it, and Demons never attack without a reason. Basically, they don't kill unless they're ordered to. Phagos is different; he has a mind of his own. I remember him on the front lines of her army. He purposely pinpointed your parents." Cryis paused, gathering his thoughts. "I want to hear your side of the story."

Dylan folded his hands, digging his nails into his skin. He was shaking. Dylan had never told anyone about that night. He and Jay had sworn to keep it a secret. He took a deep breath in, exhaling out. "Five years ago, my parents died. I was twelve and Jay was eleven. She had been living with us for nearly six years. It was around this time . . ."

Chapter Twenty

Snow fell, sticking to the windows. A black lab barked loudly outside, yanking at its leash. Dylan's mom watched from the nearest window, her hands wrapped around a mug of steaming hot chocolate. Her husband trekked across the snowy yard, shielding his eyes from the blizzard. He was layered in a coat, a snowsuit, thick boots, and leather gloves. She smiled.

Moments later, the door opened. Dylan's dad walked in with the lab bounding at his feet. The dog pranced over to Dylan's mom as she entered the room. She bent down, greeting him with a rub behind the ear.

"Hi, Buddy, who left you outside in the snow?" She used a babyish voice while talking to the dog. "Russell!" she cried. "You're leaving snow all over the place."

Dylan's dad continued shaking off his winter gear, a pile of snow forming on the floor beside the door. "Terrie, I'll clean it up!"

"Two years later!" She placed a hand on her head exasperated. "I'll just clean it myself."

Dylan's dad kicked off his snow boots, leaving them by the door. He walked over, pulling his wife into him. He parted her brown hair and kissed her temple. "Honey, don't worry, I've got it," he whispered in a low, husky voice.

"Buddy!" Jay exclaimed, rounding the corner. She fell to her knees with a wide smile. Buddy licked her face, entertaining her laughter. She rubbed him, coaxing his fur.

"Hey Jaynie, did you leave Buddy outside?" Dylan's mom asked.

"No, ma'am." Jay grinned.

"Would you like some hot chocolate, then?"

"Yes, thank you, Missus Terrie."

Dylan's mom cringed at the formality. "You can always call me . . . aunt," she suggested with a forced, but playful, smile. She and Jay's mother had been best friends, more like sisters, before she left for good, leaving her only child behind.

Jay nodded, losing some of her free spirit. Terrie nodded back, though her eyes were tinged with sadness. "Alright, I'll go make some hot chocolate, but then it's off to bed with you both. It's late."

"Okay."

"Where's Dylan?" Dylan's dad asked, looking around. The rooms he could see, the living room and office, were dark.

"Upstairs."

"Here," Dylan yawned from the steps. He had been standing there the entire time, observing them all.

"Did you leave Buddy outside?" Dylan's father asked suspiciously.

"Yeah, Buddy likes the snow." Dylan patted Buddy's back, and then ruffled Jay's hair.

"Hey!" Jay shouted as she ducked.

"Dyl, want hot chocolate?" Dylan's mom asked, heading to the kitchen.

"Yeah, thanks, Mom!" Dylan stole a glance at Jay. She was glaring at him. "What?"

"Don't ever touch my hair," Jay warned with an icy tone.

Dylan crouched until he was at eye level with Jay. "But it's cool."

Jay stuck out her lip, rising to her feet. She flipped her hair over her shoulder. "I know," she said as she stalked into the kitchen.

The hot chocolate was already waiting on the marble island. Whipped cream and marshmallows topped Jay's mug, nothing extra in Dylan's. Jay climbed into the nearest chair, grabbing the mug, but instantly set it down when she found it was still hot. She blew on it lightly.

Dylan's mom finished up with the last dish in the sink. "Alright, you two, hurry and drink up."

"Can we watch the Christmas Special on ABC?" Dylan perked up. A rim of chocolate created a mustache above his upper lip.

"Do as your mother says." Dylan's dad kissed them both on the forehead.

Chapter Twenty-One

Dylan lay in bed, staring at the ceiling. His room was small and messy. Superheroes and army soldiers lay strewn across the carpet floor. A closed door led to his bathroom. Dark blue curtains hung over the two closed windows. Pictures of his previous accomplishments along with medals and trophies lined the mounted ledge on the back wall.

Dylan pulled the comforter up to his shoulders. He continued to watch the tassel tied to the light switch swing round and round with the fan. He thought that if he counted its turns, he'd finally drift off to sleep. His eyes began to grow heavier.

The house shook, jolting Dylan from what little sleep he had managed to find. His eyes flew open. The clock beside his bed read 12:13 a.m. He had only been asleep for about two hours. Dylan rubbed his eyes, adjusting to the darkness around him. He listened for the sound again, but it never came. He stretched, turned onto his side to face away from the door, and closed his eyes again.

"Dylan!" Jay tapped the lump under the covers. "Dylan!" she called out pleadingly.

Dylan groaned as he glanced at the clock, 12:34 a.m. "What?"

"I'm scared," Jay said in a small voice.

"Clearly." Dylan rolled back over, facing her. Immediately, he regretted his words after seeing the terrified expression on her face.

"I keep hearing strange noises," Jay whispered, playing with the ends of his blanket.

Dylan recalled the sound he thought he had imagined. "It's probably the blizzard blowing a tree up against the house." He could tell she wasn't convinced. "Come on." Dylan scooted over to make room. He pulled back the blankets, patting the empty space. Jay crawled in, tucking herself close to him. "Go to sleep, Jay."

Chapter Twenty-Two

12:48 a.m.

A scream erupted throughout the house, pulling Dylan out of sleep again. His heart sped up as he searched for the problem. Jay grabbed his hand, sliding deeper under the covers. Dylan reached for his lamplight. His bedroom door swung open, and the main light flicked on, momentarily blinding him.

"Dylan!" It was his dad, still in his pajamas, his dark hair disheveled and his gray eyes wildly searched the room. "Is Jay in here?" Panic laced his voice.

"Yeah, Dad, what's going on?" Dylan asked. He could hear Jay's muffled cries.

Another sound tossed the house. "What's going on?" Dylan repeated.

"Son, get out of bed and follow me!" Dylan's dad peered out the door.

Dylan jumped out of bed, disregarding shoes. He pulled Jay from his bed and dragged her behind him as he followed his father. "Where's Mom?" Dylan's own panic settled in as he asked. He was afraid of the answer.

"I'm not sure," his father whispered, his voice faltering. "Come on!"

The moment they slipped away from the room, they were hit with an awful stench. Dylan pulled up his sleeve, covering his mouth to keep from gagging.

Jay screamed as she pointed to a shadow lingering just inside Dylan's parents' room. Jay tried to break free from Dylan's grip on her arm. Dylan's dad quickly clamped a hand over Jay's mouth, silencing her screams. The shadow grew taller as the beast stepped out into the hallway.

Dylan took a couple of steps back. The creature was indescribable, but it had a face he would never forget. It rose, touching the high ceiling. Its body was a different amalgamation of dark purple and black. Its face was that of a rabid wolf standing on two hind legs. It snarled, showing sharp teeth stained with fresh blood. Its shoulders hunched over, spikes jutting from its shoulder blades. Two rusty bronze horns curled up on its temples. It stared at him with razor-cut red eyes.

Dylan froze. His body wasn't responding to the logic of his mind. His father's cries grew distant, fading into the background. The beast's eyes seemed to focus past him, but at the same time, not behind him. Dylan willed himself to follow its gaze. His breath hitched—Jay.

Jay was being tugged from Dylan's grasp. He tried to hold onto her and regain control. It was his dad that calmed him. "Dylan, I need you right now." Dylan's dad set Jay down, focusing on Dylan. The Demon advanced forward. Dylan's father placed his hand on his son's shoulders. "Run, and do not look back." His dad paused, taking the time to stare into Dylan's eyes. A swarming storm brewed within his father's irises. "Your mother and I love you, always."

"W-where are you going?" Dylan asked.

His dad smiled as he hugged Dylan. "I have to go find your mother."

The dorm room was eerily quiet except for Cryis's constant pacing. At some point, Taybeith had gotten up and had decided to sit on the edge of Cryis's bed. The sun outside was setting, casting a golden glow across the floor of the room. Part of the sun lit half of Dylan's face, leaving the rest of it in shadows. Every time Cryis crossed in front of the window, the sun would make his white hair look like it was sparkling.

Dylan hadn't moved from the edge of his bed. His body had grown numb from sitting for so long. "It didn't register to me at the time, but the screaming . . . it was hers. My mom had already died—no, she suffered. Dad was trying to buy us some time." He clasped his hands together. "Sometimes . . . sometimes I wonder how he died. Did the Demon suck his soul, or was it a slow torture?"

Cryis and Taybeith remained silent. They didn't have the words to offer comfort to the pain Dylan felt. Still, Taybeith tried. "Look, Dylan, I know saying sorry won't—I mean if you need a friend—"

"Pain makes the heart stronger. Everybody dies," Cryis stated bluntly, interrupting Taybeith. He stopped pacing and took the seat at the desk across the room that Taybeith had been sitting at earlier. He turned the chair around and sat so that the back of the chair was facing the other boys, his legs straddling either side.

"Thanks," Dylan replied half-heartedly. "You've heard my part."

"Right," Cryis began, holding the word out longer than it deserved. "Like I said earlier, Phagos was after a specific target. From your story, I realized I was right. Phagos was after Jay. Somehow he knew she would inherit the Immoralist abilities and the Princess would awaken within her." He waited a bit, then continued, "He was seeking revenge on his fallen master." Cryis rested his chin on the back of the chair. "The Headmaster brought me in because he believes that I can teach Jay how to control her powers and use them in the right way, since I am one of the few who witnessed the last Enchantress seal away Aturdokht nearly half a century ago. I'll do my best to help but—"

"But what?" Taybeith interrupted.

"I don't know if she is ready. The Princess isn't entirely good, and it's the strength of the host that defines its character," Cryis explained. "And I don't know if her heart and mind are in balance yet. She must come to terms with her destiny. And if she fails, both Aris Magica and the outside world will fall."

Dylan took a deep breath before letting it out. "All I need from you is to promise that she won't do this alone."

Cryis sighed, staring up at the ceiling. Eventually, he held out his hand, and Dylan firmly grasped it. "Deal."

"Wait!" Taybeith interjected again. "Earlier, you mentioned a . . . uh . . . a serum. What serum? We don't have anything like that at the Institute. And even if we did, what does it have to do with all this?"

Cryis gave a sideways glance to Dylan, who shook his head. Of course—Cryis wouldn't know that Taybeith wasn't a part of the mission and was completely clueless. Only a few days had passed, but Dylan had completely forgotten the time he and Jay went on the mission to retrieve the item Cryis spoke of. With so much going on, finding out the meaning of the serum had been the least of his priorities. Cryis exhaled, leaning back. Then he opened his mouth to explain.

Chapter Twenty-Three

"Who does he think he is?" Jay snapped at Riley. They were back in his office. Weapons of all sorts lined the walls, illuminated by a ray of sunlight. Jay collapsed into the armchair facing his desk. She kicked her legs up, using the desk as a footrest.

Riley took a seat in the main chair.

"He has no *idea* who I am or what I can do! No duh, I knew I wasn't the only Immortal. Then making me look like a complete fool? What a mind invader! I want absolutely nothing to do with him and I *don't* need his help. He reminds me of—arghh! I can't stand him. He's an old, outdated loser who's going to *ruin* everything. And the Headmaster! I'm hoping you don't *ever* use that inferior tone on me, like I'm a child. And Taybeith! How could that wimp just stand there? He's supposed to have my back when—" Jay paused before finally breathing and turning on Riley. "No! Riley, *you're* supposed to have my back. So what the heck were you doing?"

"You done?" Riley casually flicked a speck of dust from the corner of his desk. During her ranting session, he had taken the liberty to clean his desk, putting away his paperwork as well as his textbooks. He didn't wait for her answer, the color of her eyes was enough to tell him she wasn't done—they were still a raging red. "Look, I'll give ya advice, free of charge. Faith told me you would be experiencing . . ." Riley cleared his throat before continuing, "emotions like menstrual emotional changes. So maybe you're confusing these emotions for something else."

"Huh?" Jay interrupted, annoyed. "Are you—are you talking about love?" she assumed. Her mind automatically wandered to Dylan, causing her to blush profusely. "No, just stop. No. I know the difference. I hate Cryis. This isn't love at first sight. Gross."

"Yes, well, maybe . . . ah, damn it, I'm not good at this stuff." Riley rubbed the back of his neck, rolling his head to the side. "Didn't your parents ever teach you about this?"

Jay immediately grew silent.

"Oh yeah, shit." Riley remembered long ago Jay saying something about her parents leaving on a trip and never coming back. He continued, as if his slip-up never occurred. "Let's just say your hate is actually . . ."

Jay held up a hand, stopping him with the buzz of magic tingling at her fingertips. "No."

Riley lifted his hands in the air, surrendering. "Alright!" he growled, just as irritated. He opened the drawer to his right, carefully pulling out a manila folder in a plastic covering. He tossed the package onto the desk, sliding it toward Jay.

"What is it?" Jay arched an eyebrow, glaring at the folder suspiciously.

"The real reason why I called you here," Riley grunted. He picked up the folder and handed it to Jay. "Do not open it, you'll need it to get the test results." He ripped off a small piece of paper from the notebook on the side of his desk. He quickly scrawled something onto it in black ink.

Jay grabbed the slip of paper—an address was written on it in sloppy handwriting. "Test results?"

"Remember that serum I had y'all get? The test results are finally ready."

Jay turned the manila folder over and saw the words *Doctor Herron* written in rushed writing on the other side. "Who is Doctor Herron?"

"Doctor Herron," Riley began, exasperated. From the tone of his voice, Jay instantly got the hint that this doctor and Riley were not on the best of terms. His voice held a slight disdain. "She is a close contact of the Headmaster. She used to be a professor at the school, and from my understanding, she's now a scientist who occasionally dabbles in Aris Magica affairs."

Jay arched an eyebrow. "I thought you were the only one who could approve these missions." She knew the Headmaster could too, but it was very rare for him to interfere, from what she had gathered from her past missions.

"Well, you know what they say, not everything goes your way. Now, be a sweetheart and get the hell out of my face and go get them for me."

Jay began to leave but stopped herself. "Hey, Professor Riley." She hesitated before turning back to his desk. He looked at her impatiently. "How long has Taybeith been a student here?"

Riley relaxed a bit, but Jay could tell he was shocked by her question. "Not long. He joined at the beginning of last semester." He laughed as he said, "Honestly gotta say I was surprised to see how well you two get along. Finally got yourself a friend other than Dylan."

Taybeith had lied to her. He'd only just got here, and it couldn't have been by coincidence. "Yeah . . . hey!" Jay shouted. She stuck out her tongue, turning to leave.

"Take someone with you!" Riley shouted to her as she left the room.

Jay made a pit stop at her dorm and was surprised to find her roommate, Rella, lying on the bed, reading one of the latest fashion magazines. Rella had been visiting her family in the mountains. With only two weeks left of the holiday break, even more students were beginning to return for the start of the spring semester.

Rella was a Therianthrope, a special breed of the Hybrid gene. Unlike Dylan and Riley, who were a masters of weapons, Rella was half animal and half human. She could control her animalistic instincts and make herself more powerful that way. Her magic showed itself in the form of a wolf. Jay had watched her train before, and her favorite offensive harnessing word to use was *Ungues*. Magic shaped in the form of a wolf's paw would cover Rella's hands and strike her opponent, leaving behind claw-like marks. Like other Hybrids, she could choose to live as a human by retracting her wolfish features, but she was too proud of her powers to do such a thing.

Rella's wolfish tail sprawled out behind her, her golden-brown ears laying lazily to the side. She barely glanced up as Jay walked in. Jay crossed the room to the closet. She pulled out her black pants and shirt with a leather jacket and took her black combat boots from the top shelf, switching the laces to a warm pink. Jay threw on the new set of clothes. She moved to the drawer hiding at the base of her bed and pulled out a box full of various weapons and ammunition stacked in numerous rows. She grabbed her silver gun and her favorite dagger with an orb-like stone on its hilt.

"Where are you going?" Rella asked, flipping another page.

"Out," Jay said tucking her hair under a baseball cap. She preferred to avoid any conversation with the wolf. The two of them didn't even really get along. They had their moments, but Jay wouldn't say the two of them were friends.

"Let me guess, you're going on another one of those little missions." Rella glanced up from her magazine and gasped. "Not like that!" She closed the magazine and walked over to where Jay stood.

Jay threw up her hands, exasperated. "Why is everyone so suddenly concerned with my hair and how I look? Especially you!" *You don't even like me.*

Rella picked up the comb on her bed, knocked off the hat, and combed through Jay's curls. When she was done, Jay's hair was soft and fell in elegant waves hanging from a high ponytail. "Look, I know the two of us haven't exactly been each other's dream roommate, but I think we should at least try to be nicer to each other this semester. This is my version of an olive branch." Rella smiled. "And trust me, you'd be surprised at how much the world has changed."

Chapter Twenty-Four

Jay gathered her bearings and knocked on Dylan's door. For once, it was locked. It was a moment before Dylan opened it. He stood in the doorway, momentarily taken aback.

"Jay!" He looked at her up and down. She was combat mission ready. "Where are you going?"

Jay forced the package into his hands, shoving past him. "We're leaving in five minutes."

Dylan turned the manila envelope over in his hands. It was sealed shut with a red stamp. "What is this?"

Jay ignored him, noticing the other two boys. Cryis sat up straighter, waving from his bed. "Yo!" Cryis smiled. Taybeith nodded shyly. Jay was shocked to see them both, and even more shocked that Dylan had allowed Taybeith into his room.

Her eyes narrowed and her teeth ground against each other, meeting their gazes. "Jay, focus," Dylan cut in. Her hair whipped the air as she turned to face him. He held up the envelope again. "What is this?"

She shrugged. "Riley said we need to give it to Doctor Herron in exchange for the test results on the serum we collected."

"Another doctor?" Dylan asked.

Jay shrugged again. "I know. When I asked Riley, he said something about her once being a professor here. But there's obviously some bad blood between them. He wasn't happy about the thought of our mission including her."

"Weird," Dylan said. "Fine, give me three minutes." He dropped the package into her hands. He pulled off his shirt, tossing it on the bed as he limped past her. Jay gasped, unable to look away. His shirt had been hiding toned muscles and a lean figure. His shoulders were broad and strong, and his back muscles were just as defined as his abs. She resisted the urge to reach out and touch his back. He looked like the athletic models in one of Rella's magazines.

Jay struggled to get her breathing right. She had seen him shirtless plenty of times, but when he turned, the stitches covering his scar brought shivers up her spine.

Taybeith tripped over his words. "Um, Dylan, Jay, you might want to—"

Jay sat down on Dylan's bed, crossed her legs, and closed her eyes. Dylan glanced at Taybeith and laughed. He grabbed his change of clothes, disappearing into the bathroom.

Cryis smirked, shaking his head.

"What?" Taybeith said defensively.

"Hope you're ready for your first day of training, Princess," Cryis said, capturing her attention.

"Tomorrow's Christmas," Jay mumbled, opening her eyes.

Cryis leaned forward, falling onto his elbows. "Christmas will come again. This won't."

Jay mockingly pursed her lips. "Certainly, you wouldn't disregard the day Jesus was born."

"He'll forgive me."

"For such selfish reasons, I wouldn't think so." Every word out of Jay's mouth dripped with sarcasm.

Cryis threw up his hands, reluctantly agreeing. "Okay, I'll give you a day of grace, but the day after, we start. No exceptions."

"Class starts." She had a retort for everything.

"Well then, I guess I couldn't have picked a better time." Cryis smirked, keeping pace.

"You ready?"

Jay looked at Dylan closely. He had chosen a pair of worn black jeans with a red t-shirt covered with a black leather jacket, no doubt concealing his weapons within the deep pockets.

Jay frowned, noticing the cast around his ankle. "I'll drive."

Dylan suppressed the urge to laugh. "Yeah, right." He knew she had never learned and didn't feel comfortable with her behind the wheel of his motorcycle. "We'll walk until we see a bus or a taxi. The town's not too far from here."

Now it was Cryis and Taybeith's turn to share the joke. "Why not use magic to transport yourselves?"

"No magic unless we have to," Dylan proposed gravely, passing his crutches to Taybeith. "Let's go."

Chapter Twenty-Five

Luckily for them, it wasn't snowing. Jay let out a deep breath of air into her hands, rubbing them together. Beyond the Institute was a dark forest that opened up to a vast city. The forest was oddly silent and bare. All the leaves were stripped from the trees, leaving their barks covered in a glistening frost. The snow was a white blanket over the forest floor. Their footprints left deep craters in the earth. The sky was clouded gray, casting a shadow over the forest. The deeper they went, the thicker their surroundings became, offering hardly any light. And the farther they were from the Institute, the less of a connection Jay felt to the magic there. She knew magic existed in the outside world, hidden in pocket dimensions like the one inside the mansion, but she felt even less connected to that side of Aris Magica than she did whenever they talked about it at school. She knew it was a part of her, but sometimes she still felt like an outsider.

"It's Christmas Eve," Jay whispered, shivering. It was strange how the holiday didn't seem to matter much to her with everything else going on.

Dylan nodded as he kicked up snow, making a right. Jay followed closely behind. "You forgot gloves," he pointed out.

"Yeah, stupid of me." Jay's teeth chattered. She tried to think of something else to say but being alone like this with him made it difficult to think.

Dylan grabbed hold of her wrist, sliding his hand down until his hand met hers. "I'll keep you warm," he mumbled.

"T-thanks." Heat flared in her cheeks, but not because she was cold. She looked ahead, trying her best not to glance down at their hands. Her eyes wandered to his face. His hair was hanging just above his thick eyebrows. His skin was pale from the cold, but his hands were warm and strong as he held onto hers. He was staring ahead as well, his gray eyes appeared deep in thought. She wondered what he was thinking. Her eyes fell to his lips. *I wonder what it would be like to kiss them . . .* Jay gasped bringing her free hand over her mouth, embarrassed she even thought about something like that. She dared a glance at Dylan.

"Something wrong?" Dylan asked. His eyebrows were scrunched together.

"Hey," Jay dropped her hand. "Do you think it's possible for childhood friends to become something more?" she asked nervously. She had to be honest with herself and to him. Maybe if it were possible, then she could finally tell him about how she had started to feel toward him. That she believed she was starting to fall in love with him.

"Like what?"

"Lovers," she said, barely above a whisper. Dylan seemed to choke on air at her question. "You okay?"

"Yeah . . . um, why are we even talking about this?"

Jay couldn't tell if he was as nervous as she was or if he was teasing her.

She frowned and sighed, regretting her question. The past couple of days had been a lot on them both—he didn't need the burden of her feelings adding to that. Her heart sank. "Never mind," she said.

They continued walking for a long time in silence, the wind whistling around them. Jay stared up at the sky. The sun was high above them now. They had been walking for over an hour. Jay smirked to herself, *Guess the taxi had been a lie.* She was happy to be able to spend more time with him like this.

They came upon a pond frozen over with ice. Tall trees leaned over the sides, surrounding the frozen water. Jay's thoughts wandered back to everything that had happened. The Princess would help lead this world from its fatal destruction. Maybe it was time for them to come out and reveal themselves once again to the humans residing in the other world. Since the last war, Aris Magicians kept themselves hidden, either amongst humans, living their lives, or in pocket dimensions, like the Institute. As far as humans knew, magic didn't exist. It was just a fairytale, and the war that had taken place had been buried and lost to history. The idea scared her to death. In her past life, the outside world and her abilities always found a problem to fight about. Even if she saved them all, humans would only find something else to hold against Aris Magicians. *Maybe they should burn.* Jay's thoughts began to resemble Aturdokht's. *They don't even deserve my help.* Jay instantly regretted the thought of abandoning the humans who lived without magic when the outside world was no doubt oblivious to the nearing battle.

The weight of it all fell on her shoulders. She felt utterly alone, even though Dylan was right next to her. Thinking of this brought her attention to him. In a heartbeat, Jay felt as if she was looking at an entirely different person than the boy she knew when she was eleven. His skin was a tan shade, despite the lack of sun. His dark brown hair clung in damp strands, sticking to his forehead. His jaw was set, and his storm-colored eyes stared straight ahead, focused on nothing in particular. Everything about him was marvelous.

"They can." Dylan continued to stare ahead instead of looking at her. He flipped the collar of his coat up, hiding his mouth.

"What?" Cold air formed a cloud before her lips.

He stopped in his tracks causing her to do the same. He finally looked over at her, meeting her gaze. "Friends can become lovers," he said. Jay felt her heart rise to her throat. "But it doesn't always mean they should," he finished. He continued walking, pulling her with him.

"Oh!" Jay squeaked. She cleared her throat and looked away. Was he talking about them? Her heart sank to her stomach. "Oh," she whispered. Jay decided it would be best if she changed the topic. "How far?"

Dylan pulled his hand away from hers. He stopped, letting his feet sink deeper into the snow. Jay took a couple of steps before doing the same. She faced him, unsure of what caused the delay.

Dylan was staring at her dead on. "No. That's not what I meant."

She gazed at the trees around them. She sighed, "Maybe we should just drop it." She couldn't even justify to herself where these new emotions came from. Admitting them to him now would only cause them more problems.

Dylan shoved his hands in his pockets. He grinned, taking a step toward her. He bowed his head in a bashful way. "Your cheeks are red."

Jay huffed, "Way to point out the obvious. It's cold."

He took another step. "Wait? Are you finally seeing me as a man?"

She was caught off-guard. Even now, Dylan was able to read her like a book. Her head whipped in his direction. He was close, too close. Jay stumbled back. Dylan caught her by the waist, saving her from the bed of snow. She collided into his firm and steady chest. It wasn't the same as when she was being held close by Taybeith. This time, she felt nervous, but also delighted to be this close to Dylan. Heat radiated off his body. She breathed heavily into his leather jacket. Her palm rested flat on his shirt, feeling the drum of his heartbeat. *What is happening to me?*

"Thank you." She managed to be even more embarrassed.

Dylan continued to hold her close. "Yeah, no problem." His voice was as stiff as ice. "A few more minutes and we should be there. Just listen."

She did. Having been distracted by these new emotions, she hadn't even heard the cries of the busy streets. A feeling of dread fell over her.

Dylan kicked away the dead branches of the frosted hedges that bordered the forest. In the process of doing so, he also knocked a wooden trail sign to the ground. He sighed and lifted it up, putting it back in its rightful place. The sign read *Salem City Limits* in scratchy lettering.

Suddenly, the first glimpse of the city came into view. Skyscrapers stood tall in the distance. Long lines of cars took up the crowded streets, zooming past in both directions. Groups of people flooded the sidewalks with hardly any room to breathe. The city had a light, upbeat feeling to it. Brightly decorated lights strung along the smaller buildings' entranceways. The taller, more sophisticated structures had expensive décor outlining the faces of their buildings, with blow-up reindeer and decorated Santa Clause animatronics waving at passersby, and flashing lights spelling out holiday phrases. A sweet, candy aroma filled the booming streets. Signs with the words *Happy Holidays* or *Merry*

Christmas were strung up on the billboards or hung outside store windows. Every so often, a stranger dressed in a red suit with a white beard stood on the corner ringing a bell and gesturing to a half-filled bucket.

Jay pinched her nose. It had been a long time since she had stepped foot on these sidewalks. So long that she had forgotten which city they lived in. None of that had really seemed to matter after all the years they had spent living in the Institute.

Dylan unfolded the crumpled piece of paper:

Doctor Herron
Biochemist Level UP Company
W 13th Street, Salem, OR

It was written in the most unreadable handwriting. Dylan refolded the paper, slipping it back into his pocket.

"Jay, let's go."

She didn't move.

Dylan gently tugged on her sleeve. Her eyes lit up like a deer in headlights. It had been a long time since Jay had been surrounded by so many humans all in one place. Usually for their missions, Riley would drive them or drop them off by helicopter, supervising their entry into humanity. Whenever she and Dylan would sneak off to visit Eugene, there were always fewer people on the road they took. He pulled harder. She blinked, finally snapping from the trance. "Look, I promise you can do it."

They took the first opportunity presented and darted across the street through an open gap. Stage one complete. Dylan pushed their way to the side of one of the buildings, pressing their backs up against the glass. Hordes of people walked by, not giving them a second glance.

"Do you know where we're going?" Jay hissed, attempting to stay close to his side as they began walking again. She was afraid she'd lose him in the crowd. And even if she did, it wasn't like she could disrupt society by moving everyone out of the way to find him. Part of her studies was learning how to blend in with the other world when she visited it, which wasn't often. Co-existing with the humans also meant hiding who they were unless absolutely necessary. There wasn't any way to tell an Aris Magician or Hybrid from a regular human unless one chose to make a spectacle, and usually an Aris Magician didn't. Hybrids, on the other hand, were even harder to spot than Pure breeds, even when using their magic, because often times it was barely noticeable, much like Dylan or Riley's gifts at being masters in weaponry.

"No, but we'll walk until we find it." He took a chance in the crowd, moving with the current, keeping his head down.

"No." Jay used all her strength to yank him back behind the building. "We don't have that kind of time. Ask someone."

"Whatever."

Jay could tell he wasn't happy with the idea, but he relented and tapped the next person that passed them. It was a woman wearing a long fur coat. Her eye shadow was odd shades of gold and blue. Her thick hair was braided up into a fancy style full of tiny braids. Her chin came to an angular point and her lips were compressed in a thin line. She gave him an irritated glare, holding her purse tightly to her chest.

"Can you help us out?" Dylan thrust the paper up so she could see the address.

The woman hastily looked down at her watch and let out an exasperated sigh. "Of course, you have one minute and fifty-four seconds of my time." Her features softened. She took the paper from his grasp and studied it. "Alright, do you know where West Thirteenth Street is?"

Jay shook her head, but Dylan nodded. He had been here plenty of times. "Then you'll take a turn on West Bottoms until you see that Italian pizza shop and turn left. After that, keep going until you get to the second light and cross over to Main. It should be along that strip there." She gave the paper back.

"Thank you," Dylan grumbled. She flicked her hand in an indifferent wave, continuing past them.

"Come on," he mumbled, shoving past the next person who crossed his path.

Chapter Twenty-Six

The building was nowhere close to the standards of the skyscrapers that surrounded it. It barely reached half of the glass structure's length. The color had faded from the outside of the building, and thick wooden boards were nailed over the rows of windows. The sign read *Herron's Biochemistry Lab* in bolded letters on a half slanted rusted plaque.

Jay pushed open the glass doors. Everything within the building looked recently renovated, the opposite of its exterior. They stepped into a brightly colored lobby. Orange sofa chairs sat in a maze-like pattern facing a long fish tank and a flat screen TV mounted high on the wall. The carpet was a checkered white and blue pattern with orange blocks centered in every other square. Besides three other people, the lobby was empty. The TV displayed an ongoing football game between the Kansas City Chiefs and the San Francisco 49ers.

Dylan and Jay bypassed the game, rounding the corner to a half-circle desk on the back wall. Two closed doors were on either side with a *Do Not Enter* sign in bold, flashing red letters. A smiling receptionist stood behind the desk. Her dark brown hair was twisted in a tight bun. She wore a navy suit that buttoned all the way to its collar. She flashed them a perfect smile.

"How may I help you?" Her words seemed rehearsed.

"We're here for a Doctor Herron, she's expecting us," Dylan explained.

Sherrill, Jay learned from the name tag she wore, continued to type away on the computer at a rapid pace. She carefully eyed the long list of appointments. She began to shake her head. "No, sorry, but Doctor Herron isn't seeing anyone today."

Dylan slid the manila folder forward. "I'm sure she'll make an exception for us."

Sherrill's smile quickly vanished as she noticed the red seal stamped on the envelope—it was of a steel hawk chasing a ball of fire. Her hands shook uncontrollably as she picked up the phone and quickly dialed the numbers. She whispered into the phone, covering her mouth.

The phone was placed back on the receiver. Her smile returned on full blast. "Ah yes. She will be with you shortly." Sherrill grabbed the folder, tossing it in the bottom drawer without a second thought. "Please, have a seat."

Jay collapsed in the chair. Dylan sat in the one beside her. He grabbed the first magazine he saw from the coffee table and flipped through its contents. Jay closed her eyes. It was the first time in days she felt this much at peace. It was as if the oncoming war didn't exist, and nothing else mattered outside these walls. She still felt the tug of magic pushing to come out of her, giving her a queasy feeling in her stomach.

"What made you wear your hair like this?" Dylan flicked the tail of her ponytail with the edge of the magazine.

Jay shook her head, irritated by the gesture. "Change."

"Change?" Dylan repeated with concern, turning to the next page.

The receptionist rushed over. "She's ready to see you. Please follow me." She held out the envelope for Jay to take.

Dylan and Jay followed Sherrill through the door to the right of the desk with the big *Do Not Enter* sign. A blinding white light lit the single hallway. Their shoes clinked against the tiled floor, the sound echoing off the walls. At the end of the long hall was a tall metal door. Jay glanced nervously in Dylan's direction. She could see tiny beads of sweat lining his forehead. His limp was getting worse.

Sherrill held herself in a slightly unsettling state. Jay could tell Dylan felt nervous, and so did she as they walked further down the hall. His hand fell to his gun. They stopped at the door. Sherrill knocked three times. Jay examined the door. It was four widths thick of steel—no sound could be heard on either side. Surely bulletproof, but not fireproof. She smirked. If it came down to it, she could easily burn right through it.

The door swung open. A tall, bald man in a black suit with a white undershirt and black tie blocked their passage. Solid black sunglasses shielded his eyes. An old scar slashed across his brown skin, trailing from under the left side of his glasses to midway on his cheek. A curled, corded earpiece wrapped around the end of his glasses, looping around his right ear. His jaw was set, and his lips formed a thin line. Even without the appearance of his eyes, the man was intimidating, standing over six feet tall.

"It's okay, Doctor Herron asked for them personally," Sherrill explained. Apparently, that wasn't good enough. His arms crossed over his chest. "They brought the rite of passage." She gestured to the folder in Jay's hands.

The tall, daunting man nodded, stepping aside. Sherrill turned and held out her arm to stop them. She plucked the package out of Jay's hand and gave it to the guard. The guard looked down at Jay and Dylan before disappearing into the room. "Do not talk unless spoken to." Her words were final.

"As long as she gives us what we need, then there won't be a problem," Jay promised.

The room was similar to a lab. Cases of rats, frogs, and other dissectible species stacked in glass containers lined a rack pushed to the back of the room. Tubes filled with bright, bubbling liquid fizzed and popped on the far back table as they continued to drip and rotate through a handmade contraption. At its center was a large foam mat lying on a clear table. A woman in her late forties with wild, curly red hair and green eyes as bright as emeralds hiding behind thick rimmed glasses stood behind the table. The light above her reflected a glare that cast a shadow over her face. The woman was dressed in a long, white, stained lab coat. She wore a huge, unexpected smile. Men dressed identically to the man at the door surrounded every inch of the room.

"Doctor Herron?" Jay asked hesitantly. She crouched into a ready position, palming her dagger. Out of the corner of her eye, she could see Dylan reaching for his gun.

"Put your weapons down," the man standing nearest to the doctor instructed. He was the only suited man in the room not wearing sunglasses. His skin was dark brown as well, as were his eyes. His hair was freshly razor-cut. Dark beads of hair traced his jawline and wrapped around his chin, as if he hadn't shaved in days. An identical earpiece was attached to his ear. An American flag pin rested on the right side of his chest. He stood with his arms behind his back, reflecting a demanding presence.

Doctor Herron laughed hysterically, apparently finding the sight of the two students to be the funniest thing in the world. She waved folder in the air. "Your Headmaster sent children!"

"Tell them to stand down," Dylan commanded, raising his own gun.

Jay gripped her dagger tighter. The man locked eyes with Dylan, seeing an unwavering threat. He gave a subtle nod. The men lowered their weapons, taking three strides back. Dylan slowly followed.

"Who are you?" Dylan demanded.

"The CIA." When Dylan didn't respond, the man shook his head, slightly disappointed. "That stands for the Central—"

"I know what CIA stands for!" he snapped with a low growl.

"What are your men doing here?" Jay asked. She wasn't about to lower her guard yet. She kept her focus on the man beside the doctor. He seemed to be the one in charge, while the others were just waiting blindly at his back.

"If you want answers, put down the weapons," the agent bargained. Dylan rested his hand on Jay's arm, gently pushing it down. He pried the dagger from her hands.

Doctor Herron slapped down the letter and crouched behind the table. Seconds later, she hauled a thick, familiar briefcase out into the open. "This here what the old man wants?" she barked out in a southern accent.

Dylan cautiously scanned his surroundings, making his way over to the table. Doctor Herron lifted the case up, tossing it behind her back. Her red lips puckered into a pout, mocking him.

The man cleared his throat, offering his hand. Dylan took it with a strong grip. "My name is agent Luke Kanon. I work for the CIA under the President of the United States," Kanon gloated, giving a brief, but formal introduction.

"Are you human?" Jay asked, confused why CIA agents would be interfering with their mission.

Kanon looked at her confused and slightly taken aback. "I am."

"Dylan McCoy." Kanon's eyes flickered to Jay. "Her name is irrelevant," Dylan noted dangerously.

Kanon agreed, facing Dylan. "Doctor Herron has debriefed us on what's happening." Dylan's eyes shifted. The look on Kanon's face showed that he suspected Dylan knew more than he was letting on. "She informed us of a war raging."

Jay's eyes widened. Dylan's expression remained neutral. Kanon seemed slightly disappointed, as if he had been expecting more of a reaction.

He scoffed. "The legendary long-lost history of the war between humanity and—I believe I'm saying this right—Aris Magica." Dylan and Jay exchanged a long glance. Jay gripped her dagger even tighter than before. She'd never met a human who knew about the war unless they were involved with Aris Magica in some way. Kanon began to smile as he went on. "A dark curse will befall the land and all the wicked will rise in its true form. A woman on fire will paint the world red, riding it as her vessel." The deeper he went into the story, the more unnerving things became. Kanon suppressed a smile upon seeing Jay's tension grow with every word.

"Does any of this sound familiar?" Kanon asked, humoring himself.

"No," Dylan denied.

"Interesting." Kanon pulled out a notepad and pen from his suit pocket and jotted down a couple of notes. Jay watched with anticipation.

"She also mentioned an Immortal with white hair and strange abilities. She could either be our savior or our destroyer." Kanon pointed the end of his pen in Jay's direction. "I assume that's her."

"Ancient." Jay whispered, not loud enough for anyone but Dylan to hear. He shot her a warning glare. "How do you know all of this?" she asked louder.

"She's an Oracle." Dylan said, pointing to the scientist.

Jay had heard of Oracles—fortune tellers who sat in sacred shrines with a glass orb and spirit senses. Warlords and kings would communicate their problems and greedy intentions with them and abuse the power of an Oracle. It was another nasty time in Aris Magica history. Oracles descended from the Purist race of Aris Magicians. It was a rare power to be blessed with; very few had it, and even fewer were able to control it. Usually, glimpses of the future could come with just a simple touch. The best could control when visions of the future came.

"Now son, I'm sure you understand. If this is true, then the wellbeing of America falls into the President's hands. And this situation becomes official government business."

"You can't stop what's coming," Jay warned. "And you can't do anything to help."

"Maybe so, but we have more control and power than two teenagers," Kanon stated.

"Why help us now?" Dylan challenged.

Doctor Herron spoke, answering his question. "They help because it matters to them, boy! They, too, are caught in the crossfire to come. If our kind doesn't survive, neither will theirs."

"You don't get it," Jay said, trying her best to remain calm. Kanon arched his eyebrows. "I've seen what she can do, what she *will* do! And your machine guns don't stand a chance." Aturdokht would destroy anyone who got in her way, and with power like hers, humans could not stop her. Only Jay could.

Kanon chuckled a dry, certainly fake, laugh. "You don't actually expect us to believe in magic, but I do believe in a threat. And that is what this sounds like. You can't expect us to stand by and do nothing."

"Millions of people will die," Dylan said, his voice remaining calm. "Just give us the serum."

"No can do, kid," Doctor Herron said. "I told your professor the same thing when he called asking about it. I called the CIA for a reason."

"You called them?" Jay asked, alarmed. But why would she do that? Jay caught herself looking at Dylan again. He seemed just as confused as she was.

Doctor Herron handed the case to Kanon. He sat it on the table and flipped up the locks. He pulled out the small syringe filled with a green liquid. "I've been meaning to ask, what do you know about this?" He turned it over in his hands. Dylan's eyes narrowed. "Doctor Herron has already told us what she knows, but I want to know what you know."

Jay straightened and crossed her arms. "It's a serum. And we don't know what it does. Our mission was to bag and tag. No extra information, but I suppose it might be somewhat important," she lied.

"I see." His voice was cynical. He took out an odd gun. In the ejection part of the barrel was an empty slot fit for a tube. The barrel of the gun was longer than most. He slid the serum into place, locking it down with three clamps. He laid the gun on the table.

Dylan took a step back, automatically recognizing it—a tranquilizer gun. "What are—"

"Show me magic. You all seem to know more about it than me, and obviously believe in it. I think if we are to work together, we will need to be on fair ground."

"Work together?"

"Precisely."

Dylan gave Jay a nervous look. She sighed, throwing her hands up in surrender. "Fine," she said. "But I can't guarantee your safety."

Jay exhaled, cracking her knuckles. She concentrated on her power and what she wanted it to do. A small grin played at the corner of Dylan's mouth. Jay knew he felt her power coursing through his body. Kanon looked around for any abnormal changes. He frowned; nothing obvious had changed.

"Well," Kanon asked impatiently.

Dylan bent down, taking Jay's dagger and driving it through the cast around his leg. He ripped the rest of it off with his bare hands, tossing it aside. Dylan flexed his ankle, rotating it around left and right. His ankle felt brand new. Even better than the first time she had tried to heal it. The crack Faith had seen must be gone. She had gotten better—her power was growing quickly.

Kanon rounded the table. Dylan raised up the bottom of his pant leg, exposing his skin.

Kanon remained suspicious. "How do we know he wasn't faking it to begin with?"

"He wasn't!" Jay snapped just as Dylan said, "I wasn't."

Kanon didn't believe them. Doctor Herron yawned, growing bored. "He wasn't. I felt her magic from over here."

"What is the extent of this power?"

"I can't bring people back from the dead or save those on the verge of death," Jay clarified. "But I can heal or subside the pain in wounds, scars, bruises, and broken bones."

"What else?" Kanon asked, pressing for more.

Jay hesitated. She didn't trust him enough to expose all her cards, so she decided to just tell him one other ability she had. "I can control the equilibrium of things, to an extent. Move things with my mind. You guys give it a cheap name—telekinesis."

"What do you prefer we call it then?" Kanon irritably asked.

"Moving things with my mind," Jay sarcastically stated.

"Show me," Kanon insisted.

Jay felt the air crackle with the energy she was eager to get her hands on. She took a deep breath, her fist clenching at her side. "No."

Kanon frowned. "And are you this world's doom or its savior?"

Jay didn't respond.

"None of this will help you—" Dylan shouted.

Kanon cut him off. He motioned for one of his soldiers to come over. The silent, intimidating man from earlier handed Kanon a letter. He extended it to Dylan. "Give this to whomever may be in charge. We would like to meet with him and discuss what's best for both parties involved."

Dylan took the letter, pocketing it. "And the serum?"

"We will be keeping it under protective care along with the girl. I never got your name."

"Over my dead body," Dylan threatened, and a malevolent shadow came down over his features.

"It's not your decision to make, son." Kanon picked up the tranquilizer gun and aimed it at Jay.

Dylan pulled out his own two guns, tossing Jay her dagger. The other agents rushed at him, aiming but not firing. Dylan cursed, dropping his twin guns for his own knife. He flipped the blade so that the blunt end was facing his opponents. He lunged at the first agent approaching. The knife grazed the man's suit but didn't injure him. Dylan whipped around, swinging his dagger left and right.

"Dylan!" Jay shouted. He ducked another lunge from the agents, meeting Jay's eyes. He was completely unaware of the agent aiming what looked like a stun gun to the back of his neck.

"Shoot!" Jay cursed. She wouldn't make it in time.

She spun out of reach from the agent she was fighting and jabbed the one behind her in the throat with the butt of her dagger. She twirled the dagger in her hand, so she held the blade and threw it. The instant it released her fingertips she flicked her wrist in a swift motion. A golden glow illuminated the dagger, weaving it through the other agents and past Dylan. He followed its motion, seeing the agent behind him. The blade of the dagger cut through skin, causing the agent to drop the stun gun. Dylan instantly reacted, kicking the gun out of reach and driving an elbow to the agent's stomach. If they wouldn't play fair, neither would he. He pulled out his twin magnums.

"Jay!" he shouted. A band of colors danced through the air, gliding over to Dylan. The light wrapped itself around the barrel of the gun, disappearing inside. When he shot, instead of bullets hitting the agents surrounding him, darts did. Four of the agents fell but were replaced by four others.

Kanon watched wide-eyed and amazed.

"Sir!"

Kanon held up a hand. "It's all under control."

Doctor Herron appeared behind Jay. She gasped, feeling the doctor's cold fingers press against her skin. The scientist had stabbed her neck with a needle. Jay couldn't move. Doctor Herron whispered into her ear and the world around her spun. Jay reached out but found nothing. A growing fog covered her vision.

"Dylan!" Kanon shouted over the commotion.

Dylan stopped, withdrawing his weapon before it struck his opponent. The agents surrounding him lowered their guns. Dylan faced Kanon with just as much control in his eyes as Kanon had. Kanon's mouth fell into a dark smile, his gaze shifting. Dylan's eyes followed. He froze. Jay's body was hauled over the intimidating agent's shoulder. She wasn't moving, and her breathing was short. Dylan took a step toward them—the guns surrounding him rose.

"I give you my oath that no harm will come to her." Kanon raised his right hand. A couple of the other agents cracked amused smiles.

Dylan shot them all a deadly glare. "Like hell."

Kanon nodded at the other agent. Sherrill opened the door. The agent carrying Jay left the room, with Sherrill following close behind. Dylan cursed, enraged. Strong hands clasped over his arms, holding him back.

Kanon rounded the table, approaching Dylan. They were almost the same height, Dylan's head meeting his chin.

"What are you going to do to her?" Dylan snarled.

"Nothing. We will provide her with the protection she deserves," Kanon replied. "When we meet again—my apologies—when the Headmaster and I meet face-to-face, then we can discuss what happens next."

Kanon raised the tranquilizer gun, placing it on Dylan's neck. He jerked back only to be pushed into place by the agents holding him. "I'm really sorry about this, son, but it's for the greater good. This is going to be a lot bigger than you and me."

Dylan felt a short, tingling sensation shoot throughout his body. The liquid mixed into his bloodstream. His body grew heavier as if his systems were shutting down. The blood inside him turned into hard needles, poking him from the inside out. Kanon straightened and said something that Dylan couldn't make out. The hands holding him back pulled away and he dropped to his knees. Dylan struggled to keep his eyes open, but failed. A silent oblivion took over.

Chapter Twenty-Seven

Dylan drove his fist through the wall, creating a hole and leaving debris that fell to the ground and clouded the air. He punched the same spot again, driving his knuckles into it until they bled. This was the second time he had lost her.

Doctor Herron pulled the cigarette from her mouth, holding it between two fingers. She puffed out smoke, watching it dance in spirals, disappearing into the air. "This place is already a rundown dump that doesn't need any help from nobody." She tapped the butt of the cigarette into the ashtray.

Dylan pushed off from the wall, striding over to the small table. When he awoke, he had been in a candle-lit, single-celled room with one couch, an old television set without cable, and a high table with two chairs, the redheaded doctor occupying one of them.

Dylan yanked the chair back and sat down. He rubbed his hands over his eyes. He let out something between a sigh and a groan. "Sorry, I'll fix it."

Doctor Herron waved more smoke in his direction, holding her nose up high. "Don't bother." She held out her box of cigarettes.

Dylan narrowed his gaze, staring at her. "I don't smoke," he stated distastefully, and then snatched the box away from her angrily. He tossed the package somewhere off into the dark. "And you shouldn't either! It's bad for you!"

Doctor Herron stared at him blankly. She put out the cigarette she had been smoking, tossing the remains into the ashtray. She ran her fingers through her frizzy hair, tossing it around. "Fine, whatever."

"Where am I?" Dylan crossed his arms, scooting closer to the table. He leaned his torso further, pressing into the edge. "What did he do to me?"

"Just sedated you," she explained with an uninterested demeanor.

"With the serum?" he asked quizzically.

"Hah! That serum? What a joke." Doctor Herron laughed dryly, shaking her head. "That wannabe monstrous doctor only created an anesthesia. Like what humans use to knock the patients out in surgeries." Her fingers tapped constantly on the surface of the table. "It's no cure."

"What does it do to us?" Dylan kept his voice level.

Doctor Herron raised her eyes, meeting his. Dylan's eyes shone with determination. She took a deep breath, heaving out an exhausted sigh. "You're one of those?"

"What do you mean?"

Doctor Herron sat up straighter, her eyes studying him. "A Hybrid. You have an extraordinary ability, yet there is nothing truly *magical* about you. Just something off. You might be one of those special Aris Magicians, but—"

Dylan shook his head, interrupting her. "Answer my question." He didn't have time to figure out whatever nonsense had just spewed from her mouth. He had a checklist: one, find Jay. Two, figure out how the serum ties into the puzzle. Three, kill Kanon.

"Alright, geez," she huffed. "For your friend and me, since we're Purist, the drug acts pretty much the same. It will nullify our powers and put us in a daze. It varies, depending on the amount a person is given. One third of a dose knocks us out and temporarily dulls our powers. Half gives us cases like amnesia or internal damage, and also drains our powers."

"What about a full dosage?"

Doctor Herron bitterly laughed again. "You'd have to either be really stupid or have done something worth the punishment to go there."

"It kills you?" Dylan inquired, sucking in a sharp breath.

She waved her index finger clicking her tongue. "Not exactly, more like putting the person in a coma. When we wake up, if ever, all our powers would have been stripped from us, leaving our souls bone dry. In my opinion, it's way worse than death, and it's only ever been done once, to a man named Sylvester Stone."

Sylvester Stone. The name sounded familiar, but Dylan couldn't place from where. "Why are you working for them?"

"Huh?" Herron glanced away. "Look, kid, I work for no one. But that meeting had to happen."

"It had to happen?" A weighty moment of silence passed between them. Dylan groaned when she didn't elaborate. He ran his hand over his face in frustration. "You mean you go where the money is. Right?" he challenged, using a different tactic. Her eyes returned to his. "Will you help me?" he asked, even though she was the reason they were in this mess.

"For what price?" she tested suspiciously.

"Any price. You name it," Dylan gambled.

Doctor Herron considered his proposal. His expression was unreadable. "A new house," she said, gesturing to the dump they were in.

"Deal." Dylan extended his hand. He made a mental note to explain the situation to Riley once he returned and prayed he wouldn't kick him out for bartering on behalf of the Institute. Dylan knew he was way out of his jurisdiction, but getting Jay back came first.

Doctor Herron hesitated but grabbed his hand. She dug her nails into his skin. "Don't play me for a fool, boy."

"I wouldn't dare."

Chapter Twenty-Eight

Jay groaned, tipping her head up to the ceiling.

"Again!"

She was bound tightly to a metal chair—again. Thick brass handcuffs locked her wrists behind the chair. A set of chains wrapped around her body, cutting into her skin. Another electrical pulse shot throughout her body, causing searing pain. It was like her powers were being temporarily controlled. Jay kicked, hitting one of the legs of the table in front of her. She closed her eyes, attempting to harness her power. Her heart rate increased and her breath turned raspy. Her body was beginning to ache and was begging for a break.

Jay rolled her head to the side. She needed to focus on something else. The room she was in was small. There were four blank concrete walls and a cold draft blowing from the vents. A single light dangled from a chain above her. Jay searched the room for a door, a window, cameras, anything, but found nothing.

Jay rocked the chair back with the heels of her feet. It inched back ever so slightly. In three days or so, she might reach the farthest wall. She gave up, and the chair clambered back into place with no progress made.

"Hey, at least tell me what the deal is!" Jay shouted. She knew someone had to be listening or watching. Minutes later, the door opened, and Kanon stepped in, followed closely by one of the agents from earlier.

"Finally. I just about gave up on you two," Jay snarled.

"I don't think we got the chance to properly introduce ourselves last time we met." Kanon came closer, taking the empty seat across from her. His partner stood in the corner.

"Guess not, but I don't think I can lay all my cards out just yet." Jay smiled wickedly.

Kanon forced a smile. "I'm guessing you've been through this sort of ordeal before?"

Jay laughed, letting sarcasm seep through. "Yeah, this does seem familiar. Let me guess, you ask the questions, and I pretend not to know what the answers are. We dance around that same routine for about—hmm—say an hour, until one of us cracks. You'll hold me at gunpoint or something else supposedly excruciatingly painful to get me to talk. Should I go on?" she asked, mocking him. "Oh, and I bet it'll end the same way, too."

"How's that?" Kanon insisted.

"All of you dead with a bullet in your head." Jay looked at Kanon and then the man in the corner.

Kanon clenched and unclenched his sweaty palms. Jay could tell that his patience was running thin. "Let's just start with names. As you know, my name is Luke Kanon, head agent of this investigation." Jay rolled her eyes. "My partner is agent Darius Vastille." The man gave a small nod.

Jay weighed her options. She had no idea how long she would be here. Any background they would try to trace from her would result in little to nothing. Her parents had liked to keep a low profile before they left her, and after they did, she made sure to do same. She took a deep breath. There was nothing to lose with a name.

"Jaynie Raremore. Call me Jay. I would extend a hand, but mine are tied." She wiggled her fingers under the cuffs.

"Jaynie—" Jay cringed. Kanon quickly corrected himself. "Jay, is there anything you'd like to tell us about this battle to come?"

"Nope."

Kanon tensed. "I didn't think so, but I still asked. Are you positive?"

Jay smiled daringly. "One hundred percent. I won't speak until my Headmaster tells me to—face-to-face, of course," she added.

She had to get out of here. If she could call on her powers, she knew she could easily knock them out with a bit of magic. Jay felt her eyes begin to turn red.

Kanon couldn't stop himself from laughing. "I would have never thought any of this were possible if Herron hadn't shown me what she could do for herself. But the eyes, interesting indeed." Kanon's smile only grew wider. "Careful now, you're treading on very thin ice."

Jay glared at him. "How so?"

"As far as I can see, Aris Magica is a threat. If your kind suddenly decided to stop hiding and expose themselves to all of humanity, I doubt everyone would be as accepting as I am."

Accepting. Jay scoffed. She could tell Kanon distrusted magic.

"I can tell you're quite the handful." Kanon rose to his feet. "Jay, you're not a prisoner, even though it may appear that way. But as our world's savior, you cannot continue to hide in the shadows while letting us humans live obliviously."

Jay looked away from Kanon. He had a point. Maybe her being here was for the best. The CIA had connections to the President. If she could speak with him, then maybe they could reach an agreement that benefited both Aris Magica and humanity in the upcoming war. If she knew where the Aris Magica council was—the leaders of Aris Magica—then maybe she could let them know too. After all, everyone deserved to know that death would be looming on their doorstep if she failed to stop Aturdokht. Jay sighed. *Why me?*

"Darius will see to the things you might need in order to make your provisional stay endurable until your Headmaster arrives." He turned to leave. "You're not a prisoner," he repeated.

"I'm not? Then what are these for?" She gestured her head toward her cuffs. Kanon sighed and reached for the door, not answering her question. "Wait!" Jay croaked, some of her confidence dwindling. "Is he okay?"

There was no question as to whom she was referring. Kanon nodded, stepping out of the room. He whispered something to Vastille, who glanced at Jay before nodding in response. He closed the concrete door behind Kanon. Vastille walked over. He pulled a key from his chest pocket. The small item clicked inside the keyhole as the locks fell to the floor. The chains followed, rattling to a crash on the ground. Jay rubbed her wrists.

"Thanks," she mumbled, feeling weak all over again. Vastille nodded. "Do you ever talk?" No response. She stared hard at him, not getting past the black sunglasses. "Fine, whatever." She couldn't afford to waste any energy on trying to figure out the mysterious agent.

Jay stood to her feet and stretched out her body. A tight, tingling sensation quickly exploded inside her, spreading and numbing the rest of her body. She shook herself and did a couple of air punches and kicks before settling back in her chair. She could really use a nap. She yawned, folded her arms on the table, and rested her head on them.

"What did you guys do to me, anyway?" Jay asked with a yawn, already closing her eyes.

Chapter Twenty-Nine

This time, the pond was on fire. Black clouds of heavy smoke rose from the forest surrounding her. The water was once again colored blood red. The souls of lost Demons marched toward the edge of the pond. Jay looked around, invisible to them all. Her spirit produced a dim blue glow that covered her body. The water lapped at her feet. She jumped, only feeling a cold chill. She took two steps back into the grass. A ghostly fog encompassed her surroundings, lifting from the surface of the water and rolling through the trees. Jay glanced up at the red sky, searching for the moon—one side was entirely fractured into scattered pieces across the crimson sky. The air around her thickened and the wind picked up, ruffling the fallen leaves. A low hum erupted, trembling the earth. The Demons were singing an ancient song from the old world of Aris Magica, a haunting melody.

A dark silhouette emerged from within the fog, rising from the water. Ripples pulsed underneath the figure in silent waves, caused by the magic she used to hover slightly above the surface. A blazing orange fire erupted across the lake, engulfing the sky's reflection. Wavy black hair danced in the wind, framing her face. Bits of flame spiraled up her arms until they covered her body entirely. When her hands rose, so did the fire surrounding her.

The Witch was staring directly into Jay's spirit. Jay panicked and turned to run, only for her foot to get caught under the hem of her dress. She tripped, falling forward. Jay looked down to find that her hair was inches longer than it should have been, decorated with golden beads. Her clothes had been replaced with a long white dress with a red trim wrapped around the edge of the sleeves and through the middle. A red satin sash was tied around her waist with a silver pendant hanging from her hip. Her breath hitched, astonished at the transformation. She felt different, as if her body were no longer her own, yet it was familiar.

Jay met the Witch's cold gaze. A stream of fire raced behind her, and she stopped just a few feet before Jay at the edge of the pond. The Demons surrounding them grew closer, stopping at the edge of the grass before they walked into the water. Jay glared at them as they mindlessly stood there, still humming. Suddenly, a golden staff appeared in Jay's hand. Ancient text was engraved in the metal, spiraling up the staff. At the top was an open claw holding a red opal. Once again, a sense of familiarity washed over her. She knew what to do. Jay lifted the staff into the air.

"Who are you?" Jay shouted, demanding an answer. A strong manifestation of magic surged inside her chest. Jay held the staff higher.

"This is how it will begin," the Witch vowed with confidence. "When the sky bleeds, and the moon fractures, and the water is set on fire."

"What is your name?" Jay asked, moving steadily forward.

"Mirama Aturdokht, daughter of fire." Jay pursed her lips. Aturdokht continued, "I will give you one last chance, Princess, one last chance to save humanity."

At the sound of that name, another much stronger and wiser voice seemed to conquer Jay's own. "My answer remains the same."

The fire in Aturdokht's eyes grew with hatred. "Why help them? They have done *nothing* for us!"

Jay's free hand unwillingly extended out to Mirama. Her voice was a gentle whisper laced with another. The second voice that followed Jay's was not her own, but still felt like a part of her, as if her past life was speaking through her. "Mirama, things do not have to be this way. We can start over, and you can live again. Together, we can unveil the true light belonging to this world. You, too, once saw the beauty it possessed."

Mirama laughed. "I woke up! The beauty that was once here is no more. All humanity has to offer are lies, secrets, and treacheries. They do not deserve a second chance."

"Mirama, you must let go of the darkness that corrupts your soul. It's using you as a vessel, and when it's through—"

"Then it shall make me its queen!" Mirama screeched. "The Blood Moon approaches, and your successor is nowhere close to having the courage to deny me what I desire. Your *beloved* humans will perish. Heed my warning."

Aturdokht's voice faded off into the distance along with everything else. Jay felt her soul ripping from the dream and into a cold and dark emptiness. She hit hard, solid ground. A cold shiver ran along her bare skin. Jay examined the dark pit, rubbing her hands together and blowing in them. She could feel the icy air in her lungs each time she took a breath.

Jay recognized where she was instantly; she was in someone's soul world. Every being had one, including humans. A world that lived inside of everyone, where the essence of them thrived. Beings could visit their soul world through dreams, although often humans would not remember it for long after waking up. Jay just didn't know whose soul world she was in.

A single blue flame flickered midair. Somewhere in her heart, Jay felt as if she knew exactly whose soul the flame belonged to. It felt like it was a part of her. Jay concentrated on it, willing her spirit to embrace it. Suddenly, the darkness wasn't as dark. The soft glow from the flaming soul enveloped her in warmth. Jay took the heat in and gladly crept closer to it.

Jay's voice echoed off into obscurity. "The Blood Moon? Is that when she will return?" The next Blood Moon was only four days away. Panic started to rise in Jay. "Who are you, and why did you show me that?"

The voice that responded emitted from the flame. Each word sent a pulsing beat through the blue soul. "You need to understand what you will be up against."

"But I don't want to fight your battles." Her entire life had been centered on fighting. She realized long ago that all fighting led to was destruction.

“Neither did I,” the flame replied, flickering.

She took a seat, sitting cross-legged on the cold ground. “Was Atur—Mirama human?” Jay asked hesitantly.

The voice chuckled, and it sounded like ringing bells. “No, she was much like you and I.”

“An Ancient.”

“No, lost.”

A sadness swept over Jay. She knew the feeling all too well. The more she learned, the more she felt as if the line between her and Aturdokht was blurring. Maybe they weren’t so different. “Can you teach me more about who we are?”

“Perhaps another time. I don’t have much remaining and I have a lot I need to cover with you,” the soul sighed. “Where to begin. Mirama, or as you know her, Aturdokht, was one of the most powerful Ancients I’d ever known. This was during the time when humans knew we existed, but after the time when there was peace. During my time, humans hated us. During your time, they have ignored your existence, but fear still remains.”

Jay only knew a small part of the history of Ancients from what she had discovered from the book, but a lot of it was still a mystery to her. She hoped that the blue soul was prepared to rectify her ignorance. Jay took a deep breath. Before the soul could continue, Jay asked her question again, “Who are you?”

“I am the first version of you.”

Chapter Thirty

"I met Mirama by accident," the soul began. "At the time, my powers had not yet been discovered, and I was still a regular girl. During my time, the forest had been home to otherworldly creatures, and it had been a forbidden act to travel into their territory, one punishable by death. Humans had shown great fear toward them. I was only six and did not fully understand the feud that lingered between humanity and Aris Magicians. My mother had always taught me to love everyone because God created us all equally. Because of that, I was the target of the village children's abuse and teasing tricks." The soul briefly paused, allowing Jay to process its words.

"One time, they took it too far, and I found myself running without a destination in mind. I found myself deep within the forest. The sun was setting, hidden behind the thick leaves of trees—"

Suddenly, through the soul's words, Jay felt like she was there in the forest, witnessing the events of the story.

I knew someone had been following me. When I turned to face them, it was only a girl. Aturdokht looked as she always had, with fair, pale skin and black hair. Her eyes were an unreadable emerald. It was like her entire self was carved from the heavens—a girl of pure innocence and made of marble beauty stood before me. I didn't dare breathe, let alone have the voice to speak a word. There was something special about her that I could not comprehend.

Her eyes grew big, that all-too-familiar look of concern filling them. "You shouldn't be here!" Her voice was light. The girl was dressed in an elegant, soft, red and orange dress. The silk cloth hung loosely on her, too big for her small figure.

My bare feet dug into the forest floor. I tugged at my rags, feeling self-conscious. I was nothing compared to her, with my brown, nearly black, tangled hair, dirty skin, and brown eyes. I felt out of place; I didn't belong there.

"A-are you a Princess?" I stuttered.

She blinked in surprise. Her expression softened, settling into a Faery-like laugh. "I'm nowhere close."

"Then what are you?" I asked, curiosity taking over.

"I'm a girl." She hesitated. "What's your name?"

"Emilia Prestain," I responded, embarrassed.

"I'm Mirama." She smiled. "But Emilia Prestain, you should not be here." Mirama glanced around before grabbing my hand and dragging me behind her.

I watched the forest. The lack of light played tricks on my eyes, and I thought I saw a shadow weave in between the trees. "Then why are you in here?" I asked, stumbling behind her. She moved as swift as a fox.

"I live here." She gave me a weird look, as if I already should have known.

We had already made it to the edge of the forest. I could see dim fires and candlelight shining from my village. Mirama stopped, not daring to venture further. She released my hand. I looked back at her, confused.

"This is where I leave you, Emilia Prestain."

"Just Emilia. Will I ever see you again?" I beamed, hopeful. She was the first person who had ever helped me, let alone talked to me as if I were a normal person.

Mirama smiled, but it was filled with despair. "I hope you never will, but if we do, then I would be most happy," she whispered. I squealed, embracing her in a warm hug. She tensed, but then slowly relaxed and patted my back.

"Now go!" She gently shoved me onto the dirt road. When I looked back, she was gone.

The little clearing in the forest became our own little secret. I continued to meet Mirama whenever I could. I would teach her about the world beyond the forest, and she would expose hers to me. We both knew our meetings would not last long, but we still tried to hide the danger with the happiness we found.

I had been right in thinking she was special. Mirama was gifted in the art of fire, and she had so many more talents I'd never heard of. I was always impressed by her gifts and willingness to show me. She even told me she could sense some rare and powerful magic within me.

In Mirama's world, she was one of the most respected creatures amongst Aris Magicians. Mirama explained to me about all the mighty Ancients and how they had been the first to lay the foundation for Aris Magica. Long ago, her ancestors, other Ancients, had helped keep the evil at bay from attacking humans, but now, she was the last one. For that and more, I respected Mirama like a child should respect her mother. Mirama had never hated humans—she pitied them. And yet, she would never venture further than the edge of the forest. I tried many times to invite her to enjoy what she imagined humans were like. Each time, I failed. She said she knew what dark desires they possessed.

Mirama set her mind to teaching me magic. She could feel the power within me begging to be awakened. I was gifted in spirit work. Most of my time was spent in the forest, dedicated to honing my new skills. Mirama taught me how to heal the sick and bring back those on the verge of death. I was making quick progress, and slowly, my power grew. Soon, the power of life wasn't my only talent. Mirama saw endless possibilities to my magic, if trained correctly. She offered for me to come live with her, but at the time, my mother had been dying of an incurable disease. I felt obligated to stay with her until the end. Mirama understood, but warned me not to use my magic on my mother. I wanted to badly, but if the others found out, my mother would be in danger.

I was fourteen when the changes started to reflect on the outside. My eyes saw outside of the human barrier and into the dark auras shadowing many of the villagers. When I looked in the mirror, my eyes would sometimes appear red. My hair was gradually taking on the color of snow. Mirama warned me that my powers would soon awaken and there would be nothing I could do to stop it. The daily teasing grew worse. The night my mother died, I remember the house being ablaze with fire. She had been too weak to move, so I ran.

Tears stung my cheeks, blood stained my rags, and the forest floor stabbed into the soles of my feet. I wanted to scream for all that I was worth. I ran deeper into the forest, shouting her name.

"MIRAMA!" I shouted, my lungs still clogged with smoke and raspy breaths.

A familiar hand grabbed my wrist, yanking me back into darkness. I yelped, falling into her arms. I sobbed as she stroked my now white hair and rubbed my back. "She's dead. They burned her—they killed her," I choked. Flashes of the villagers, the fire, and my mother's burned body crossed my mind. I quickly pushed it away; I wanted to forget.

Mirama was strangely silent. The feelings of compassion and kindness seemed to leave her. Her actions were still gentle toward me, but there was a coldness to her. After that night, something about her changed. She had grown more distant, more secretive. Her patience was running short. In the days that followed, Mirama became aggressive and adamant about me leaving the human world behind and falling into the depths with her. I even noticed her magic had taken on a new feeling of hatred.

"Mirama, stop this!"

She was pacing back and forth before me. We had been practicing in the clearing, as we always did, at a vast opening that dipped down into a wide pond surrounded by a thicket of trees. The water I was manipulating fell back with the rest in a splash.

"Stop what? Breathing?" she teased. "Again!"

I pushed off the boulder and stepped into her path. She stopped abruptly, turning her hate-filled eyes on me.

"Stop trying to decide my future," I told her.

"The future with those that won't ever accept you!"

"They will!" I was sure one day both races could once again unite in peace.

"They will kill you! How do you not see that?" Mirama pleaded with me. She grabbed my shoulders. "Emilia, you are my very best friend, and together, you and I can create something—"

"Dangerous," I finished her sentence and shook my head. "We can carve our own path and bring forth peace."

Mirama's face fell, and she stepped away.

"What happened to you? Where's the light I'm used to seeing?" I reached for her.

Mirama turned her back on me. "It was put out, and yours should be, too. You should be even more enraged than I am."

My eyes darkened, changing to a deep red. When my mother died, I wanted revenge—I craved it—but I knew revenge would only bring about another war. The dream Mirama had worked so hard for would have been destroyed because of my anger. She wanted the humans to see the potential of her kind.

"Should I?" I challenged her with a clear mind.

"You should! My dream about humans is over! There is nothing more to understand about them!"

"Mirama, there is so much mo—"

"No! They have shown their true colors. All humanity has to offer is hate, deceitfulness, death, and sin. There is nothing in this world to love."

"You haven't experienced it how I have. Humans are so much more than you make them out to be. You just need to give them a chance."

"Humans had their chance. I will die before I sell my soul to understand them."

I stamped my foot, even more frustrated. "So, you'll sell your soul to the darkness."

"If that's what it takes—"

I gasped, taking a step away from her. "You aren't going to harm them!"

"There is a war coming, Emilia Prestain, and I suggest you figure out which side you're on." Mirama stood her ground.

"Then I have." I did not hesitate. "I will protect what you wanted to protect for so long."

All at once, Jay realized that her eyes had been closed. She slowly opened them to find the soul in front of her.

"I never regretted my decision. I pressed on to protect and warn the humans about the things to come."

"What did you do?" Jay quietly asked, hugging her knees. She needed to know.

The laugh the flame gave seemed distant. "I walked into the village and announced it . . ."

Everyone had been gathered in the center of the village, around the fountain with stone cupids spewing water from their mouths, their bows and arrows pointed toward the sky. I climbed onto the stone platform that circled the base of the fountain.

"Please hear me out before you decide to pass your judgment." Things were quiet. "There is a war coming!" A burst of mumbling conversation erupted. "But it can be prevented! I have seen what the Aris Magicians can do. I have met them. They want peace just as much as we—"

"She's a Witch!" someone shouted, and hell broke loose.

"What?" I scanned the crowd, trying to find the voice's match.

"Look at her hair!"

"Yeah! I've seen her eyes change red!"

"Her mother was an odd one as well!"

"What about her father, is he one of those diviners?"

"No, her father was a drunk!"

"Please, wait! Listen to me!" I shouted.

"Are you here to kill us? Bring us into submission?" an older man barked and waved his cane at me.

"No, I would never—" I shrieked, ducking just in time. A huge stone flew over my head, chipping one of the cupids' elbows. I watched the chunk of stone fall into the water, cracking the marble at the bottom.

Something squished against my face. A fleeting pain pinched my cheek. Out of the corner of my eye, I saw a tomato fall to the ground. Another one followed, slamming into my arm. More food pelted my body, soaking me from head to toe. Sharp shards of stone and glass pierced my skin, tearing at my flesh. Blood trailed into a puddle, slipping into the fountain. Villagers shouted profanity while throwing anything they could get their hands on. My vision blurred, and my heart took its final beat."

"I still don't understand why you're telling me this." Jay blocked the image of Emilia's death from her mind.

"Because I want you to understand why Mirama is the way she is."

"But why?" Jay rose to her feet. "What good will it do to understand the enemy?"

"So you do not become like the enemy," the soul fired back. "I want you to fully understand your past and the reason why you were reincarnated into this life. You need to know what your lineage has been fighting for from the start. Your mind must be as strong as your powers."

"What if I don't want to protect what you did? Just because your powers are passed down to the chosen one does not make me you." Jay paused. "All of the humans I love are dead or gone. Why should I care about the rest?"

"Think of all the ones you haven't met. All the ones you haven't begun to love."

Jay laughed bitterly. "Yeah, that's why I'm stuck in an interrogation room right now."

The flame snapped, "You will not trouble my lineage with revenge. You were chosen to be a part of this for a reason."

"I know . . . I know this story isn't for the weak minded," Jay interjected. Then, her voice softened. "I just wanted you to know, your fantasy of a relationship with humans is long lost."

The soul sighed, depleted. "Nothing is ever lost . . ."

Jay felt an outside presence pulling her back. Jay did her best to resist, but the force pulled harder. "Wait a sec! What about that thing you mentioned earlier? What are Ancients?" The flame began to flicker, along with its response, fading away.

Jay's fist banged on the table, rattling the legs. She raised her head up slowly to find Vastille sitting calmly across from her, reading a nameless book. Jay stared long and hard at him, but he paid her no attention. She ran her fingers through her hair, turning away. That had been the longest vision she'd ever had, and yet she still had so many questions. It was frustrating. She was still nowhere close to solving anything.

Jay rolled her eyes, leaning back in the chair. She wasn't going to think anymore. Pulling her chair closer to the table, she asked, "So, what's your backstory, Vast?" She had forgotten his full name. He flipped through another page, ignoring her.

"What? Am I a disgrace just because I'm a freak? You're too normal to talk to me?"

Vastille looked up from his book. She couldn't see anything past his sunglasses. He held her gaze for a moment longer. Vastille shook his head, slowly returning to his book.

"Fine, whatever. You're too much of a loyal dog for me, anyway."

"And you're too much of a child with a big mouth."

Jay pretended to nearly fall out of her chair, dramatically surprised. She gripped the edge of the table, balancing herself. His voice was deep. "He talks!"

"Just not to you," he grunted.

Jay scoffed, "What? Is it out of your jurisdiction?"

Vastille closed his book. He pinched the bridge of his nose, then casually glanced around the single room. He leaned over the table. Jay did the same. "I advise you to give Luke what he wants," he whispered.

"I'm still mulling it over," Jay said stubbornly.

Vastille groaned, "Listen." He pushed down his sunglasses until his eyes could be seen over the top rim. One was a stormy silver the other a dark brown.

"What's wrong with them?" Jay asked, leaning in closer. She could feel a small surge of magic within the silver eye now that he had removed his sunglasses. "Wait! Are you an Aris Magician?"

"Hybrid. Emag Master. Now keep it down," Vastille hissed, pushing up his glasses. "If I wanted the entire department to know, I would have told them myself."

Jay covered her mouth, unable to control her excitement. Electromagnetic Master, Jay thought happily. She knew that they were distant cousins to their Pure breed, Tekhne. While a Tekhne's powers were limited to only the internet, an Emag user could master any technological application with an electromagnetic wave. "B-but aren't they watching?" she asked frantically, scanning the room. He had become her best asset for getting out of here; she couldn't lose him.

"They aren't. No one is operating the cameras. It's lunch hour." Vastille was staring at one of the empty concrete walls.

"Seriously?" Jay asked, unconvinced. "How long have you been here? Do they know about Aris Magica? How long have I been here?

Where are we? Is Dylan really safe?" Rapid-fire questions shot out of her mouth.

Vastille cut her off. "No, and fourteen years," he answered casually, relaxing in his seat.

"Fourteen years! Oh my gosh!" Jay laughed, amazed. "Wow," she whispered to herself. An Aris Magician successfully living among humans. Her smile faded. "But you're hiding your identity." The excitement she felt faltered. There were plenty like him living among humans as if they were one of them. It felt entrapping, knowing how her kind had to keep their magic a secret for fear of history repeating itself. Aturdokht was right, and it angered her.

"I am. But by choice," Vastille said, catching her last comment. "It's not because I'm scared of what they will think. It's just easier this way in my line of work. There are people who would try to abuse my powers if I told them about it."

Jay snorted. "Kanon."

Vastille smirked. "It is possible."

Jay looked up at him, hopeful and doubtful at the same time. Vastille smiled. "My late wife. She worked as an educator, and she wasn't afraid to show her magic at times. It was quite unique." Jay smiled as well, hearing the joy in his voice as he spoke of his wife. "She could create things out of light. She'd use them to make the stories she told her students come to life. Of course, most humans thought she was using some sort of updated technology. Magic is a hard thing to believe in."

"What about the ones who did believe?" Jay asked.

"The good ones kept her secret. But like anything, there will always be people who are intimidated by you and just look for one thing to hate. She had her enemies, but they never dared to act. Magic can also be scary for humans who don't have the mindset to understand it."

Jay's heart tightened. She was filled with an unlikely joy at his wife's experience. She chuckled to herself. It was possible. Just because Jay couldn't see it, didn't mean that all humans were monsters, and not all Aris Magicians should be feared. Aturdokht had been wrong. She swallowed tears threatening to build. "Thank you."

Vastille shrugged as if it wasn't a big deal for him. "And about your boyfriend . . ."

"He's not my—"

"To my knowledge, he's safe."

Jay scoffed, clicking her tongue against the roof of her mouth. She shook her head, annoyed. "What about you? What can you do?"

"Thought we pinned that discussion?" His dark brow arched.

"Not even close. Now I'm interested."

Chapter Thirty-One

The car rolled to a stop outside the looming black gates. Behind them was a winding pathway leading up to the building. It was at least three houses long, with ten levels. The building looked like something out of the Victorian era, with drapes of frozen ivy that suffocated the walls. The windows remained dark with the early lift of a morning's fog. The field surrounding it was covered in white snow with bare trees spread throughout the yard. An empty fountain split the pathway in two, covered with icicles.

Doctor Herron looked out of the passenger window. "You've got to be kidding me." Her mouth fell open as she stared through the glass, dumbfounded. "The old man turned this into a—" she cut herself short, shaking her head.

Dylan blew hot air into the palms of his hands. His body was rigid and cold; the doctor's car didn't have a heater installed. "What, did you used to live here?" he asked curiously. She turned the car off and stepped out onto the winter ground, the soles of her boots crunching against the ice.

"Oh, sorry for invading your privacy," Dylan mumbled, irritated. He undid his seatbelt, opening the jeep's door.

Doctor Herron pulled her coat tighter, stalking over to the gate. She grabbed one of the metal railings and yanked hard, attempting to force the gates open, but they didn't budge. She cried out, kicking the bottom of the gate. "Shit!" She rubbed her toe, hopping on her opposite foot. "Damn metal."

Dylan rolled his eyes as he walked past her. He typed a four-digit code into the keypad on the right post of the gate. The hinges creaked as the gate swung open. Doctor Herron narrowed her eyes, mumbling under her breath.

They walked up the long path in silence. Cold air swirled all around them. Dylan tucked his chin, pulling the collar of his jacket up. Doctor Herron's hair whipped back and forth behind her like an untamed fire. When they reached the door, Doctor Herron stood back, letting Dylan take the lead. He dug in his pockets for his personal key. The small golden key clicked in the lock. The door opened with ease, welcoming them with a reprieve from the cold air.

"Home sweet home." Dylan eased himself out of his jacket. Doctor Herron scoffed, kicking off her boots and tossing them beside the door.

She briefly took in the first level of the mansion. They stood in a dome-shaped opening that extended out into numerous halls. A glass chandelier hung from the high ceiling, the light bouncing off the glass creating an array of colors. Pillars bordered the sides. Before them was a winding staircase leading up to another floor, and to the right and left were two hallways leading to separate rooms of the Institute. Doctor Herron looked down at her feet. They were standing on a circular Persian carpet with a beige and red, zigzag pattern.

Dylan watched her head spin as she tried to take in everything. Her eyes snapped to him with a fierce glare. "What?"

Dylan shrugged, breaking eye contact. "Nothing."

She gave him a glare of pure hatred. "Punk, this is why I won't have kids of my own."

"Dylan!"

He glanced up in time to see Ami, followed by a sullen Taybeith, bounding down the steps. Her hair bounced with every step. She was already dressed for the holidays, wearing a festive white sweater. When she got close enough, she pulled him into a hug. "Merry Christmas!"

Dylan didn't return the gesture, keeping his arms at his sides. He gently shoved her off in annoyance. Dylan sniffed, smelling the faint scent of apple cider and roast ham being prepared for dinner. Christmas lights and candy decorated the railing, strung up above the doors and hallways, no doubt adorning the rest of the Institute.

Taybeith made his way down the last of the steps. He was dressed in his usual black attire. "Merry Christmas." Dylan nodded at him, giving him a suspicious stare. Taybeith looked at him, confused.

Taybeith frowned. "I hate Christmas, I was forced to come." He glanced at Ami.

Ami placed her hands on her hips, giving Taybeith a resentful look. "You sure are a gothic downer. Not even I was going to let you spend your time locked up in the library."

Dylan placed a warning hand on her shoulder. "Everybody has a reason behind the things they hate," he reminded her gently. "Let him be."

Ami reluctantly zipped her mouth. Taybeith's frown deepened as he looked from Dylan to Doctor Herron. "Where's Jay?" His voice rose in panic. Dylan wouldn't meet his gaze. Taybeith took a couple of steps toward them. He kept the tone of his voice level as he repeated, "Where is Jay?" Dylan took a deep breath, raising his eyes to the dark, violet, withdrawn stare.

"Yo," a familiar voice waved, entering in from the side hallway. A Santa Claus hat sat slanted over Cryis's white hair. With one quick look, he noticed the tension in the room escalating. "What's going on?"

Taybeith's eyes dilated before he lunged at Dylan, snatching him by the collar. "Where is she?"

Dylan was taken aback, but only for a moment. He wrestled with Taybeith's wrist. "Let go," he growled.

"Not until you tell me what happened," Taybeith pleaded, but slowly began to release him. Dylan straightened out his shirt.

Doctor Herron cleared her throat. The others turned, finally acknowledging her presence. "Dylan, don't you have shit to do, so I can get the hell out of here?"

Dylan sighed. He patted Taybeith on the shoulder, attempting to slip out of the situation. "I'll tell you later."

Doctor Herron walked past Taybeith, gently brushing against his arm. She froze moments after passing him and looked back at Dylan. Dylan gave her a quizzical stare as he began to walk toward her. She looked as if she had seen a ghost.

Taybeith seized Dylan's arm, yanking him back around. Dylan stumbled over his own feet but regained his footing. "No, you'll tell me now!" Cryis and Ami looked at Taybeith, who was becoming more unhinged by the second. Veins started to pulse in his forehead, and his eyes started to become bloodshot.

"What's with you?" Ami shouted.

"Careful," Dylan warned, yanking his arm out of Taybeith's grip.

"Careful!" Taybeith spat back, his hands balling into fists. "I bet that's what you told her too. Don't you know what's at stake if we lose her?"

Dylan's nostrils flared. He reacted blindly, landing a punch square on Taybeith's nose. Taybeith's head whipped back. He quickly recovered, wiping away the smear of blood that exploded from his nose. He retaliated, throwing a punch back at Dylan. He hit him right in the shoulder, shoving Dylan back.

"Whoa!" Cryis yelled. He ran over, grabbing both of Dylan's arms, holding him back. "Ami!"

Red smoke appeared from Ami's arms, transforming into hands as they extended out from her. They gripped Taybeith's shoulders, locking him in place. "What the heck is wrong with you?" Ami shouted while restraining him.

"She should have never trusted you! Everywhere you go, bad things happen to the people closest to you! You're not good enough for her!" Taybeith fired back.

"Trust? How dare you talk to me about trust. So, help me, Taybeith, if another useless word comes out of your mouth, I'll—" Dylan bared his teeth, puffing out his chest.

"Dude, calm down," Cryis shouted over them. "Taybeith, what's gotten into you?"

Taybeith turned his attention to Cryis. Strands of his hair hung in his face, and his eyes were bloodshot and wild.

Taybeith snarled, showing his teeth. "What? So whenever he lashes out, it's okay, but if I do it, there's a problem?"

"No, man, that's not what I meant."

"Don't lie to me! Everyone that follows him or even is around him has died. And you know it."

"TAYBEITH!" Ami roared furiously.

Taybeith's words were an invisible punch, smacking Dylan in the gut. Dylan stopped struggling against Cryis. "No." Dylan gritted his teeth. "I lost her. It was my fault." He lost his fire, relaxing against Cryis. "I know bad things happen to those around me. That's why I always push people away. Even those who are in my life aren't really there," he admitted. "I don't trust myself to keep them safe."

Doctor Herron yawned as she watched the scene on the sidelines. She had finally regained her composure. "Pathetic," she whispered.

Doctor Herron glanced at Cryis, who was watching her out of the corner of his eye. She walked over, stepping under Ami's mist. She placed her palm on Taybeith's forehead. Taybeith's eyes widened, and his body crumbled to the floor. Ami's mist dispersed, and Cryis slowly released his hold on Dylan, letting him fall to his knees. She stepped over the broken boy. "He needs to get him purified. He's been tainted."

"How did you—" Ami asked.

"Another one of an Oracle's abilities. If I've seen a vision about the person, I have limited access to their mind."

"What did you see?" Cryis asked.

Doctor Herron mischievously smiled, "If I tell you, then certain events I've seen that need to happen will not happen."

"What's wrong with him?" Ami asked, concerned.

"Seems like his heart was being controlled by a malevolent force." She made her way to him. She tousled Dylan's hair, and he didn't resist. "Whatever that kid said wasn't the truth." He nodded, unconvinced. She cleared her throat, returning to her usual gruffness. "Get up."

"A malevolent force?" Cryis repeated. "How do you know that?" He glanced at Taybeith, his eyes widening. "By whom? And for how long?"

Doctor Herron shrugged. "I don't have those kinds of answers, kid. But if I had to guess, maybe for a year or so now. I felt a pretty strong vision of one of the nasty ones looming."

"Aturdokht," Dylan said, his voice barely above a whisper. "Jay saw him talking to a raven in the library," he said, louder, as he faced Cryis. "After that, he stared acting more weird than usual."

"Aturdokht?" Cryis helped Dylan to his feet. He turned toward Doctor Herron, "You're an Oracle, aren't you?"

"Smart boy," she teased.

"Intuition," Cryis corrected. "What did you see?" Cryis asked, referring to her vision.

The room was silent for a moment as an eerie feeling settled in. Doctor Herron sighed, "Nothing good will come from me telling you."

"Tell us anyway," Dylan said, just as curious.

Doctor Herron sighed again, "Fine. I saw a glass tower covered in flames and vines. Above it was the woman I wager you were talking about—Aturdokht. Four orbs of light surrounded her, while she scorched the ground beneath her."

"A glass tower . . ." Cryis mumbled, his face deep in thought. "The council building?" Cryis asked, confusing Dylan.

Council building? Dylan looked between Doctor Herron and Cryis. Neither one gave an explanation. "Four orbs?" Dylan said aloud. Her vision made no sense.

Doctor Herron shrugged. "The future's not always clear. It's ever changing. You asked what I saw, and like I said, knowing now would do you no good." She tossed her curly hair over her shoulder. "Perhaps it'll make more sense to you in the coming time."

"That's it? There has to be more. What kind of half-assed explanation was that? The other Oracles I've met were so muc—" Cryis ranted only for Herron to wave him off.

Herron sighed, "Look, kid—"

"Kid?" Cryis scoffed.

"Just take me to the Headmaster so I can get what I came for."

"And what matter am I obliged to discuss with you?" A stone-cold voice rang out. The Headmaster stood at the entry of one of the doors leading to another hall. Riley stood behind him, looking not the least bit happy. His usual black and gray was substituted with a dark green shirt with red lettering spelling out "Who's Your Santa Clause."

"Maverick," Doctor Herron spoke with as much cold locked in her own voice. "Riley," she said with even more disdain.

"Herron." Riley rolled his eyes.

"Virginia." The Headmaster turned to leave. "My office, now. Riley, please deal with the matter downstairs." Riley nodded, keeping his eyes on Dylan. Doctor Herron begrudgingly followed.

Riley walked past Taybeith, shaking his head disapprovingly. "He needs a purification," Ami explained.

Riley grabbed Dylan by the forearm, ensuring he wouldn't run away. "I want every damn detail."

Dylan and Cryis were locked in Riley's office. The window's blinds were pulled down. Ami had taken Taybeith to the infirmary. Cryis leaned against the wall with his arms crossed and head bowed. Dylan was seated in one of the chairs facing Riley's desk. Riley sat in the big chair behind his desk, beyond outraged—his lips were pursed, and the creases in his skin pinched even tighter.

Riley's voice was calm, yet dangerous. "First, you're gone for an entire day, and when you show up, you're not only without Jay, but you're with that wretched woman. And then, you have the audacity to start a fight."

Dylan sunk deeper into his chair. He didn't feel like hearing this right now. "Yeah, whatever. I thought Doctor Herron was a friend."

"A loose term. But you don't get it, do you? People do care what the hell happens to you," Riley stated, teetering on the edge of his calmness.

Dylan rolled his eyes. "Enough." He couldn't bring himself to listen to this. "I'm still on a mission."

"Authorized by who?" Riley's voice rose. "Because last time I checked, aside from the Headmaster, I'm the only one with that power. And these little so-called missions end now. I only brought them into the picture to help train you kids about coexisting with the other world."

"Coexisting? You really think that's going to happen? Especially after the stunt they pulled today? Cut the bullshit, Riley."

"Watch your tone, I am still your professor."

Cryis peeled himself off the wall. By the expression he wore, anyone could tell that he was fed up. "Enough," Cryis said, stepping in front of Dylan before he had the chance to say something he would forever regret. "You messed up. We all mess up, but what's pissing us off is your inability to grasp our concern and forgiveness." Cryis paced forward pointing at himself. "Heck, I don't even know—"

"The serum," Dylan interrupted, changing the topic.

Cryis stopped mid-sentence. "What about it?"

Riley raised his eyebrows, closely watching Dylan pull something out of his pocket. He tossed him a wrinkled letter, throwing it onto Riley's desk. "What's in it?" Riley picked it up and ripped it open.

"Did you get the serum?" Cryis continued as Riley quietly read over the letter, a range of emotions playing over his face.

"Doctor Herron betrayed us. The CIA was there. They knew."

"They took Jay?"

"And the serum," Dylan finished. "We still might have the upper hand."

Riley crumbled up the letter in his fist after he finished reading it. He looked annoyed as he tossed it the direction of the trashcan at the foot of his desk.

"How?" Cryis asked.

"You said the serum is part of this big puzzle," Dylan confirmed.

The letter hit the trashcan, bouncing in. Riley rejoined the conversation. "The government is full of bastards; never cares for us until shit starts hitting the fan. Hell, I doubt they even knew we still existed. Now they want us to work together?" Riley barked out a rough laugh, amused by his own words. "Those bastards can go to hell."

"Wash your mouth out with soap!" Cryis pointed a finger at Riley. "Dylan, finish telling me what happened."

"Herron explained the damage the serum could do if used against us," Dylan began to explain.

"Which is?" Cryis pressed.

"For Hybrids, nothing serious. But for any Pure breed, half a dosage will sedate them and temporarily take away their powers. A full dosage will put them in something resembling a coma, but when, if ever, they awaken, their memories would be gone along with their powers."

"A modern version of the sealing spell the previous Princess had used to contain Aturdokht," Cryis mumbled.

"A seal is temporary, breakable, if some fool is powerful or dumb enough to open it," Riley added.

"Do you think the CIA knows this?"

"They didn't seem to. Do you know Kanon?" Dylan asked, directing his question toward Riley.

Riley ran a hand over his bald head. "Nope, but the handwriting did look familiar."

"There was someone else who managed to put me off," Dylan recalled the daunting agent. "Then there's Taybeith." Dylan wanted to ask if they could use the serum to strip Taybeith of his powers and perhaps whatever was possessing him, but he refrained from asking.

Cryis sighed. "I haven't seen anything like this in a long time. But he's either possessed by a Demon or half-Demon."

Riley scoffed, "But the kid's a Tekhne. That's not possible."

Riley was right, Wizards and their sub classes were the only Pure breeds incapable of being possessed by a Demon's powers. Before the possession could take its full course, the Wizard's magic would alert them of it. Wizard magic worked hand in hand with being in the know. Although a Tekhne's magical knowledge ranged only to the internet, Taybeith still should have been able to pick up on the signs of a Demon's acting power, unless he had allowed it to happen.

Dylan frowned at Riley. It was unlike him to not believe in the impossible. "Tell that to the raven Jay saw him talking to."

Riley had to know what Dylan was talking about. After all, he was there as well when they'd seen Aturdokht shape-shift. Riley banged his fist on the desk. "We let the enemy slip right in," he sighed. "But I won't give up on the kid. He's just as much a victim in this as we are, I'm sure."

Dylan clenched his jaw. How could Riley be so confident that Taybeith was innocent? He could very well be a main player in Aturdokht's game. Dylan shook his head, shoving the thought from his mind. They had bigger problems to take care of rather than discussing Taybeith's loyalty. "And we have another problem."

"What?" Riley growled.

"I might have made a deal with Doctor Herron, but it was only to help get Jay back." He quickly rushed the words out, knowing he had crossed the line by the look of anger written on Riley's face.

Riley dragged his hand over his face. "Don't matter now. If we want her back, we're going to have to play their game."

"Consult the Headmaster," Cryis clarified.

"What other choice do we have?"

Chapter Thirty-Two

The story would have to wait. Kanon strolled in, relieving Vastille of his duty. Kanon took his seat in the chair opposite Jay. He sat, placing a loaded weapon on the table.

Cryis. Jay tried to reach him, but was unable to. She still wasn't sure how their mind connection worked, or if she would be able to reach him from this far, but it was worth a shot. She needed to let him know what she'd found out. Especially about the upcoming Blood Moon. They were running out of time.

"Do you know what this is?"

Jay crossed her arms, leaning back in the chair. "It's a twenty-two pistol with an easy enough recoil for beginners." She rolled her eyes as if it weren't obvious enough.

"Precisely. Now impress me."

"What?" Jay exclaimed, shocked.

"Show me I can trust *magic*," Kanon bargained, but the way he said "magic" told Jay that no matter what she did, Kanon would just use it to prove how dangerous magic was.

Jay inhaled sharply, every muscle in her body screaming in pain. She was not going to give in easily. "So restate everything you already know," Jay affirmed. Kanon's smile dropped; his entire demeanor shifted. Jay smirked. "I can do a lot with a gun, even break it down and put it back together again, but everyone should know how to do that."

Kanon narrowed his eyes and opened his mouth, but Jay beat him to it. "Even break out," she teased.

"You won't," Kanon assured. "You're too smart to take such a risk."

Jay smirked, leaning closer to the table. "Something simple then?"

"In your terms, then yes." Kanon took a deep breath. "I know it sounds like an unusual thing for a child to be helping the CIA, but in order to present this idea of magic to other empowering authorities, I need your cooperation." He paused, then added, "And to save this world we live in. If this being is a strong as you say, then I highly doubt her powers will stop at just your side of this universe—if you can't stop her."

Jay sighed, bored. "If it hits *my world*, then it would hit your world too. Our worlds are merged together, not strung in separate universes."

"You do still care for this world." It wasn't a question, but a statement.

Jay nodded. "Of course, I do. I *still* live in it."

Kanon leaned forward. "Then help me help you."

Jay looked from him to the gun, then back at him. The choice to shoot him and opt out was tempting. She shook her head, took a deep breath, and released it. It felt as if the fate of both worlds rested in her hands. One wrong move and she could make an enemy other than Aturdokht. She squeezed her hands together and rubbed them back and forth.

"Alright, I'll help, under a couple of conditions."

Jay saw the corner of Kanon's mouth twitch as he visibly suppressed the overwhelming satisfaction growing inside him. "Wonderful."

"One, you let me call Dylan, at least to let him know I'm okay," Jay demanded. "Two, if we decide to work together, then Aris Magica will not be at risk because of your world's curiosity." Jay knew it was a far-reaching promise for her to demand, but she had to be sure. Despite Vastille's hopeful story about coexistence, Jay knew that humans were just as capable of betrayal as Aris Magicians. "Third . . ." Jay thought about it only for a quick moment. "I want Vastille as my personal guard. As dark times approach us, I should be under constant protection." Regardless of how much control Kanon believed he had over the situation, Jay had accepted that in the end, it would be her against Aturdokht. She was the only one who could create the seal and find a way to destroy her once and for all. She was the last hope for the world.

"Absolutely," Kanon agreed.

"Hmm," Jay mumbled skeptically.

Kanon gestured a hand toward the pistol. Jay waved a hand over the gun. "*Libero.*" The item instantly disabled, and the bullets dumped into a small pile on the table.

Jay slammed her hands on the table, causing the scraps of metal to jump. "Four, don't you ever point a loaded weapon at me again, or next time, you will die."

Kanon was too baffled for words. He rose, adjusting his tie, then cleared his throat before continuing, "I'll see to it that your accommodations are met to the best of my ability."

Chapter Thirty-Three

Cryis rounded the corner, carrying a wrapped present, a troubled look on his face. He hugged the present tighter. "Cryis?" Dylan stopped midstep. Dylan rubbed the back of his neck, intending to ask if everything was okay, but he didn't get the chance.

Cryis lifted his head. "Hey." He waved the present, his smile brightening. "Are you coming?"

"Where?" Dylan leaned against the wall. Then it hit him. "To the Grand Hall? Nah, I'm headed to the library."

Cryis laughed, anchoring his free hand on his hip. "Everyone's going to be there, plus, there'll be cookies, coco, and an extravagant feast to follow. Oh, and get this—the Headmaster got us presents." Again, Cryis waved the gift in the air.

Dylan shook his head, his hair falling just before his brows. "Yeah, I know. He does it every year." They both were silent for a moment, letting the awkwardness pass. Dylan sighed, pushing his hair back, leaving behind strands that stood on end. "How's Taybeith?"

Cryis blew out a strained breath. "He's managing." He rubbed a hand through his own hair before shoving it into his pocket.

"Yeah, fighting the Demon inside of him," Dylan recalled.

"Yeah, I know, but I wonder how he got like this. He's a good kid from what I've seen."

"What do you mean?" Dylan asked, concerned.

"I don't know. In the past, Demons would align themselves with Aturdokht. Demons love destruction and are called to it. That's why they could never fit into Aris Magician society today. But to be possessed by one is rare. The last time that happened was during the divide between light and dark within Aris Magica," Cryis admitted, followed by a long sigh. "Look, go do what you do, and I'll go check on Taybeith." Cryis pointed in Dylan's direction, backing away.

"Thanks," Dylan said. Cryis waved his present over his head, walking away.

Dylan peeled himself from the wall, taking the next turn to the library. The room was practically empty except for the helper behind the front desk, typing frantically away on the computer. He was a student. His skin was a dark blue, and his eyes were bulbous green orbs. Little rough stubs protruded from the sides of his temples. His hair was a pasty red, sitting on his head like a mop. He looked around the age of either sixteen or seventeen. Before break, Dylan had seen him behind the front desk, substituting for their missing librarian, who was away on sabbatical. He'd never paid much attention to him.

Dylan went to the back corner, logging onto one of the computers. He couldn't do anything to help Jay. The Headmaster said he would personally see to it, so he decided to take a page from her book and do some research. He recalled how Jay had said that her trident scar had given her more control over her powers. Dylan still wasn't sure how much he believed that it did, even though he'd seen it in action. Still, the trident had come from Aturdokht.

What game could she be playing? he thought.

Dylan typed the word "trident" into Google. Results pertaining to the Greek god Poseidon covered the page. Dylan scrolled down, moving to the next page, and then the next. Nothing.

Dylan banged his fist on the desk, holding the monitor. "Damn it." He rubbed his hand over his face.

The blue-skinned kid from earlier paused in front of Dylan's computer. He was carrying a stack of books. He sat them down on the corner of the table. "Need any help?"

Dylan peered up at him, not saying anything. "Okay, then." He leaned over, just enough to see what Dylan was searching. "A trident?"

"Yeah."

"Doubt you mean the Trident of Poseidon." He had a slight accent. Dylan couldn't quite place it, but knew he was certainly not from the city.

Dylan began to relax. He leaned back in the chair. "Far from it."

"Hmm . . . Do you think you could describe the trident for me?"

"It has three points with a short staff. It's just a regular trident." Dylan stressfully massaged his temples.

"Maybe it leans more toward the Devil," the boy suggested.

"The Devil?" The trident could mean that; it wasn't as if Aturdokht was the daughter of good.

"There is another thing I can try," the boy added. "But it would require an object of some sort, or something that resembles what you have envisioned." His voice dropped as he doubtfully looked around, seeing nothing that resembled the trident.

Dylan extended his left hand, palm up. He didn't have anything to lose by letting this boy try to help. "Will a symbol work?"

The boy leaned over the desk. He grabbed Dylan's wrist. Dylan felt cold, scaly imprints rub against his skin. The kid looked closer, seeing the faint remnants of a trident burned into his skin. Dylan wasn't sure what the kid was about to do. He wasn't even sure what breed of Aris Magician he was. Dylan only knew the boy wasn't a Hybrid because he couldn't pass for human. "This will sting," the boy warned.

"What will sting?" Dylan asked, but the boy had already begun.

The boy's green eyes turned to two black orbs. Dylan watched as needles grew from the boy's hands and pierced into Dylan's skin surrounding the trident. He was right, it did sting, but even that was an understatement. The needles dug deeper, grabbing hold of blood and tissue, and pulled in every direction around the scar. It was as if Dylan's skin was being torn from his bones. Dylan allowed himself to be absorbed by the pain.

The boy blinked his eyes, and a soft glow shone from them. Quick glimpses of pictures flashed across Dylan's mind. Within a black space, the trident turned gold, shimmering in the dark. The two tails pointed up on the outside, extended up, and curled inward on each other, forming a heart. The middle rose slightly below the two and flattened out into a small circular mount. The base extended, transforming into a staff. An illusion of a red opal stone appeared in the center of the heart, hovering over the top of the staff. It gleamed there, reflecting a spark of light.

The discomfort subsided as the boy pulled back. The needles returned into the scaly imprints on the palm of the boy's hand. Dylan dared to open his eyes, facing the boy.

"Wow," was the only word that managed to leave the librarian's mouth.

Dylan stared at him for a moment, impressed by the magic he had performed. The boy was a Seer. Unlike an Oracle who could see people's futures, a Seer saw supernatural insight on objects. His powers fell into the Purist class.

"Yeah, wow," Dylan agreed. All the pieces were gradually beginning to fall into place. The only thing that was missing was the person who had to embrace it all. "I never got your name." Dylan reached out a hand to his new friend.

"Oh, I'm—"

Suddenly, a loud scream pierced the air, followed by a deep tremble from the ground. The windows shattered and books fell to the ground as shelves toppled over. Dylan shouted at the boy, commanding him to take cover. The boy rushed around the table and slid under it with Dylan.

More screams followed from the library as a couple of other students came out from their regular spots toward the front and hid behind the nearest desk or chair.

"What was that?" the boy asked, searching Dylan's eyes. The lights above flickered off and on.

"*Who* was it, is the question we should be asking," Dylan stated. Another crashing sound shook the mansion, followed by more cries. Dylan tugged on the boy's sleeve. "Come on," he whispered.

They rose from their hideout. The library was trashed; fallen shelves lay on top of torn books. Glass was shattered on the ground near the stained glass windows. A couple of students helped lift a bookcase that had fallen on another student's leg. A fierce wind swept in, ruffling the pages of the books. The sky had turned deep purple and black, with hideous laughter echoing in the wind. Dylan could feel the dark presence gliding in the air. He rushed to the door and pushed it open. Outside, the screams amplified, and the two of them ran in the direction where most of the shouts were coming from.

"DYLAN!" Ami collided into him, knocking him back.

Dylan held her at arm's length. "Ami, what's going on?"

Her breathing was coming out in short, heavy breaths. Dirt covered her body. Blood soaked a small part of her sleeve where her shirt had been cut open. "Demon attack! They're attacking the Institute!'

"Wait, what?" As if on cue, a serpent with two heads attached to a Minotaur's body smacked against the wall rounding the corner. It cast a looming shadow over their small figures, taking up the entire opening.

Dylan took a step back, dragging Ami behind him. "Where's Riley?"

"I don't know!" Another explosion rang out from below, rattling the walls. Debris fell from the ceiling above them. Ami screamed.

The serpents began charging at them. Dylan took out the blade he kept stashed in his back pocket. He brought it down in a swift arc, slicing one of the heads in half. The remaining head hissed in anger and retracted. The arms of the Minotaur hefted an ax with a curved blade. He brought it up, arcing it back behind itself. Dylan cursed, shoving Ami into the boy, and rolled to the opposite side, dodging the blade. Dylan hopped to his feet and pressed himself against the wall. The beast turned, drool slithering from its tongue. Dylan lunged again, drawing his dagger into a cross rotation. He barely missed, sliding to the ground as the ax came down again. Dylan slid beneath the monster, slicing at its hind legs. A hideous cry came from its parted mouth. Distracted, Dylan hopped to his feet, now behind the Demon. With one swift movement, his dagger crossed through the middle of the Demon, cutting it directly in half. The monster froze, stunned. The serpent head recoiled on itself before turning to ash like the rest of the body.

"First priority," Dylan wiped blood from the side of his mouth and black goo from the blade of his dagger. "We find Riley."

"Dylan, no!' Ami whimpered. She looked at his companion, then back to Dylan. "They're Demons!"

Dylan understood her distress. Every student that attended the Institute was trained in how to defend themselves, not so much against monsters, but against humans from the outside world who would try to do them harm. No one had ever predicted a Demon attack, or an attack from an Aris Magician.

Dylan grabbed her by the forearm and slammed her hard against the wall. She shrieked, unprepared. His new friend hesitated, but stood back. "Get it together. Where are the other students?" More of them had started to return with the break nearing its end, and depending on their numbers, they might be able to organize a strategy, or at least get everyone out. Dylan knew that at least half of the students had probably returned by now. Christmas Day was a huge event at the Institute that most students hated to miss. He didn't wait for her answer. "Find them and fight your way out," Dylan seethed in a dangerously calm voice.

Ami took in a rattled breath, nodding her head. She sniffed, wiping the tears from her eyes. "Okay."

Dylan turned to the boy. "Your name?"

"Ah, yeah, Lyid."

"Dylan. Let's move!"

The Institute was a madhouse. Monsters had managed to breach the school, crawling all over the premises. Most of them were no taller than the average man; the bigger ones hadn't made it into the mansion yet. The remaining Demons scattered as kids battled their way through the chaos. As Dylan pressed on, things felt more like déjà vu—like the night when Phagos had broken into his house. Amid it all, that's who Dylan continued to keep a look out for, but there was still no sign of him.

"Dylan!" Ami shouted. Mist shot out of her hands, swarming past him. The sword in the monster's hand fell to the floor in front of him.

"Thanks."

"Don't mention it," Ami yelled, going in for another strike. Lyid backed her up, stopping one from behind. "We got this, go!" Ami instructed.

The entire building was falling to pieces. Dylan barely recognized the main level as he approached the stairs. Some parts threatened to catch fire, while others were caving in. An enormous hole was burned through the front entrance, leaving a gaping hole where the door once stood. Parts of the mansion were packed with piles of rubble, exposing both the higher levels of the Institute and the setting sky.

Explosions created by both the students and Demons continued to erupt around him. Dylan took the barely-intact steps two at a time down to the lower level. He needed to find Riley.

Groups of towering Demons hovered together in large masses near where the Grand Hall should have been. The tiled floor was cracked, with jagged marble pieces sticking up from the disaster. The whole east wing had been knocked to a pile of ash and debris. Snow gently fell into the mansion, covering the ground in white. A mixture of blood and black goo splattered the stone hedges that collapsed from the walls and ceiling. Dylan took a hard step forward, ready to engage.

A familiar, callused hand grabbed hold of his collar, yanking him back. Dylan fell to the ground behind a fallen stone column, the dagger dropping from his grasp. "What the—"

"Shush!" Cryis pressed a finger to his lips.

Riley and Cryis were both there. Riley peered over the top of the column at something far outside. Bruises and nicks crossed his brown arms. Parts of his shirt were slashed open and stained with blood. Cryis appeared unharmed, although there were still rips in his clothing. Blood stained the ends of his white hair. His skin was covered in a thick layer of dust and dried blood, no doubt belonging to another, staining his face and hands.

Dylan kicked aside debris, making room for his legs. He leaned against the fallen column, releasing a long sigh. Dirt and dust shook from his hair. The ceiling above him seemed to be on the verge of sinking in. "What happened?" he whispered, composing himself.

Cryis's voice was hushed. "Taybeith. Turns out the Demon possessing him triggered the attack." His fist banged on top of the stone. "And now, she shows up."

Dylan creased his eyebrows. He angled his body, lifting his head until he could see the damage inflicted. He followed Riley and Cryis's gaze, leading outside. Dylan concentrated hard, trying to see what they saw. A long line of Demons continued to march past the gate; the line went all the way to the forest. The clouds in the sky were a deep shade of purple and black, circulating in a fixated spot directly above the Institute.

Hovering several feet in the air was a silhouette of a woman. Black hair shielded her face. She wore the same fiery-red, skintight dress that fanned out around her calves in flames. The torso portion of the dress was decorated with curlicue designs of orange and gold that spiraled up the left side of her chest and crossed over her visible stomach. Her arms were folded across her chest, and one leg was crossed over the other, as if she were sitting in an invisible chair. Her expression was too hard to make out from where they were hiding.

"Damn. Is it her?" Riley asked with caution.

Cryis nodded. "Yeah, it's her," he replied, but he didn't sound entirely sure. "In a manner of speaking."

"Forget about her," Dylan hissed, pushing away his confusion. The awakening was still days away. "We've got to secure the premises." It made no sense how she could be here in the flesh now.

Cryis pulled out two loaded, silver magnum guns, passing them to Dylan. "Where's the Headmaster?" Cryis turned to pick up the long, silver staff behind him. Its blade was curved sharply, wrapping around half his body—a scythe.

Riley answered, "He left some time ago with Doctor Herron." He clicked his mortar into place. "Let's do this," he growled.

Cryis stood, attracting the attention of many Demons. He twirled his scythe above his head, a fast wind developing with each stroke. "Buy me some time!" Cryis's eyes were glowing red.

Dylan rolled into the open, firing his guns on one knee. The closer Demons he attacked with his dagger, doing a single tag team with himself. Two Demons rushed at him, and Dylan crossed his guns down, diagonally blasting through both. Riley repeatedly fired his weapon, sending the tiny bombshells into the large group of Demons ambushing the mansion. They flew back on impact, turning into ash.

A Demon with razor-sharp teeth, taking the form of a tiger with the hind legs of a bison, swiped one of the guns from Dylan's hand.

Hot, sickening breath hit his face, causing him to gag. Dylan ducked under the claw coming at him and ripped his blade through its thick hide. Black goo oozed from the beast as it let out a bloodcurdling howl, falling to its knees. Dylan kicked up his second gun, firing just in time as another beast pounced from behind. Its head rolled off to the side. Another Demon that resembled a green goblin approached. Dylan fired his gun, but only a click sounded. He dropped the guns, exchanging them for his dagger. The goblin grabbed the blade, unfazed by it piercing into its hand. The Demon tore it from Dylan's grasp, swallowing the dagger whole. It cackled in delight as it was joined by others, encircling him. Dylan balled his hands into fists, now weaponless.

"Cryis, time's up!" Riley barked, throwing his own empty weapon over his back, preparing for hand-to-hand combat.

Cryis stopped twirling the scythe and slashed it down diagonally across his body. A light blue trail of light followed. His eyes glowed deep red, and his teeth sharpened into fangs, giving him a monstrous look. "That's all the time I need," he growled. The butt of the staff slammed into the ground. A fierce wave jolted from it, pulsing through the mansion. Once the wave hit, the Demons began to turn to ash where they stood. The group leading up the spiraling steps vanished with one last, long cry. A visible force field sealed the opening, blocking the rest of the existing Demons from entering.

When Dylan looked around, it was quiet, except for the screeches from the beings trapped outside. "We've got to move," Dylan commanded.

"Round up the kids—injured and alive!" Riley instructed, heading for the steps.

Dylan looked around. There weren't that many kids left; he counted less than fifty. "What about the dead?" Dylan shouted.

Cryis raised the staff up with both hands. "Let their souls be purified and the gates of the heavens open wide," Cryis whispered. The staff dug into the stone. Blue streams of light branched out from it like roots on a tree. All around them, blue wisps began to appear, rising out from the walls above and beside them. Dylan counted at least 122, maybe more. Dylan watched in awe as the souls of the fallen students began to rise into the sky. It was the first time Dylan had experienced an

Immortal's reaping abilities. Cryis was providing safe passage for the souls as they moved on to their next part of existence. Humans believe in religion, but for some Aris Magicians, living was only the first part of life, while death held another journey. Dylan closed his eyes as tears began to fall down his face.

"The rest is up to them now," Cryis whispered.

Chapter Thirty-Four

Fortunately, Jay had been alone in her cell when it happened. First came the seething, white-hot pain that started from the trident on her wrist and soared up the full length of her arm. It was unbearable, bringing her to her knees. With her opposite hand, she cradled her burning wrist against her chest. Quick flashes of images formed behind her closed eyes—the golden rod from her dreams with a stone glittering its center. She attempted to grasp at it to keep a solid hold on the vision, but it continued to slip away from her. The pain subsided as quickly as it had come, leaving her gasping for air.

Something inside of her was unraveling, she could feel it. And because of her lack of control over her powers, she couldn't do anything about it. Tears fell from her eyes. She was afraid of losing what little control she did have. Jay held back even more sobs, hugging her knees to her chest, and rocking herself back and forth against the wall.

Jay.

Her head was buried, resting on her knees, and her hair cascaded over her legs, hiding her expression. She gave off the impression she was sleeping. The voice had been a quiet, delicate whisper.

Jay, come on. I feel you breathing.

"Cryis," Jay whispered, her voice muffled against her knees.

Hey, Princess. How are you holding up?

For once, the absurd nickname filled her with joy. *Good—for now.*

As you should be.

*Cryis, what happened? Something did happen, didn't it? He's not . . . You're not—*Jay swallowed down her fears, fighting to break through the panic arising.

Whoa, calm down. His voice sounded weak and plagued with sadness. *Are you alone?*

His voice was like a jab in the gut, never answering her questions but demanding an answer to his own. Jay lifted her head, tossing her hair back. She found the camera, making eye contact with the lenses. She could feel them watching her.

No.

I'm going to need you to maintain a neutral expression. They cannot know you are able to have connections with us. Can you do that?

She suppressed a confident smile. *You're asking because . . .*

His laugh tickled the nerves in her brain before he grew eerily quiet. *The Institute was attacked.*

Jay did as she was told and kept an emotionless mask.

Demons invaded, striking us where it hurt the most. They used Taybeith as the trigger.

She took in a shaking breath, not losing her composure. *Did any . . . did we lose anyone?*

Out of the two hundred and thirty students that resided here, ninety-eight of us survived; forty of that number were injured.

Taybeith . . . and the Headmaster?

Both are okay. The Headmaster was said to have left earlier that evening. He's on his way to you now. Cryis paused to let Jay let the information sink in before continuing. *One more thing, Aturdokht was there.*

Jay's body went rigid. *I thought you said she couldn't physically leave the boundary, she's not strong enough.*

She was strong enough to raise an army and rally them into invading our forces, Cryis retorted. *But yeah, she's not strong enough to be in a solid form. I think it was just another illusion.*

How could you tell?

I can't. He sounded defeated. *But there are more myths, rumors really, of her once being able to manipulate the souls of animals and shape-shift through them, but it's temporary. The fact that we should be worried about is that she was able to leave the boundary, which means she's getting stronger.*

Makes sense, I think. I saw something like that with her and a raven back in the forest when we fought her. Jay hadn't said anything about it at the time, thinking she'd sound crazy. Soul-possessing and shape-shifting was a weird combination, even among her kind. *Cryis, there's more. We're running out of time!* Jay cried. *In my vision, I found out that Aturdokht will be revived with the next Blood Moon. The next Blood Moon is in four days.*

Three.

What? Jay exclaimed, shocked.

Look, I've got to go, Princess, but Merry Christmas.

Cryis—

His presence was stripped from her soul, leaving her feeling bare and exposed. Jay tasted blood in her mouth; she had been biting the inside of her bottom lip. She sighed, pushing her hair back behind her ears. It had grown to be longer than it had ever been in such a short period of time. Jay pushed herself to her feet, her hair falling to the start of her hip. She lifted a small chunk of it, letting the pieces slip through her fingers.

Just then, the door on the wall across from her slid open. Kanon and Vastille walked in uninvited. Vastille gave a curt nod in her direction. Jay dropped her hair, flipping the strands over her shoulder with a forced smile.

"What's up?"

Kanon did not return the pleasantry. He marched over to her, stopping a few feet away. Vastille hovered near the closed door in his normal stance—arms crossed, chin tucked, shades on. Jay smirked as Kanon approached her. "Do you happen to have a pair of scissors?"

"Where is the entryway into Aris Magica?" Kanon spat.

"Who knows?" Jay lied.

Kanon bent down inches away from her face. He lowered his voice. "I am losing my patience. Now, I've waited patiently, playing your game, but frankly, I've grown tired of it. You need to give me some answers."

Jay rolled her eyes, side stepping him. "Kanon, no matter what I tell you, you'll never be able to trust it!" She pointed a finger at him. "I could tell you that Aris Magica is all around you, but you'll still question everything I say."

Kanon seized her by the hair, yanking her forward. Jay yelped, stumbling over her own feet, and smacked into Kanon's chest. He snatched her by the arm, releasing her hair, and twisted her body around, snapping a pair of handcuffs on both of her wrists.

Jay snarled as Kanon dug his fingers into her skin, pulling her close once more. "What the hell?"

"Luke." Vastille pulled out his gun, aiming it at Kanon's back. The sound of the revolver clicking into place was familiar to her. He slowly glanced over his shoulder at his partner.

Kanon's grip loosened, but he didn't release her. "I know," he snapped. He reeled her around, pushing her forward. She stumbled toward Vastille.

Vastille noticed her blue eyes changing to a red. He nudged her in the ribs with the barrel of the gun. "And you, don't try anything funny."

Vastille kept his gun trained on her back, directing her out of the room. Kanon followed closely behind. "Think of it as a late Christmas present," Vastille whispered, wary of Kanon's ears. Jay hardly glanced at him, continuing to glare ahead. "Just keep walking," he demanded, louder.

Jay obeyed, keeping her mouth shut. The outside of the room she had been locked away in led out into a gray hallway that eventually led to more cellblock halls. These cells had bars, and prisoners could be seen crouching in the corner or laying in cots. The prisoners leered at Jay, and in return, she gave them a look that shut most of them up. Guards in navy blue suits were stationed at every corner. They stood perfectly silent, like statues. Vastille rested a hand on Jay's shoulder, moving her behind him as they neared the end of the hall. The farther they went down the hall, she saw prisoners who just stared, or mumbled and laughed hysterically to themselves. Jay shuddered, feeling lucky to be in between the two men. They neared the section of the prison where men in orange jumpsuits were contained behind concrete walls and metal bars. The panels on their doors looked reflective. Some continuingly stared in her direction with a sinister gaze only to snap their teeth and look away. They couldn't see past the wall.

Vastille punched a quick set of numbers into the keypad. The sound of metal gears turning against each other grinded in Jay's ears as the door slid open. They entered a much brighter setting. Numerous cubicles swarmed the sunlit room. Tall glass windows opened to a bustling city below. There were very few employees left, and the ones that were still present typed away on computers. As Jay entered, everyone stopped and stared at her. She felt oddly shy, heat rising in her cheeks. Jay kept her head down, her hair shielding her face.

"Is that her?" someone whispered.

"Yeah, the covert, special operation Agent Kanon was assigned. Oh yeah, it's one of 'em."

Jay tensed. *One of them?* She took offense to his statement. She was a person too.

Vastille gave her another push, and Jay snapped her head forward, walking past them. "Where are you taking me?"

"Turn right. He should be right through those doors," Kanon insisted with an unreadable tone.

Vastille punched in another set of numbers, opening the door. The room was much like one of the smaller cubicles, apart from there being no windows. One light flickered above a single table with two occupied chairs.

"Headmaster!" Jay gasped, jolting forward. Kanon reacted instantly, grabbing her forearms, and holding her back. "What are you doing?" she cried. Jay kicked her foot back into his shin. Kanon grunted but maintained a steady restraint.

The Headmaster rose from his seat. He held up a hand, warning her to stop. Jay obliged, reluctantly ceasing her fighting. The woman beside him yawned, obviously bored. Jay recognized her instantly—it was the traitorous doctor from earlier. Jay narrowed her eyes and bit down hard on her lip.

"Agent Vastille, Agent Kanon, it's a pleasure to finally meet you," the Headmaster said, reaching out his hand.

Kanon extended a hand, keeping the other latched onto Jay's arm. "Likewise, Headmaster." He glanced at the woman. "Herron." She scoffed, rolling her eyes at his hand. He clenched his fist, letting it fall to his side.

"Now, as we discussed," the Headmaster began.

What had they discussed? Jay looked between the two with curiosity.

Vastille took Jay's wrist and stuck a key in the handcuffs. Kanon waved his hands at Vastille. "Wait a minute. How do I know you'll uphold your end of the bargain? As far as I know, you'll blast me where I stand, escaping with us looking like fools."

"When the Headmaster makes a promise, he never breaks it!" Doctor Herron assured.

Kanon's dark eyes met the Headmaster's. They never faltered. He snapped his fingers. Vastille turned the key, removing the handcuffs. Jay shook out her hands, taking turns rubbing each wrist. Creases in her skin showed where the cuffs had been locked too tight. Jay glared up at Kanon before making her way across the room to stand next to the Headmaster.

"And the serum?" Doctor Herron added.

Kanon hesitated but took out the tranquilizer gun, placing it on the table. Jay smirked, meeting eyes with him as she picked it up.

"Now for my part of the deal," the Headmaster explained himself. "The Witch will not be revived until the Blood Moon. No man-made weapon will stand the slightest chance against what is to come. Your best chance to save these people is to evacuate from Salem to Eugene. It is the safest route I'd suggest you take. The tragedy will spread, no doubt, but this will give my students and me enough time to pacify the problem. As much as I would love to see our kinds come together as we have before, it just cannot be done to pacify this enemy we face. This is Aris Magica's problem, and we shall handle it with care."

Jay's eyes widened. *How did he already know about the Blood Moon?* Her eyes shifted to Doctor Herron; she must have told him.

"Your students," Kanon repeated sarcastically.

The Headmaster did not find it funny. "Only a select few."

Kanon displayed his anger, using his hands to project his words. He slammed his hands on the table before pointing at Jay. "Students, are you mocking me Headmaster? You think a bunch of teenage outcasts stand a better chance in handling this impending threat rather than trained—much stronger, might I add—military personnel?"

"I do."

"Look, Kanon, that's the deal. Take it or leave it." Doctor Herron slammed her hand on the table. "You saw the future I showed you. Don't be a fool."

"Luke," Vastille began. "Let them go."

The color drained from Kanon's face. "You're making a mistake," he announced.

"We acknowledge the good you have accomplished, and under different circumstances, I would be grateful to help mend a broken relationship between our two worlds." The Headmaster thanked them before guiding Doctor Herron and Jay to the door. Kanon took in tight breaths as he watched them leave.

Jay stopped in front of Vastille. "Hope to see you in a different light, Vast."

Vastille gestured with his head to the door. "Get out of here before my partner changes his mind."

"Kanon." She stiffly nodded her head.

"Get out." Kanon scowled darkly.

The Headmaster, Jay, and the doctor descended the stairs to the garage at the base of the tall building. Doctor Herron led them to her old, beat-up jeep. She unlocked the doors. Jay opened one, ready to climb in. "Nuh-uh, hand over the serum first, kid." Doctor Herron gripped Jay's shoulder tight enough to leave a bruise.

The door slammed shut and Jay whipped around, pointing the tranquilizer gun at Doctor Herron. She backed away, hands held high above her head. "I'm not giving you this. Are we clear on that?"

"Jay, put the gun down," the Headmaster ordered.

"Headmaster, she's a traitor!" The words rolled off her tongue like ice.

"You can trust me, kid," Doctor Herron said. "You don't have the full story."

"Shut up!" Jay shouted, keeping the gun trained on her.

"Listen, you little imbecile! I'm the one that got your boyfriend to safety and helped save your pathetic skinny ass." Doctor Herron's voice softened. "You can trust me."

Jay glared at her then looked back to the Headmaster. She slowly lowered the gun. "Fine, but I'm still keeping it. Eventually, you would have to give it back to me anyway. I'm the one that has to fight her."

Doctor Herron sighed, pinching the bridge of her nose. "Just get in the car," she grumbled, sliding into the driver's seat. Jay took the back. "To your little school, I suppose." She started the car.

"You guys haven't heard?" Jay was surprised. *Of course they haven't.* "Headmaster, the Institute was attacked by Demons."

"What?" Herron shouted, befuddled.

The Headmaster remained calm. "I feared this would happen."

"What do you mean?" Anger crept into Jay's voice.

"Do you know where the survivors are now?" the Headmaster asked, dodging the question.

Survivors! Jay held her tongue. "No."

"Look, you two can do this later, I need to know where I'm going," Doctor Herron interrupted, pulling out into an intersection. Cars behind her honked, impatiently waiting for her to decide.

"Most of them were probably sent back home. I'm sure their parents are concerned," Jay suggested rather sourly.

The Headmaster ignored her. "Drive back into the forest in the direction of the Institute."

"Are you crazy?" Doctor Herron protested.

"There is an emergency shelter that was built for situations like these." He paused, meeting Doctor's Herron's credulous look. "Hurry."

Chapter Thirty-Five

Riley kicked away the boards blocking the doors to the small wooden cabin. It swung open, greeting them with a cloud of dust mixed with the smell of cold, damp air. The cabin had been a twenty-minute hike through the Willamette Forest behind the Institute's grounds, farther into the mountains. They had crossed underneath the waterfall not too far from the Institute, before breaking through to the last clearing and hitting the mountains, which provided a wall of protection. Dylan had come across it once or twice but never knew what it was for. Up until now, most of the students had believed it to be haunted.

Riley stared at the small group of kids who were left, at least seventeen of them—the rest had been given the chance to go home. He had used one of the many orbs the Headmaster stored to open a pocket dimension back to the council's headquarters. Some of the teachers who had returned from break had also gone through with a handful of students that lived in Aris Magica. They would alert the Aris Magica council of the events that had transpired today. He ushered the remaining group of students inside. "Watch yourself, it'll be dark for a while."

Each student ducked under the doorframe, swallowed by darkness. Dylan and Cryis were the last to go inside. They both lingered on opposite sides of the door. "That all of them?" Riley asked, checking out the distance behind them.

Dylan stared out into the open woods where the falling snow was already covering their footsteps. "Yeah."

Cryis shook his head, turning inside to go. "Worst Christmas ever."

Riley patted him on the back, walking the two boys inside.

In the center of the room, Lyid was cupping a small flame, doing his best to illuminate the shelter. The space was a small, square box. There were ten bunkbeds lining three sides of the walls. Some of the students had already claimed a bunk, while the older kids attempted to comfort the younger ones. There was barely enough room for them all. Dylan found Ami leaning against a wall, alone. He made his way over, taking the empty bunk beside her. She shifted from one foot to another before sitting down next to him. Dark smudges covered parts of her body, and her hair was clumped together with a mixture of dust and black blood.

"Hey," she whispered.

"Ami, what are you still doing here?" Dylan asked. "Go home." He knew her parents had to be concerned for her.

Ami squeezed her hands together. "I am home." Dylan shook his head, frustrated. "I'm willing to fight even if it means I have to die. Dylan, what I saw back there, what she did . . . I had to watch classmates I've grown up with die! People who took me in and accepted me when the world wouldn't! If there's a chance to spare the people out there from the destruction we witnessed today, then I will fight. I'm not going to abandon my family."

"Ami . . ." Dylan began.

"Dylan, look at me." Her voice was pained with regret. He glanced up at her, seeing her eyes drift deeper into sadness. "I know in the past we haven't seen eye to eye, but you've never known what it feels like to have your own mother look at you with disgust because you're different. A father that tried to kill you because he thought something was wrong with you." She gestured to the few students left. Dylan followed her gaze. "We are all here because we want to be, and nothing you say will make us leave." She smiled. "I guess that's why I chose this school, because everyone here is like family to each other, something I had but never really felt." She grabbed his hand, leaned in, and gently kissed him on the cheek. Dylan watched her get up and leave to go console one of the students who were injured.

"Yo." Cryis approached Dylan, replacing Ami's spot.

"Hey," Dylan mumbled.

"What now?" Cryis asked. He stretched out his arms above his head. Dylan remained silent.

"Where's Riley?"

Cryis scanned the room, finding him in the far corner. Taybeith was resting on one of the bottom bunks. Ami pressed a cold towel on his forehead.

"We fight," Dylan said, watching them as well.

"How? Our main source of power is being held captive," Cryis reminded Dylan.

"It doesn't matter, I'd rather not have her involved in th—"

"Stop it! She's already involved in this, we all are," Cryis groaned. "Look, you keep trying to act like someone's savior, but you're not! You're just a kid, one with a lot of baggage. If Jay was here, I'm sure she would want you to lean on her. We're here in her place, and we've got your back, so for her sake, lean on us."

Dylan nudged him in the ribs. "Corny is not your style." He grew serious. "But I know what you mean."

Cryis patted Dylan's back. "Good. Now get off. You've got top bunk."

Chapter Thirty-Six

"Park here," the Headmaster stated darkly. "We will pursue the rest on foot."

Doctor Herron parked the jeep outside the once grand gate, now leaning off its hinges and ripped from the ground.

Jay was the first to get out of the car. She looked at what was once her home, speechless. The mansion was destroyed. Its dark brick blasted through with holes, slowly crumbling to the ground. Snow fell into its interior. Dark piles of ash smothered most of the broken landscape. The fountain that stood in the center of the path was cracking in various spots; the heads of the cupid statues were missing. Jay took a hesitant step forward, then marched on toward the Institute. She climbed the steps up to the wide hole meant to be the front door. She ducked under, careful not to harm the fragile structure. The roof above her was gone in most areas, leaving long walls stretching up endlessly. Some of the higher floors were caved in, making it impossible to climb to the upper levels.

Jay cursed under her breath, kicking up the dirt and debris around her. Under the wreckage, her foot hit a softer object. Jay stopped, bending down to move the rest with her hands. Light, sandy strands of brown began to expose themselves. Jay brushed away the dirt and screamed.

She fell back onto her hands. She felt as if she had forgotten how to breathe. Her chest heaved in and out. Rella, her roommate, laid beneath the wreckage, staring up at a nameless fate, her mouth parted as if she were about to say something. Her skin was cold to the touch. Doctor Herron and the Headmaster rushed to her side. Herron knelt to her level, embracing Jay. Jay wouldn't allow herself to cry but didn't try to push her away either. The Headmaster knelt before Rella's body. He placed two fingers on her forehead and mumbled a spell of condolences. Delicate, light blue wisps emanated from Rella's body until all that was left was her shining soul, soaring up to the heavens.

"May she rest in peace."

"Are there anymore?" Jay choked on her words as she spoke.

"I'm not sure," the Headmaster confessed. "Cryis would have sent them on their way, the only ones who he couldn't have reached were the ones still dying."

"Still . . . dying."

The Headmaster did not respond.

"Let's go, I'm sure the others are anxious enough," Doctor Herron reminded them as she helped Jay to her feet.

Chapter Thirty-Seven

Everyone grew silent at the first sound of a knock. Dylan set aside the knife he had been wiping clean and reached for one of his twin silver pistols. Riley sat up from his perch near Taybeith. He strode across the room, silencing anyone who dared to speak. His heavy footsteps made the floorboards creak beneath his feet. He clicked his mortar into place, resting a steady finger on the trigger. The door swung open.

Jay obnoxiously rolled her eyes. "Put the gun down, Riley."

A wide grin broke out across his face. He barked out a laugh that turned into a whistle. "This here is my baby!"

Jay once again rolled her eyes, a habit she had formed when holding a conversation with Riley and shoved past him. "It's a toy."

"Headmaster." Riley's back straightened as the two adults followed close behind.

"Good to see you." The Headmaster congratulated him by placing a firm hand on Riley's shoulder.

All the muscles in Dylan's body relaxed. Her eyes instantly found his. A small and relieved smile took over. Dylan hopped from the bed, not caring who saw him, and sprinted into her outstretched arms.

"Jay!" he breathed her name into the side of her neck. She giggled, burying her face into the nook of his shoulder. Dylan lifted her, spinning her around twice. Jay's hair flattened against her body.

"I missed you!" Jay cried. They both squeezed tighter, afraid to let go.

"I'm sorry . . . I broke my promise to protect you—" Dylan whispered.

Jay cut him off, "It's okay."

Dylan pulled away just enough to cup her face in his hands. He examined her face, staring into her deep blue eyes. Jay grabbed his wrist, stopping him. "I'm fine."

Cryis seized hold of the back of Dylan's collar, dragging him back behind him. Then, he reached for Jay's hand, pulling her into him. "Hey, Princess."

Jay shook her head in disbelief. "Hey, you."

Cryis smirked mischievously. "Glad you're back," he replied in a hushed voice. Cryis delicately brushed his lips over hers before pressing his mouth to her cheek in a swift kiss.

Dylan fumed behind them, his mouth hanging wide open. Cryis patted him on the back and shrugged. "She's all yours now." Cryis smiled, rounding back to where the Headmaster stood. Dylan and Jay met each other's gaze. Heat rushed to their cheeks and the air grew intense around them. Jay was the first to pull away, finding herself staring at everything except Dylan.

Cryis glanced over his shoulder and shuddered. Dylan was giving him a threatening glare. Cryis looked like he was suppressing the urge to laugh. "Too slow man, too slow," Cryis whispered softly.

Chapter Thirty-Eight

The younger students were finally asleep, along with a team of third years, led by a girl named Shelby, who was monitoring the kids. Ami sat quietly off to the side attending to Taybeith, leaving Lyid, Cryis, Dylan, Jay, Riley, and the Headmaster sitting in a circle on the floor in the center of the cabin. Doctor Herron had excused herself to light a cigar outside. The tranquilizer gun holding the serum sat at the center of their circle.

"What have we learned?" Riley started the conversation off, looking at each of his companions.

"And what do we still need to learn?" Cryis added.

"I discovered the past legend of the original Princess and why the evil spirit inside Mirama was born. Also, that the serum might be our only hope in permanently eliminating Aturdokht. But I also learned my actions cannot be because of vengeance," Jay explained.

"Look." Dylan held out his wrist. Everyone leaned in for a better look. "Remember the trident we had imprinted into our skin?" Jay nodded. "Lyid and I figured out it somehow transforms into a staff." Lyid shook his head in agreement with Dylan's statement.

"Yeah, I saw it too," Jay said.

The Infinity Staff, Cryis thought.

Jay didn't answer or look his way, but she had heard him. It was the same staff she had seen in her dreams. The power the staff contained held the ability to seal Aturdokht and perhaps destroy her.

"The Witch isn't too far off from gaining power then. Having that much strength to control an entire damn army," Riley cursed.

"What we don't know is how to combine these visions and dreams to make them a reality," Cryis noted. "Things are different from before," he sighed. "In the past, it wasn't a mystery to the next reincarnation as to what must be done. Once awakened and reunited with their memories, they all just knew what to do—where to find Aturdokht and how to renew the seal."

"When does she revive?" Jay was hesitant about the answer she sought.

"In three days." Cryis folded his arms across his chest.

The Headmaster had kept to himself, oddly put out, not saying a single word. "You know we're asking these kids to lay down their lives for a world that doesn't even see them as equals?" Dylan said, staring at the Headmaster.

"We know." Riley shook his head. "This fight will eventually affect them someday anyway if we can't stop it now. It's not going to be small scale."

"I think they're ready, otherwise they wouldn't have followed us to this shelter," Lyid said, speaking for his classmates.

Cryis snapped, "They followed us to this shelter because they didn't have a choice! Shelter and death or vulnerability and death, which would you have chosen?"

Jay rested a calming hand on Cryis's forearm. She glanced at the Headmaster, who seemed to be speculating about the situation and weighing its outcomes, but not offering any advice. Jay sighed, watching the stress eat away at each of her friends. Her eyes wandered to Ami, who was pressing another cool towel to Taybeith's forehead.

"We can't force them to do anything," Jay began. "That's not how we do things, and it's not how we're about to start." She pulled one knee up to her chest. "Look, we are at war. I get that, and the bad guys pretty much have a lifetime jump on us." She paused, waiting for someone to interject. No one did. "This is my fight, and I'm not expecting any of you to die along with me; I don't even plan to die. I don't want to do this alone, but I don't want anyone to feel as if they are obligated to help. I know this world has done nothing to help us, but that doesn't mean we can't rise up and do something for them!" Jay pointed at Riley and then Dylan. "They're both human and they've set their lives aside to help freaks like us."

The Headmaster applauded. Everyone looked in his direction. "Very well said, Miss Raremore," he said proudly. "*What has this world done for us?* Thinking like this is exactly how Aturdokht wants us to think. She controls us by using that fear against us. Once we know what scares us the most, the better prepared we will be able to face her."

Every last person in the group was still overlooking the main problem. Jay ran her fingers repeatedly through her hair. They had all these clues with no clear sense of how to use them. Suddenly, the door squeaked open. Doctor Herron walked in, shivering from head to toe. She rubbed her hands together. Her cheeks were rosy red, nearly the color of her hair. At this rate, it didn't matter how much of a plan they could devise to defeat Aturdokht. If they couldn't get their hands on a weapon powerful enough, all their planning would fall down the pit.

"I think that's enough for today. Obviously, we're all tired and stressed out over this." Riley yawned, rubbing the back of his neck. Everyone followed his lead, getting up. The air between them remained somewhat somber.

Jay debated checking on Taybeith. She needed to know the full story of what had happened to him, but was it something she could bear? She stood up, offering Dylan a hand.

He stared at it for a moment before shaking his head and rising on his own. "I need space," he mumbled, brushing past her, straight for the door.

Jay cringed as the door slammed shut. She glanced back at Riley then gestured to the door. "Make it quick and be careful!" he warned, turning on his side.

Ami handed her a small, loaded gun and a dagger. "Here, you'll need it . . . just in case."

Jay gave her a quizzical look, pocketing both weapons. She grabbed the hoodie draped over the end of the nearest bunk bed before following Dylan's path out the door. She shivered, throwing on the hoodie. A cold whip of air spiraled around her. His footsteps ran deep into the snow, circling around back. She followed them, careful to keep her steps in sync with his. Dylan paced back and forth, completely oblivious to the frost building up on his arms.

"Dylan," Jay exhaled. She came closer. "Get back inside, please, you'll freeze to death."

Dylan briefly stopped pacing and stared at her. Jay shifted from one foot to another under his gaze. She couldn't tell what was going through his head nor read his expression. He shook his head looking away. "I'm fine," he snapped.

Jay approached with her arms shoved deep in her pockets. "I thought we were done with the lies and secrets," she sighed. Jay stood inches away from him. She peered up at him, smiling.

She wasn't sure what the next couple days would bring. All she knew was that before the end were to happen, she didn't want to leave anything unsaid between the two of them.

"What?" He began to back away, but Jay caught him in a tight embrace, only to be dragged forward with him as he fell back under her weight and his momentum, gravity sending them crashing down. Snow flew up, soaking their clothes. "What the hell, Jay!" Dylan shouted, holding onto her with one arm. "Geez, you're such a—"

Jay ducked her head, grabbing his collar. Instantly, their mouths met. The world was taken away—the cold, the pain, and their worries all drifted into a state of peace. It was just the two of them, held closely together. Jay felt the warmth of her body escalate into his, and an array of powerful, yet ancient, magic moved between them. She felt as if she could do anything and everything. She could see the past and future developing within and around their kiss. Jay wasn't sure if she clung to him in desperation or love, but she wouldn't let go. She couldn't. She was afraid he would pull away, but Dylan kissed her back, more fiercely. Jay relaxed in his embrace. He released her arm, grabbing the waistband of her pants, holding her body into place against his. He must have felt the magic surging between them too. She slowly drew back, sucking in the refreshing cold air. She had forgotten how to breathe, and now the air stung her throat as it entered her lungs.

Dylan's hands slipped away, falling into the snow. "What was that for?" he asked, taking in heaving breaths. Jay could hear his heart pounding against his rib cage.

Jay shrugged, falling back onto her hands. "I don't know. I wanted to try it before . . ." she trailed off, but then quickly added, "Plus, it shut you up, didn't it?"

They were silent. The snow began to fall once again, adding a thin layer to the already frozen ground. Jay knew exactly why she had kissed him. She was more afraid of losing him than losing herself in the days to come, but she wasn't ready to admit those feelings out loud just yet. What if he wasn't ready? What if he didn't want the same things she did?

Dylan rubbed his arms, hugging his body. Jay could tell the cold was starting to get to him. "I didn't like it." His teeth chattered, but his face was still a warm red.

Jay wouldn't meet his eyes. "Yeah," she huffed. "Well, neither did I." Jay remembered the way he held her against him and how cold she felt the moment she pulled away. "Dylan, I . . ." Jay groaned putting her head in her hands. She still couldn't bring herself to say that four-letter word, even though the two of them had said it plenty of times before to each other.

"I know." Dylan said, barely above a whisper. He laughed and threw up snow with his hands.

Jay peeked through her hands at him, wondering if he really did know what she meant.

"Come on!" He stretched out his left hand and Jay grabbed hold with hers. Their fingers laced together, sending a spark of energy through their bodies. Jay screamed, jerking her hand back—she was still on the ground, and Dylan cursed. Her wrist was burning. Jay stuck her hand in the snow, soothing the pain. Dylan looked down at the inside of his wrist. The trident scar was outlined with a strange glow.

"What happened?" Jay asked through gritted teeth while cradling her hand.

Dylan looked down at his hand as the light was already fading. "It can't be," he whispered. "Jay, your hand!"

She drew back.

"I know it hurts, but I have a hunch. I just need to see if it's real."

"Are you crazy? You want me to risk my hand on a hunch!"

Dylan nodded, completely serious. "I want you to trust me."

She couldn't argue with that. Jay groaned, reaching out her hurting hand. "Fine." Dylan hauled her up once again, and she felt the start of the spark. "But if I lose a hand for this, I'll kill you," she proclaimed.

The pain was intense. With each jab, the pinpricks became angrier and hungrier. She could feel them moving up and down, back and forth under her skin. Jay wanted to scream, but held it back to refrain from anyone inside coming out to investigate.

Something heavy fell in the space between Jay and Dylan, causing the connection to end. Jay was forced to grab the hot rod. She blinked back into reality upon noticing what was taking place. They were both holding up the bronze staff with the curled end housing a red stone at its center. Jay gasped, dropping her end. The rod fell to the ground, burning a deep hole into the snow. Steam rose, clouding her view of Dylan. Dylan kept a secure hold on his end, careful not to damage the core—the stone.

"It's the staff," he said in a daze.

Jay pressed both hands to her ears, shaking her head back and forth. "This is more magic than I can handle. It's too overwhelming. I can't control this! And they want me to fight her with that!" Thousands of doubts came rampaging to the surface of her mind.

With the staff came a much stronger force. From where she stood, she could feel its power, even without touching it. Her fingers twitched with the electrifying zing of magic. The staff was leaking it into her system, and her body absorbed it greedily. Suddenly, a huge weight settled in her soul, attempting to drag her down into darkness. Negative energy stirred around her heart and for a moment she felt as if there would never be light or hope again, just darkness and an unveiling evil. Jay looked up to see Dylan's grip on the staff had tightened to the point where his knuckles turned white. She wondered if he felt the same way she did.

The stone was glowing with a dark, mesmerizing light. A hazy, electrical mist emitted from it. Jay noticed Dylan's failure to take deep breaths—he was suffocating. Sweat dripped down the sides of his face and his knuckles had lost their color. She could see the magic was too much for his state and the energy was eating him away.

"Dylan! Drop it!" Jay shouted. "Drop the staff!" He didn't seem to comprehend what she was saying because when he looked her way, amusement crossed his face. "I'm not going to ask again," Jay warned, already reaching for the loaded gun in her pocket.

Dylan didn't respond, only a mischievous smirk played at his lips. Jay took aim, her fingers resting on the trigger, but she had no idea where to aim. Dylan consciously blinked his eyes, still not in total control. His face was strained in agony. Through gritted teeth, he managed to say, "Help me!"

"Working on it!" Jay mumbled, settling on a target. The gun fired, sending the bullet inches away from the inside of his arm. It was enough to jolt him back to his former self and into reality. His hands fell away, and the staff crashed into the bank of snow. Dylan relaxed, the tension leaving his body.

They met eyes. "Not exactly how I thought I'd spend my day, but . . ." Jay sighed, bending over to pick up the staff. The moment she touched the metal, her eyes changed to crimson red. Her two side canines grew a tad sharper and longer into fangs. An ancient-looking text of many symbols in golden writing spiraled up her arms like tattoos. Jay felt the weight pull down, and she resisted. All the hate built up from the past centuries coursed through the staff and into her soul, but it wasn't overwhelming. She was wrong, she could handle this.

"We need to figure out what to do with it. Clearly, it's not a toy to leave lying around." She glanced back at Dylan, who hadn't moved. He nodded rigidly. "What's wrong?"

"Are we going to talk about how you kissed me?" Dylan asked.

She ignored him, walking toward the front of the cabin. "Maybe it's possible to get it back into our markings or something." When they had conjured the staff, Jay's trident scar had glowed.

"Jay!" Dylan snapped.

Jay closed her eyes and extended her mind out to Cryis.

There was an irritated groan followed by a grumbling response. *Yeah, what is it, Princess?*

I think we just found the Infinity Staff. Long story short, we have it.

What! Cryis's voice was more alert than ever. *Where are you?*

Just outside the cabin.

Don't move! I'll be right out.

A chill ran down her spine and she shuddered. The wind picked up, sending her white hair fanning out around her. Jay gazed out into the surrounding mountains and trees. The last touch of sunlight kissed the snowcapped peaks above, leaving behind a cold emptiness. A trembling howl called off in the distance. Many more would soon follow.

Chapter Thirty-Nine

Riley wrapped the tail of the bandage around a small kid's arm, giving it a final tug. The kid squirmed and the bandage loosened. "Damn, this would be a whole lot easier if Faith were here." Faith had been among the many Aris Magicians who had died in the attack.

Ami took hold of the cloth, fashioning it into a sling that draped over the student's shoulder. "I know what you mean."

The battle yesterday had taken many of the faculty and students from the Institute. Grieving started the day after. The shelter seemed smaller and more lost in despair as they prepared for war.

"Thank you," the child mumbled, sliding off the bed and disappearing amongst the small group.

Ami smiled, glancing over at Riley. His jaw was set, and his eyes fixated on nothing in particular. His shoulders slumped lifelessly forward. "What's eating you?" Ami asked.

"The Headmaster." Riley shifted his position, singling out the old man in the corner discussing something with Taybeith, who had just awakened. "I've never seen him act this way."

"What? Like nothing ever happened?" Ami asked. Riley grunted a yes. "You'd think he'd be more concerned . . . Every encounter I've had with him thus far, I thought," she paused, thinking of what to say. "I thought he was this all-powerful, indestructible force. For heaven's sake, he created a whole institute within a pocket dimension, and he's radiating with magic. But when you boil it down, he's just a wise man in his old age."

Riley harked out a laugh, slapping his knee. "I see why people think that. Don't forget, he's the most knowledgeable person in the world! Read every book at the Institute." Riley laughed sarcastically.

"Do you honestly believe that?" Ami pressed on, turning his joke into a serious matter. "Because during your little circle, he had nothing *knowledgeable* to say."

"Yeah, I believe it." Though the tone of his voice wasn't convincing. "Look, he has his reasons for what he does and how he does it. Just like me, he's always trying to teach you something in the midst of chaos. Even though I don't always agree with his methods," Riley explained, mumbling the last part under his breath.

Cryis tucked a scarf inside the borrowed coat he was wearing. Riley caught sight of him heading for the door. "Where are you going? It's past bedtime."

Cryis pulled on the pair of gloves. "Then shouldn't you be asleep?" Cryis rolled his eyes, "I'm going to check on Dylan and Jay. They need to get back inside before something happens."

Riley didn't see the need to argue on that one. "Alright, make it quick."

Cryis saluted in a mocking way. "Yes, Commander, sir!" Ami covered her mouth, snorting.

"Get out of my face before I shoot you."

Cryis smirked, leaving the premises.

"Ami!" The Headmaster's strong voice demanded her presence.

"Yes," she squeaked, rising to her feet.

The Headmaster waved her over. She kept her eyes locked on Taybeith's. He was still lying in bed, tucked under the plain sheets. He gave her an encouraging smile as she neared.

The Headmaster leaned in closer, whispering his next words. "I need to ask a favor of you." Ami nodded slowly, unsure of what she was getting herself into.

Cryis rounded the corner of the shelter. Jay peeled off the back wall. "Hey!" She waved with a bob of her head. Dylan watched her closely.

Cryis stumbled, doing a double take. Everything about her was different. The way she stood, walked, talked—she had a defining confidence radiating from deep within her. "Wow, you've changed."

A prideful smile spread across her face. "It's only when I'm holding the staff." She felt a strong sense of otherworldly power bloom inside her.

Cryis walked over to where Dylan stood. Dylan had his hands shoved in his pockets, but his body was shaking. Undeniable fear shone through his eyes. "How long has she been like this?"

Dylan shot Cryis a dangerous look. Cryis took a couple steps back, putting some distance between them. "However long it took you to get out here—" Dylan stopped himself. "Wait, why are you out here?"

"Jay called me," he said. Dylan arched an eyebrow, confused. Cryis awkwardly laughed. "I-I mean . . . urgh I'll explain it to you later." Cryis directed his attention to the problem at hand. He cautiously approached her. "Jay, honey, let's just slowly suppress this magic, alright?"

She pointed the staff at him. "Don't talk to me like I'm a child," she said pointedly. "And I know that!" Jay fired back, sticking the staff back in the ground. The moment she released it, she returned to her usual self. "I don't want to feel any more of this cooped up negative energy."

Cryis sighed, relieved. "Good." He turned toward Dylan. "I'll need your help. The staff came from both of you, so that's where it'll have to return."

"I'm not touching that thing," Dylan spat.

"I'm not asking you to touch it, just focus and hold out your hand," Cryis ordered instructively. "Focus on the magic, find its core, and bend it in the directions you want it to flow."

Jay closed her eyes, shutting out all interferences. Soon, all she could hear was a steady current of power fluctuating in an empty space. She grabbed hold of the stream, following its trail to the very center. The current of magic was slowly slipping away. She felt it easily curve into her arm, igniting the trident symbol. When she reopened her eyes, the staff was gone, and she had returned to normal. The weight lifted, giving her soul a light and airy feeling.

"We will have to start training tomorrow, you'll need to learn everything in one day, or you won't learn it at all." Jay sucked in a tight breath, understanding. "Good, now let's get some sleep—you two can share a bed because we're short." Jay stepped in one of the footprints Cryis made, tensing. Cryis looked back between the two, both of their faces were red, and it wasn't from the cold.

"What happened?"

"Aren't we a little too old to share a bed like that?" Dylan mumbled.

Cryis rubbed the back of his neck, still looking between the two. "I thought since you two are so close, you always do it."

Dylan glared at Cryis, and Jay quickly averted her eyes. "No, no . . . I'll share a bed with Ami."

Cryis gave them another quizzical glance. He squeezed the bridge of his nose, shaking his head. "Alright, I honestly don't care."

Chapter Forty

Morning came too quickly. A bright ray of sunshine spilled from the cracks under the door and into the small cabin. Many of the beds were now empty. Dylan stretched, pulling himself out of bed, careful to hit the ground without waking Cryis. He slipped on his boots and quietly pulled on his jacket. Dylan reached for his twin magnums hidden underneath his pillow. The sharpening of two blades stopped him. Dylan jumped, taken by surprise.

Riley sat on the opposite bed, staring at him with two blades in his hands. Dylan tossed his head, annoyed. "You startled me," he whispered.

"Good. It's been getting a little too quiet for my liking." Riley laid the two cross blades down. A partial stream of light caught the tip of the farthest blade, reflecting the light off at a bended angle, shining past Dylan's shoulder.

"Yeah," Dylan agreed, pocketing his guns. "Where is everybody?"

"The Headmaster thought it best to take them into the city with one of our allied forces."

"Did they have a choice?"

Riley didn't respond.

"Who all's left?"

"The ones that matter."

Dylan shrugged, figuring he was only wasting more time. He glanced around—any extra coats lying around had been taken with the rest. He grabbed the hoodie hanging from an empty bed post.

"Where do you think you're going?"

"Out. If I stay here any longer, I'm going to burst."

"I never said I'll try to stop you, but I'm coming with. I've been needing a little action since that practice at the Institute."

"Practice?" Dylan snorted. "You're pathetic. Come on, I want to see if we can salvage a few things from the wreckage before we go."

The door closed, and Jay sat up. Part of her wanted to be upset with the way Riley and Dylan were handling things, but she knew it was their way of not losing themselves to grief. Sometime in the middle of the night, Ami had moved to the higher bed, leaving Jay alone. Everyone else was still asleep. She could hear Lyid's obnoxious snores from across the room. There were a lot of empty beds.

Jay sighed. The Headmaster knew what was best. He wouldn't have taken the other children into the city unless danger was on the horizon. Jay nodded, sitting up. She pressed her fingers to her lips, remembering the moment she and Dylan shared last night. But before she could think any further, a familiar voice entered her mind.

Jay, I need to show you something. Emilia's voice tickled the corners of Jay's mind. Jay had not expected to hear from her again after the Ancient had shared her memories with Jay.

Jay's body froze. She felt her eyes change red. Her soul slipped into an oblivion as she became shrouded in darkness. Jay found herself in the soul world yet again. She looked around for the soul that brought her there but couldn't find it. "Why did you bring me here?" Her voice echoed off the dark walls of the soul world.

Slowly, the darkness began to fade away into another familiar place. Jay looked down at her body. She stood in a white gown, barefoot at the edge of the forest where she first witnessed the Witch's power. Inside the memory, the air was warmer, and the season never changed. A cluster of ravens called out above her, soaring from branch to branch.

A harsh gust of wind surrounded her, sending a spiral of leaves in her direction. Jay jumped at the touch of a cold hand on her shoulder. She spun around, releasing a shriek at the sight of the girl behind her.

She looked to be at least seventeen. The girl had dark skin and huge brown eyes. Her nearly white-blonde hair hung past her waist in a long braid. A white gown loosely hung on her small body. She smiled, obviously pleased with Jay's reaction.

"Oh, please don't tell me I'm that easy of a face to forget." The girl smiled. Her voice was coated with an accent Jay had never heard before, but she knew it was from ancient times.

Jay glanced feverishly around, trying to find a possible weapon. The girl tapped a finger on her head, her voice sounding older than she appeared. "I'm the voice in your head."

Jay squinted at the girl as she stared back. Jay's eyes widened as she began to recognize the person in front of her. It had only been a couple of days, but Jay realized she had seen her in a memory. "P-Princess Emilia!" The girl smiled, nodding. Jay began to relax as her heart rate slowed back down. "B-but how!" Jay couldn't contain her excitement and ran to Emilia, embracing her into a warm hug.

Emilia laughed, awkwardly patting Jay's back. After a moment, she cleared her throat, holding Jay back at arm's length. "I need you to listen, I have quite a lot of explaining to do before they arrive."

Jay scrunched her nose, slightly confused, but she obliged. Emilia continued slowly. "Okay. You asked me where we are, but by now I'm sure you have realized. Yes, we are where the awakening of Aturdokht may occur, but as of right now, we are in a frozen space in time within this memory. We are in my soul world." She waited for Jay's approval before moving on. "Once I release the protection I have extended over and around us, we will be wrapped in the chaos and madness surfacing—"

Jay stopped her. "How do you know all of this?"

"I have lived countless lives, and you will not be my last. My soul is spread out across this world, running through the roots of these very trees. May I continue?" Jay nodded, still not fully understanding.

"I brought you here to learn what you must do, to get a feel for the battlefield before tomorrow night. If you cannot push her to the pond, then I'd prefer it takes place here away from the city." Jay looked around; she had seen this exact forest many times within her dreams. It was where the last Princess had sealed Aturdokht. It was where the same clearing where Dylan, Riley, and Jay had last fought Aturdokht.

"But . . ." Jay's voice trailed off. Why did it matter where she fought Aturdokht?

Emilia smiled sadly, sensing Jay's hesitation. She looked past Jay and stared off into the distance, as if recalling an old memory. "We're drawn to this place for some reason," she said barely above a whisper. "Perhaps it's her doing?"

"Aturdokht's," Jay said, frowning.

Emilia turned back to Jay and quickly grabbed her by the shoulders. "Jay, you must not let your mind become vulnerable to her. Do you understand?" Jay looked at Emilia uneasily and nodded. Emilia relaxed, relieved. She slowly let go of Jay's shoulders.

"Lastly, no matter what you see, do not fear—since it's only your spirit here, you cannot be harmed by the living, but fear can damage your soul in this form. As of right now, we are observers to the events that must take place."

"Wait, what aren't you telling me?" Jay asked, her eyes widening. "Who's arriving?"

A sudden blast of cold air coursed down her body as the soul world surrounding them was lifted. Jay noticed that they were still standing in the forest from Emilia's memory. Emilia stood by her side, but she was more transparent than before. The crunching of leaves under heavy footfalls drew Jay's attention back to what was in front of her.

The forest looked pretty much the same, winter had not touched this part of the world. The trees leaned in farther, their branches brushing the ground. There were hardly any leaves left; most of them had fallen, covering the path in fall colors. The earth beneath her was silently trembling as a mad rush of energy clouded the air.

"Jay?" She spun around, catching sight of Dylan and Riley coming up the path as they crossed into the other world.

Dylan picked up the pace, running toward her. Jay met him halfway. He tried to grab her, only for his hand to pass right through her. Jay's explanation quickly tumbled from her mouth. "I'm not really here! I won't be of much use. Emilia and I are only here as observers, so don't do anything stupid!" she pleaded.

"Who?" Dylan searched the air behind her, but there was no sign of anyone. Jay followed his gaze. She was gone. Jay began to panic, waving at the empty space behind her. "Jay, calm down," he snapped.

Riley approached them, standing by Dylan's side. "We've only come here to observe, too. The awakening is in two days, and I have a feeling this place will have some answers. We're smart enough to know we can't face whatever evil is here alone." She still felt unsettled. Riley readjusted the strap of the gun he carried across his back. "There's an immense amount of energy flowing from farther down the road, we should start there," Riley pointed out.

Riley led the way, Dylan and Jay following close behind. Dylan rested a hand on the gun hooked to his hip.

"If anything happens, I want you to disappear," Dylan lowered his voice so Riley wouldn't hear. He kept his eyes focused straight ahead.

"Don't worry about me," Jay snipped firmly.

Riley came to a stop, smelling the air.

"That's not your choice, because I do worry about you, every day, and every night!" Dylan said defensively.

Jay was speechless, taken aback by his concern. Her eyes fell to his lips. The kiss they shared filled her mind. She couldn't breathe as she remembered how his body had felt against hers. Jay coughed into her hand, hiding her embarrassment. Her next words came out in a small croak. "I can take care of myself."

She watched his hands tighten and untighten as he continued in front of her. Riley came to an abrupt stop again, causing Dylan to do the same. "Just do as I say, alright?" He was clearly frustrated by her choice to resist his wishes.

Riley put a hand up, silencing them. A darker shadow loomed overhead. Riley lowered his stance, revealing a small handgun, loading it up. He aimed it at the darkened blank space before them. His finger rested on the trigger.

"What is it?" Dylan whispered, taking his own defensive stance.

Jay took hold of a steady breath, releasing it.

"Something's coming," Riley warned. His fingers tensed over the trigger.

They listened, only hearing a whistle that came from the wind. Something was certainly off. The ravens no longer sang their haunting song, but sat silently, perched up on high branches. The ground shook louder than before. Up ahead, forming within the darkness, was a silhouette of what looked like a beast drawing out from the shadows.

Jay recognized the cry the monster gave, and her body instantly chilled. Two bronze horns pierced through the dark mass. Like a bull, it charged at them.

"Shit! Move!" Dylan shouted, dodging to the side. He hit the ground, sending piles of leaves flying up into the air.

The beast slowed, missing its targets. It stood to its full height. Jay gasped, holding back a terrifying shriek. She knew the Demon before them. The familiar dark-purple coat of sleek fur on a wolf-like body. It had two spikes of armor jutting out from its shoulder blades and bronze horns curling up from its temple. The beast snarled with hunger, revealing sharp, ragged teeth. Eagerness. Pride. Jay found his red eyes promising their next victim's death. The scream was caught in her throat. Fear crept into her soul, preventing her from making a move.

The Demon ignored her, staring fixedly into Dylan's eyes. A vengeful pull of remembrance crawled into its smile. Dylan's nostrils flared, not turning from the beast's gaze. "Phagos," Dylan sneered.

Riley stepped protectively in front of Jay's spirit. He pulled out his mortar, ready for anything. Something between a howl and a laugh echoed from the Demon's closed snout. "I serve her lady and master Aturdokht, my name is Phagos." Phagos extended his right hand, pulling out a wide, thick sword from thin air. Its blade was black granite with an ivy cord wrapped around its hilt. The Demon's voice was deep, yet alluring, drawing their souls in.

Phagos sniffed the air.

"You killed my parents," Dylan said with a dangerously calm voice. Both magnums hung in his clenched hands at his side.

"I remember your soul's smell," Phagos growled, dropping into a lower stance. "I will take great pleasure in devouring it."

Jay clung to air, her scream finally breaking free. Phagos charged at them with incredible speed. One second he was there, and in a blur, he was elsewhere. Jay saw the Demon before Dylan did, it appeared right behind him. Dylan turned around, blindly firing silver bullets into an empty space. The smoke cleared and Dylan cursed. Jay looked around for Phagos—the forest had grown oddly quiet with his disappearance.

"Is it over?" Riley asked scanning the forest, just as Jay was.

"Jay, I need you to leave," Dylan demanded, concentrating on the silence.

Jay shook her head, struggling to speak. "I-I can't m-move!" Fear had enslaved her body, taking control.

"What?" Dylan shouted, alarmed, just as a wave from a sword knocked him off his feet. The force of magic sent him flying a few feet back.

"To your right!" Riley cried, throwing a grenade into the spot he thought the Demon would be.

Phagos reappeared, snapping his jaw over the airborne bomb. It split in two, falling to the ground in a puff of smoke. Riley fired his gun again, but the bullets seemed to go right through the beast.

Jay's breath hitched; it was as if Phagos was in spirit form just like her. Jay's eyes widened as Emilia's voice echoed in her mind. Only the living could not hurt her. Phagos was somehow phasing between the spirit world and the living one, meaning Jay could fight him once he entered the spirit side. Her fist tightened at her side. Unless she moved—Jay looked over at Dylan, who was rushing at Phagos while Riley reloaded his gun—they would both die. Jay shut her eyes, drowning out the sounds of the battle. She took a couple deep breaths, the fear she felt was overwhelming, but she fought through it.

"PHAGOS!" Jay screamed at the top of her lungs. As she did, the fear controlling her body was expelled into the air. She no longer felt weighed down by it. It was the first time she had confidently said his name.

His head whipped around at her. A wicked smile formed across his snout. "You." Phagos lifted his sword.

Jay held out her hand. It began to spark with electricity. A cloud of mist soon followed behind the sparks. "*Fulgur.*" The magic shot forth from her hand and toward Phagos. It wrapped around his sword and then his body, trapping him.

Dylan looked back at her, alarmed, but not for long. He brandished his guns and attacked Phagos. This time, some of his bullets hit the beast, burning through fur and flesh. Jay's magic held Phagos, causing him to phase between spirit and flesh as he tried to escape.

Her magic didn't last long. The lightening magic calmed, singeing Phagos's fur.

Phagos vanished before their eyes.

"Where did he go?" Dylan shouted.

Jay spun, looking behind herself as well as behind Riley and Dylan—her heart beat out of her chest as anxiety filled her lungs. She felt something wet drop through her spirit. It sent shivers down her spine. Jay looked at her feet to find drool on the ground.

Jay slowly looked up to find Phagos appear above her. He lifted his sword in a swift arc as he came down on her.

"Jay!" Riley shouted. A fire of bullets went off around her shooting through her body and his.

Jay aimed her hand at him as he fell toward her. "*Ik'splōd*!" The air between them ignited as if a bomb had gone off. The magic went right through his body as he returned to the world of the living. Jay screamed, throwing her hands up to block as Phagos came closer. He landed on all fours on top of Jay, his body going right through hers. He glanced over his shoulder at her with a disgusting grin. Phagos dragged his sword through the ground, kicking up dirt as he did.

He turned and faced Riley, who dropped his gun, pulling out a similarly thick sword from the sheath at his side. He swung it, making the first contact with Phagos. The Demon howled, showing razor-sharp teeth. He swiped Riley's sword away with his own, digging his paws into the earth. Riley was pushed back, losing his footing. Phagos threw himself onto him, digging his claws into Riley's side. Riley screamed, trying to fight off the beast's strength.

"Damn it!" Dylan yelled, jumping to his feet. He ran toward Riley, but he wasn't fast enough. "Damn it, Riley, move!" Dylan stretched out his hand, still too far away.

Phagos raised his sword. A satisfied grin stretched across his face. The sword came down, emitting a dark purple aura from its blade. "No!" Dylan cried, shutting his eyes as the blade went down. He pulled out his guns and fired them aimlessly at the Demon's back. He heard a piercing whimper followed by a refined silence. Phagos instantly vanished.

Dylan's breaths were heavy and labored as he came to a stop. "Dylan . . ." Jay whispered.

Jay watched Dylan gradually turn around. His eyes widened. Phagos's sword jutted out from her stomach. Dark purple particles crept into the white fabric of her dress, gathering and then expanding. Riley was on his knees behind her, with one hand gripping his side and the other drenched with blood that fell from his arm into his hand.

"What's going to happen?" Riley asked in pain. Jay shook her head. "I thought you said you couldn't be touched?'

"By the living. Phagos was in spirit form, too, so his soul can harm mine. Physically, I'm fine . . ." Her voice wasn't as convincing as her words. Jay bit her lip, straining to smile. "Just make it back home safely," she begged, pulling the sword out. It clambered to the ground. The purple faded from her skin and her dress returned to its pure, transparent glow. She began to fade out.

Jay saw Phagos before they did. He dropped down behind Dylan. Jay screamed, pointing at the Demon. She watched the sword leave his hand. Dylan stared at Jay before his eyes widened.

Chapter Forty-One

Jay screamed, shooting up from her bed. Cryis jumped on her, pushing her back down. Jay fought against his restraint. "Calm down, Princess!" Cryis said, holding her down by her arms.

"Let me go!" Jay cried, the warmth of her tears stung her eyes. "They need help, they're going to die!"

"Who's going to die?"

She didn't get a chance to explain before a searing pain struck her body. Jay screamed louder, curling into a ball. Cryis glanced down, seeing blood soaking through the sheets. He yanked the cover back. Her entire midsection was drenched.

"Oh god . . ." Cryis breathed, his hands hovering above her stomach, shaking.

Jay screamed, pulling up her shirt, exposing her wounded flesh. A diamond-like gash sliced horizontally across her stomach. Deep purple and black veins spread from the open wound, blood spilling into the cracks of her skin. Phagos had stabbed her spirit and when she had returned to her body, it appeared on her flesh as well. Emilia had been right.

"What the hell!" Cryis shouted, his voice drowned out by Jay's shrilling cries. He'd never seen anything like it.

"What's going—" Ami gasped, seeing the damage. Jay screamed louder, thrashing on the bed. Cryis seized her wrist again, forcing them back down.

"Ami, go and ge—"

Jay saw a piece of wood whack Cryis against the head, sending him into a short daze. Cryis shook his head, trying to clear up the fog enough to see who it was. Somehow, he managed to keep a tight grip on Jay.

"Dude!" Lyid shouted, jumping down from his bunk.

Taybeith stood behind Cryis, holding a board above his head. Dark rings outlined the bottom of his eyelids. A hazy film covered his irises. He wore a wicked smile that didn't belong to him.

"T-Taybeith!" Jay shouted, struggling against the unbearable pain. She attempted to reach out a hand toward him. His wild eyes shot toward her in bloodshot fury. Cryis jerked her arm down.

"Jay, trust me on this! Someone get him out of here!" Cryis demanded over his shoulder.

"Yeah, easier said than done," Ami cursed as Taybeith's heel went down on her shin. She yelped, pushing him into Lyid.

Lyid squared up, punching him in the jaw. Taybeith tumbled back but didn't appear fazed. "Grab the serum!" Lyid managed to say.

Taybeith lunged at Ami. She grabbed the tranquilizer gun from the bag beside Jay's bed. Taybeith reached her, shoving her onto the bed. Ami shouted, thrashing beneath his weight. Taybeith bared his teeth, trying to bite down on her neck.

"Ami!" Lyid cried.

Jay watched as Ami wedged the gun up into the side of Taybeith's neck, ready to pull the trigger. "Taybeith . . ." she whimpered through tears and heavy breaths.

Tears welled in Jay's eyes as she fought through the pain and Cryis's grasp. She watched as Taybeith struggled to reach Ami and fight Lyid off his back. Black wings that resembled those of a raven sprouted from his shoulder blades, knocking Lyid to the ground.

Jay tried to reach out a hand to him. *Demon . . .* She struggled to speak. "Tay-beith . . ."

His head spun to leer at Jay, his eyes glowing a wild red. The Taybeith she once knew was replaced by what began to look like a Demonic creature. Jay whimpered at the sight of her friend. Cryis pushed her hand down and stepped in between her view.

"Not a good idea, Princess." He warned.

Chaos surrounded Jay, scattering her mind; she failed to grasp a hold of a single thought.

The gash in her stomach coursed with pain. Her screams drowned out the entire room. Her body felt like she was on fire. The golden symbols began to appear on her skin. She could feel a dark magic moving further up her body, sinking into her flesh.

Finally . . . the words reverberated in Jay's mind.

"Emilia!" Jay shouted.

"What!" Cryis shouted taken aback by the name. He seemed to recognize it. "How do you . . ."

A husky female voice laughed corruptibly. *You belong to darkness . . .*

Jay felt as if a hand had grasped her throat. She couldn't breathe. *Atur . . . dokht . . .*

The world around her spun uncontrollably. The golden aura surrounding her vanished, replaced by a black aura. Jay's breathing slowed. She slumped against the pillows.

Cryis gently pulled his hands away, cautiously watching her. "Jay . . ."

Chapter Forty-Two

Jay's eyes shot open. She found herself no longer in pain, but surrounded by darkness. She looked down to find herself naked and covered in a protective golden aura fused with her skin. The shield around her body was cracking in places as a black aura attempted to seep through. The air around her had no smell. It was if everything had been swallowed by the dark abyss. Jay rose to her feet slowly. The place felt familiar to her, as if she had been here before.

"Emilia," she whispered. Jay looked around for the familiar light but couldn't find it.

The last thing Jay remembered was the stab wound from Phagos, the dark magic infused in his sword nearly got a hold of her.

"Finally . . ." The same husky voice as before echoed off the walls of the world.

Jay spun around in time to see Aturdokht step out from darkness. Her entire body was covered in flames. Her black hair fanned out around her, blending into the darkness. Bright, envious green eyes stared at Jay as Aturdokht slowly approached her.

"We finally meet, and not in a memory." Aturdokht whispered.

Jay took a step back, widening the distance between them. "What did you do to me?" Jay said calmly.

"We're in your soul world." Aturdokht said.

"No . . ." Jay staggered back once again. Aturdokht confirmed her suspicion. It looked much different from the time Emilia had brought her to hers. As if on cue, a pulse of energy went off around them, causing Jay to look up. She could see the faint heartbeat of her soul dimming. They *were* inside her soul world. Jay had carelessly left herself vulnerable enough for Aturdokht to cross into it. Phagos's sword had not been infused with just any dark magic, it had been infused with Aturdokht's soul, ensuring that this moment would happen.

"Clever girl," Aturdokht gleaned. "Now." She held out her hand to Jay. "Let's end this. Become my vessel."

Jay gritted her teeth. It was her soul world, meaning anything was possible. She could still use her magic without the use of harnessing words. In this soul world, she had complete control. Jay focused and called upon it. Her arms lit up with a golden light. "Let's . . ."

She charged at Aturdokht, and as she did, pieces of the aura surrounding her began to chip away and become dust floating off into darkness. Jay swung her arm toward Aturdokht, letting a flow of streaming Old Magic spiral in her direction. Aturdokht smirked and didn't even try to dodge as the magic came hurdling at her. Jay's attack was met with the flames and disintegrated on contact.

Fear constricted her body, threatening to immobilize her. Jay tried again. She wove her hands together and slowly separated them. A blade made purely of light magic began to form, extending to a hilt. She drew out the sword and charged at Aturdokht once again, this time getting closer. Jay could feel the heat of her flames threatening to break through her aura. Jay swung the sword. Aturdokht raised a hand, sending some of the flames from her body up into a wall, dividing her from Jay. The sword hit the wall, tearing a small rift in it. Through the hole, Jay could see Aturdokht on the other side, grinning wickedly back at her. Her body was exposed as the flames held up the wall between them. Her skin was a ghastly, pearly white. Her lips as red as the fire around her.

"How do you possibly expect to defeat me without the staff?" Aturdokht chuckled as the rift began to close. "As of now, your power does not compare to mine."

Jay waved a hand across her sword, causing it to disappear. She stepped back, creating some distance between them. She had a chance. Jay smiled to herself. If she could get Aturdokht to use the wall again and create a big enough opening in her defenses, Jay could defeat her.

The flames returned to Aturdokht's body. "My turn." She smirked.

Jay smiled back, she saw the confusion in Aturdokht's eyes, but didn't let it sway her. Jay knew she only had one shot—the minute Aturdokht caught on, Jay would lose her only opportunity to defeat her. She could not let Aturdokht have her soul.

Jay waved her hand behind her back and a gun made of magic appeared. It only had one bullet. Jay raised her other hand up and created a version of the staff she and Dylan had conjured. The fibers of magic beaded together, creating a solid figure of a staff. At the tip of the staff was a sharp blade.

The smile on Aturdokht only widened. She raised her hand toward Jay. "*Hořet.*"

All of the fire surrounding Aturdokht left her body and shot toward Jay. It came at her in incredible speed. Jay closed her eyes and focused on channeling her magic. She felt the heat of Aturdokht's power growing closer. She raised the staff in the air as she'd seen reincarnations of her do in every previous life. A rush of adrenaline exploded through her body, igniting its own fire. Jay opened her eyes to see gold flames come from her body and grab onto Aturdokht's flames. She saw fear cross into Aturdokht's eyes at the sight.

"Let's finish this," Jay said.

She slammed the staff back into the ground, drawing Aturdokht's attention to it. The golden flames infused with Aturdokht's red ones, rising above them, and creating a canopy. Aturdokht's gaze followed it. Jay pulled out the gun hiding from behind her back and fired the single bullet. It whizzed through the air between, hitting Aturdokht's body straight through her heart.

The flames began to die around them, turning into smoke. The light in Aturdokht's eyes dimmed as she looked down at the bullet embedded in her chest. The bullet melted into magic particles that quickly spread across her whole body.

Jay watched with great sadness as Aturdokht's body slowly turned to the ash from which her flames were made. The sadness of a thousand lifetimes filled Jay with sorrow as Aturdokht's spirit and soul disappeared before her eyes. Jay couldn't explain why she felt this way; Aturdokht was a great evil the world would be better off without, but in very many ways she had been the quiet voice in the back of all Aris Magicians' minds. They shouldn't have to hide in fear anymore. A world of coexistence was possible again. Jay had seen it. If only Aturdokht could have too.

Jay fell to the ground in relief. She closed her eyes, relishing the peaceful silence. "It's over," she laughed, leaning her head back. Her eyes widened and her smile quickly faded. Above her, her soul's light was even dimmer. Purple veins pulsing with magic stretched out from the darkness, encasing her soul in a web. It was the same exact ones that had been entangled on her flesh. "No . . ."

"Foolish girl." Aturdokht began to rise once again from the ashes.

"No, no, no, no . . ." Jay repeated, watching the ashes start to form into the body of a woman. She struggled to her feet. "How?"

"I already won, even before this battle began." Aturdokht laughed. The noise filled Jay's body with chills. "You belong to me now."

The final layer of aura encasing Jay's body shattered around her, but for once, Jay wasn't scared. She wasn't scared of being the reincarnation everyone hoped for, nor their savior. In this moment, she wasn't worried about what would happen to the humans or to Aris Magica. She wasn't even worried about Dylan. For once, her body felt light and free of expectations. She took a deep breath, feeling the magic that pulsed throughout her entire body leave her as a calming darkness washed over her.

Chapter Forty-Three

Jay's hair cascaded over her face as her body slumped against the bed. A deafening silence filled the cabin. Cryis slowly removed his hands from her body. The wound on her stomach had stopped bleeding, and the magic had settled, leaving purple residue floating in the air. The veins spreading from the wound had disappeared.

Ami pushed Taybeith off her, letting his slack body fall to the floor. She had managed to inject the serum in him before he had made the complete turn into a Demon.

Lyid helped her to her feet. "Is it over?" he asked.

Cryis lifted the strands of her hair, gently pushing them back behind Jay's ears. With a shaking voice he whispered, "Hey, Princess?" A few silent moments passed.

A wicked smile formed across Jay's lips. She opened her eyes. Cryis's breath hitched. They were red.

A Guide to Aris Magica

Name Pronunciations

Ami: *Ah-mee*
Aturdokht: *Ah-tour-duct*
Cryis: *Cry-is*
Mirama: *Mee-raw-mah*
Emilia: *Ee-mill-yah*
Phagos: *Fae-goes*
Rella: *Ray-la*
Taybeith: *Tay-bee-ith*
Vastille: *Vah-steal*

Word Terminology

Aris Magica: The world of magic hidden within the human world.

Black Gates: Guarded by several cloaked figures deep within the realm of Aris Magica. The doors keep the darkness of the world from escaping; most Demons and Faeries retreated there after the war.

Magicians: The racial name for those who belong in Aris Magica.

New Magic: Magic that does not come with a price. Controlled and predictable magic that can be created by spells or nature.

Old Magic: Unpredictable forms of magic. In order for the user to use this magic, the source or the user must pay a steep price. If the source the magic is drawn from has a soul, then a piece of that soul will be taken and turned into magic; if the source does not have a soul, then the user must pay the price with their own soul.

Pocket Dimensions: Created by Witches and Wizards. Makes it possible for two places to overlap in the same time frame without disturbing the other; only Aris Magicians can see and enter them.

Pure Breed: Both parents descend directly from magic.

Serum: A drug that can permanently strip the powers from a Pure breed Aris Magician.

Soul World: A world that lives inside of everyone; the essence of a person's soul. Beings can visit their soul world through dreams, although humans may not remember it for long after waking up.

The Institute: The Institute for Aris Magicians and the Gifted. It bears the same emblem as the symbol for eternity. A safe haven created long ago for students practicing magic.

The Symbol of Eternity: an S with a diagonal slash through it. Appears on the chosen before they become immortal.

Breed Terminology

There are eight known breeds in Aris Magica. Each Breed has many sub-classes that follow under each class of magic.

Demons: Dark creatures that spend their time in the shadows. Can soul possess humans and Aris Magicians; banished from Aris Magica.

Faeries: Dark counterparts to Fairies; associated with death and bad omens. Can weave, control, or walk through a person's dreams. Their magic stems from disrupting one's sense of reality and imagination; banned from Aris Magica.

Fairies: Can use Old Magic freely without paying a price; most present themselves as healers.

Immortals: Rare beings who are chosen; does not have to belong to Aris Magica or possess the Hybrid gene to be chosen. Must undergo a transformation to make them immortal. Their purpose on earth is as a soul reaper who guide the dead to the next life. Each immortal has a secondary purpose: once completed, their immortality is passed to another. *i.e., Can also become guides for an Ancient.*

Hybrids: The gene known as the Hybrid gene gives users magical abilities and mastery; user does not have to come from magical ancestry.

Weapons Masters: Can use a weapon once and master its technique.

Emags: Anything with an electromagnetic wave the user can control, *i.e., Electromagnetic Masters.*

Therianthropes: Half human, half animal; magic pulls from animal instinct.

Lost Breeds: Dangerous forgotten races and forms of magic; not much is known about them.

Ancients: Powerful Enchantresses that can create magic and bend reality. Only one can exist at a time. They watch over the seal keeping Aturdokht at bay. Often confused with Immortals because of their similar features. *i.e., Immortal Princess; Princess.*

Shape Shifters: Can take on the form of an object or animal.

Purists: One of the most powerful classes of magic. Their magic is unconventional and often rare.

Oracle: Can see the future.

Seer: Can see the supernatural insight of objects that have yet to appear; must first touch or see a similar object.

Witches: Originally aligned with evil forces before the Aris Magica Wars. Elemental users, often mistreated because of past events. Emotions strongly control the extent of their powers; do not have to use harnessing words to control magic.

Mist Casters: Uses molecules in the air to create tangible magic mist that can be dangerous to touch.

Elemental Mages: A user that uses one of the four elements (earth, wind, fire, water); can create the element of choice from nothing.

Wizards: Cousins to Witches but have always fought for the advancement of society. Magic is based on a knowledgeable aspect: it either helps others learn or teaches the user; their magic makes them very wise and close to all knowing. Can sense magic being used; cannot be possessed by a Demon unless allowed.

Tekhnes: Range of magic limited to knowing and controlling anything on the internet.

Harnessing Words / Spells

Magic words that help the user focus power.

Amuletum: Charm magic used to make a person desire the user and reveal their secrets.

Cincinno: Locking spell.

Confractus Cininno: Unlocks any lock.

Confractus: Fractures objects.

Cor Imperium: Allows the user temporary control over a person's heart and soul; Old Magic that pulls from the source of another's soul or the user's soul.

Daknɛs: Takes away sight and shrouds the area in a veil of darkness.

Forsvinne: Counter spell; deflects magic back at the opponent.

Fulgur: Trapping magic; creates a bind.

Helbrede: Old Magic used to heal injuries; the soul the user pulls from will experience death or pain depending on the extent of the injury healed.

Hořet: Ignites objects/persons into fire turning it into ash.

Ik'splōd: Creates an explosion.

Kapalina: Turns anything solid to liquid.

Neviditelny: Makes the user temporarily invisible.

Opravit: Mends objects.

Pevný: Turns anything liquid to solid.

Somnum: Puts a person to sleep.

Světlo: Creates light.

Ungues: Claw arm magic; offensive attack spell.

About the Author

Autumn Green is a debut author who first began creating fictitious worlds and characters in the fourth grade. After graduating from Drury University with a degree in animation and writing, Autumn has spent the last few years writing YA novels. In her writing, Autumn enjoys crafting characters with a tangible spark and designing an escape for readers. Autumn lives in Kansas City, Missouri, and spends her summers exploring the world with her family and friends.

Ooligan Press

Ooligan Press is a student-run publishing house rooted in the rich literary culture of the Pacific Northwest. Founded in 2001 as part of Portland State University's Department of English, Ooligan is dedicated to the art and craft of publishing. Students pursuing master's degrees in book publishing staff the press in an apprenticeship program under the guidance of a core faculty of publishing professionals.

Project Managers
Luis Ramos
Maliea Ruby

Editorial
Sienna Berlinger
Rachel Lantz
Kelly Morrison

Design
Katherine Flitsch
Elaine Schumacher

Digital
Anna Whemeier Giol

Marketing
Sarah Bradley
Sarah Moffatt

Publicity
Tara McCarron

Social Media
Nell Stamper

Acquisitions
Amanda Fink
Alena Rivas
Kelly Zatlin

Rights
Jenny Davis

Publisher's Assistants
Elliot Bailey
Dani Tellvik
Emily Villaverde

Book Production
Rachel Adams
Alex Burns
Francisco Cabre Vásquez
Jenny Davis
Rachel Done
Brenna Ebner
Alex Halbrook
John Huston
Maya Karkabi
Jackie Krantz
Savannah Lyda
Yomari Lobo
Agi Mottern
Abby Relph
Rachael Renz
Jules Roth
Alexa Schmidt
Eva Sheehan
Mackenzie Streissguth
Cecilia Too
Sumayyah Uddin
Shoshana Weaver
Page Zimmerman